These
LONG
SHADOWS

Praise for *These Long Shadows*

A book that will pluck on every heartstring! Two wounded characters desperate for a future will have you invested in their story in a heartbeat. *These Long Shadows* is haunting, powerful, beautiful, and most of all, a true testament to the victory that faith and love brings us. This one won't be letting me go for a long while!

~**Roseanna M. White**, bestselling and Christy Award–winning author of *Yesterday's Tides*

A heartachingly tender tale of second chances set against the backdrop of a city rising from the ruins of the Second World War. Vivid historical details paint a portrait of London in the aftermath of VE Day. As Jonty sought to win Katie's heart, he stole a bit of mine. Historical romance fans will savor every page of this beautiful novel.

~**Amanda Barratt**, Christy Award–winning author of *The Warsaw Sisters* and *Within These Walls of Sorrow*

Praise for *Heart in the Clouds*

A sweet and compelling romance that doesn't shy away from the difficulties of war. *Heart in the Clouds* is beautifully researched. Perfect for both World War II buffs and for those who simply enjoy a lovely story and characters who feel like friends. Don't miss this one!

~**Sarah Sundin**, bestselling and Christy Award–winning author of *Midnight on the Scottish Shore* and *The Sound of Light*

These LONG SHADOWS

JENNIFER MISTMORGAN

ISBN 13: 978-0-6458566-9-9 (Print)
978-0-6458566-8-2 (eBook)

In loving memory of
Angela Janice
(2007–2009).

Angie, this one's for you.

PROLOGUE

March 1943
Lincolnshire, England

The restaurant swam around her, but at least the nausea had eased enough for her to be out of bed. She'd pulled on her Women's Auxiliary Air Force uniform for the first time in two weeks to be here. Jonty was waiting at a table but jumped to his feet and fussed over her. She let him, unable to meet his eyes. She focused instead on the steely blue of his RAF uniform and the way it clashed with his red hair.

"Tea?" He didn't wait for an answer but let her sit while he went to place the order.

She slumped. Laying her head in her arms would feel nicer, but she tolerated being upright—just—slowly sifting through the thick fog in her mind.

Jonty returned. He'd insisted she push through and meet him here, even though they rarely saw each other outside the armory where she worked. He said he had something important to talk about.

"What's so important then?" All her manners were still back in her WAAF cot.

"I know about your condition, Katie."

She didn't need to ask what he meant. She also didn't have the energy to deny the truth. The rumor would be halfway around RAF Bottesford by now. She was pregnant. Not that it was polite to say it that way, but "being in a family way" wasn't right for the circumstances, was it?

The color must have drained from her face, already pale from a fortnight spent keeping the nausea under control with crackers and ginger tea, the only things she could keep down.

"How much do you know?"

She couldn't imagine that the instigator of her current state, Jimmy Hardie, would be discreet. Not after everything she'd learned since that night outside the pub—"Don't worry. You can't get pregnant if you're standing up."

Until then, she'd thought he was sweet and attentive, the kind of man she'd want to marry. Less than twenty-four hours later, she'd discovered their encounter had been part of a cruel game among bored airmen. The Sweetheart Sweepstakes. Her virginity won him the game. Her bottom lip trembled. She bit down on it so Jonty wouldn't see.

Jonty confirmed the worst. She was the laughingstock of the airfield. Anyone who didn't know about the baby would work it out soon enough. A waitress interrupted, placing a cup of coffee in front of Jonty and weak tea in front of her. She braced against a wave of nausea at the smell of the coffee sloshing in his cup.

"Maggie told me what Queen Bee said."

Would the humiliation never end?

When she'd become too sick to work, she'd had to tell her commanding officer. Maggie was no fool. She'd worked out the real reason and told the highest-ranking WAAF officer at the airfield. Queen Bee had offered to pay for a trip to a clinic that would end the nausea and get her back to work. The usual way to deal with a girl who was pregnant without permission. But how could Katie do that?

She stared down at the tea, unable to drink in case she retched in the restaurant. She barely heard Jonty's next words as she stewed in the shame of the situation. She wanted nothing more than to put her head down on the table, block out the world, and stay like that until the problem went away.

She closed her eyes when the sting of tears began. *Please not here.*

"I want to help you."

"How can you possibly help?" She spoke through heavy, closed eyes.

She went so far as to touch the teacup handle, wondering if she should take a sip to distract herself.

"I'm a teetotaler. I'm not a violent man."

This wasn't a solution. It was a list of credentials. She willed him to get to the point.

"I understand that I'm not a handsome man."

True. When she'd first met him, she had found it difficult not to focus on the scars that marred his otherwise handsome face. She chastised herself now for being unable to look at him properly in those early days.

"But I am a rear gunner and not likely to survive till the end of the war. Normally this wouldn't be a great selling point. But in this case, you'd be rid of me and have a pension, which I feel is relevant."

She looked up at him then, nausea forgotten. Considering how sick she'd been for the last two weeks, that in itself was a minor miracle. What was he saying?

"We never have to tell anyone the baby isn't mine. And"—his brow furrowed—"I promise not to touch ye until after the bairn is born."

His accent strengthened, as it often did when he was emphasizing a point. His resolute frown seemed so Scottish that it might have been comical if she hadn't been so sick.

"I know we don't love each other. But we like each other, don't we? And some have started with less."

She couldn't breathe. What was he saying?

"I'd like a family, Katie. And you need one. So." Jonty reached across the table and took her hand from where it toyed with her teacup. "Katie Baines, will you marry me?"

"Marry you?"

He nodded. Those gunmetal-gray eyes were serious—somber, even—not hopeful, as a man's should be when asking for a woman's hand in marriage. She held his eyes with her own.

Jonty wasn't like Jimmy and his cronies. He'd had nothing to do with sweepstakes. He'd always been unfailingly kind and good humored, even to people who mocked his scars. He was right to say that they liked each other, though she'd never thought of him as more than a friend. But he was the dearest kind of friend, wasn't he, if he was willing to give the baby a future?

Some instinct deep inside her whispered yes. But she didn't get the chance to say the words. The woman at the next table heard the question.

"Oh, how lovely! He's proposing!" she exclaimed.

Before Katie knew it, every eye in the restaurant was on them, every neck craning to hear what she would say.

A heckler called out from near the kitchen. "You're not down one knee, lad! Why aren't you down on one knee?"

Jonty's eyes went wide in horror as their quiet moment was blown to pieces. "I'm so sorry." Apology painted his face in pitiful colors. "I didn't mean for it to be like this."

"Yes, Jonty." She spoke just for him, despite the others listening. "I'll marry you."

Jonty nodded, looking relieved rather than excited, though his lips curled into an uneven smile. The crowd around them erupted with a cheer and tossed them a sea of congratulations, stealing whatever smidge of happiness they could. With difficulty, she and Jonty extracted themselves.

Jonty turned to her when they were on the street. He hadn't let go of her hand that whole time. "Shall I speak to your father?"

Suddenly the nausea swept back in full force, and she retched into the gutter. "I'm sorry."

Jonty handed her his handkerchief.

"You've nothing to be sorry for, Katie-my-love."

She frowned at the nickname that sprung out of nowhere, but ignored it. "We should tell him together. He can be . . . unpredictable."

"I can get a leave pass this weekend. But will you be able to travel on the train? You look very unwell."

"I'll manage. But you might have to let me use your shoulder as a pillow if I can't sit up properly."

He grinned. "Gladly."

He seemed genuinely happy. Even if she weren't feeling weak and slow from the nausea, she wasn't sure she was happy about what they'd just agreed to.

But there was a hope of happiness eventually, wasn't there? Which after the last two weeks was unexpected.

Before they parted, he stepped closer and took both her hands in his. She stiffened, unable to control her response. He was only an inch or so taller than her five foot four inches, but that difference allowed him to plant a simple kiss on her forehead.

"We'll make this work, Katie-my-love. I promise."

CHAPTER ONE

King's Cross Station, London
Thursday, 4 July 1945

As the bitter taste of coal dried out her mouth, Katie Ables twisted the thin gold band on her left hand and watched the train pull up in a hiss of steam. She would have preferred to come to the station alone to see her husband again for the first time in almost two years. But her mother had insisted on coming too.

"Don't fidget, Katie."

Katie hated being chided like she was a girl when she was, in fact, a married woman of almost twenty-two. But there wasn't much she could do about it when she was still living with the woman. She dropped her hands, but her insides still twisted. Questions she'd already asked herself a thousand times wove through the nerves in her belly. Chief among them: What would happen when Jonty stepped off the train?

"Boys, keep your hands to yourselves."

Mum had insisted on bringing Katie's two youngest brothers, although Katie had no idea why. At eight and six, Davy and Tim could have no idea of the significance of the meeting. They were already bored after waiting in line at a polling station this morning while she and Mum had voted. Now the boys chased each other around the platform, narrowly missing luggage trolleys. Mum's weary reprimands punctuated the sounds of comings and goings at the station.

"Are you sure he'll be here?" Mum asked.

Yes. No. I don't know.

Maybe he had changed his mind. Tightness rose from her belly into her chest. Ignoring her lipstick, she gnawed at her bottom lip, eyes tracing the alighting crowd for a flash of gray-blue. But maybe he wouldn't be wearing his uniform. She wasn't even sure if he had been properly demobilized or not. Even in the clouds of smelly steam, he shouldn't be hard to spot, with his scars and lopsided mouth.

"Boys. I've told you to stop, haven't I?"

Katie only vaguely heard the chastisement. Her eye caught on an RAF uniform. Her heart rate escalated as the man moved closer.

It wasn't Jonty.

She released the breath that had caught in her throat and tried to calm herself. She followed the airman long enough to see him drop his duffel bag and hold out his arms for a woman in a well-cut plum-colored suit to throw herself into them at a squealing run. They clung to each other for minutes on end, her head over his shoulder, before they found each other's lips. They kissed long and deep, in full view of the whole station. Just like in the novels Mum read every night.

"Oh, how romantic." Mum had seen it too, then.

A crashing sound behind her stole her attention away from her search. She spun around to see that her youngest brothers had somehow managed to topple over a luggage trolley.

"Boys! Behave!" Mum hurried over to help restack the trolley, apologizing to the glowering station attendant.

The boys stayed contrite for approximately two seconds before they began their games again, farther down the platform. Katie should help Mum right the fallen suitcases, but she turned back to scour the crowd for Jonty's face. She took out his last letter from her coat pocket to double-check the details, even though she knew she was right where he'd told her to be.

Kings Cross station. Platform two. 11.30 a.m.

What if he didn't come?

She prepared herself for the mortification of going home without him, for the conversation with Mum, for what she'd say to the rest of her siblings.

"Katie?"

Jonty's unmistakable accent came from behind her.

Time stopped.

Every muscle tightened. She took a deep breath to steady herself and turned toward his voice. For the first time ever, she was glad for his scars. She might not have recognized him otherwise. The scars on his neck seemed more pronounced than in her memory. They pulled his expression slightly to the left. Jonty had never been plump, but he'd lost even more weight since she'd last seen him. His uniform sat like it was on a hanger.

Of course he had changed. She had too. It had been almost two years since they'd buried the baby girl who had been their reason for marrying in the first place. Almost two years since that dreadful night when, numb in her grief, she'd screamed at him to leave and never come back.

Jonty moved first, shuffling to narrow the distance between them. His cheerful spirit used to fill his whole body, giving him the air of an irrepressible puppy. His slow steps now marked a stark contrast to the man she'd married. She worried she might knock him over.

His eyes searched hers, so intense she glanced at the ground to avoid them. "I'm glad you came, Katie-my-love."

She hadn't heard that in two years. Her throat tightened. She stiffened, fighting against the swirl of feelings inside her gut. She didn't realize how much she'd missed the way he'd run the words together as though they were all part of her name. Like his love, the nickname hadn't grown from anywhere. It was the result of his decision and determination—like stating a fact.

"Hello, Jonty."

She tried her best to smile but wasn't sure if she managed it. She'd conceived possible things to say last night as she'd lain awake next to her younger sister. Practiced them under her breath as they'd trooped through the rubble to get from their home in Hackney to King's Cross. But none of them came to her dry mouth now.

A smile stretched over his thin face, and he reached out to take her hand. She flinched and pulled away out of instinct, but also because she didn't want to do this in front of her mother and siblings. Jonty held his smile in place, despite the disappointment flickering in his eyes.

Mum had grabbed her youngest brother by the ear and dragged him over to say hello to Jonty, with Davy following be- hind. Tim struggled, until his eyes landed on Jonty. He stilled, eyes wide. He probably didn't remember what Jonty looked like, if he remembered him at all.

"Well, say hello to your new brother then, Timmy."

Tim remained silent, no doubt terrified of the stranger Mum told him to greet as a brother.

"Mum," Katie muttered under her breath, willing her mother to have compassion on Tim. And on Jonty. And quite frankly, on Katie herself.

Jonty defused the tension by holding his hand out to Tim. "Tim, isn't it? You were so young last time I saw you. And now look at you. Almost a grown man. And you must be Davy." He repeated the compliments to her other sibling.

She watched their expressions change from fear to awe, even

if they were too scared to speak.

She bit the inside of her lip, relaxing enough to move. It had been so long since she had thought about the future with any hope that she didn't even try to now. "It's good to have you home."

She tried with all her heart to mean what she said.

He should be dead.

He knew it. He'd even wished for it.

But somehow, incredibly, he was still here.

In the last five years, since joining the Royal Air Force on little more than a whim, he'd crash-landed twice. Three times, if he counted the occasion his pilot friend had landed without elevator control. He'd almost burned to death and, more recently, failed to succumb to both starvation and infection. And that was saying nothing about the fact that he flew every mission in the most exposed part of the aircraft.

Yet here he was. The most ludicrously lucky, statistically un-likely rear gunner to ever serve in the RAF.

Jonty had no idea why God had chosen to allocate him more than his fair share of fortunate escapes and near misses, when plenty of chaps didn't get any. But the Almighty must have a reason for wanting Jonty to grace the face of this earth. Now that he was being demobilized, he had to figure out what that reason was. Which was why he'd written to Katie.

She'd been adamant last time he'd seen her that she wanted nothing to do with him. She'd told him to leave, forcefully and at the top of her lungs. He only had himself to blame for that.

Nearly two years had passed, and he had to see if she had changed her mind. So he'd given her a choice. *Meet me at the station if you think there's any future for us.*

And here she was.

"Hello, Katie-my-love."

Chaps in the Royal Air Force had pictures of their sweethearts to kiss every night. But he'd only had memories—ones that played tricks on him during the hungry, dark hours before dawn. The Katie in his dreams was plump, even when she was sad or angry at him, but the one in front of him was thin, with hollow cheeks and hard angles across her face. Her waist, which had thickened during her pregnancy, now seemed even tinier than when he'd first met her.

"Hello, Jonty. It's good to have you home."

He chose to believe she meant it. He bent his head, attempting to catch the eyes she cast around, focusing on anything but him. She turned away then, and he followed the direction of her gaze.

Ah, her mother was here. As if this reunion didn't have enough pressure, she'd added his watchful mother-in-law to the mix. "You brought your mother?"

Martha Baines held one of Katie's younger siblings by the ear, watching them keenly, as though they were a puzzle she was determined to solve.

"She insisted." Katie looked at him then, directly in the eye. "She said that if you were going to live under the same roof as her, she wanted to make sure you hadn't become the savage, murdering kind while you were gone." She dropped her voice, and he saw the genuine question in her eyes. "You haven't, have you?"

"Not that I know of. But then if I had, I don't think I'd be likely to admit it."

Her lips tipped up at the joke. Not quite a smile. Just a softening of her delicate mouth. A hint that she might smile at him again. One day.

"Come on. We have to walk."

She reached for his duffel bag, like he was some kind of invalid who needed his wife waiting on him hand and foot. He scooped it up before she could lay a hand on it.

They walked in silence from the station, ahead of her mother and brothers. The wrinkle in Katie's brow told him about the myriad of feelings swirling just under the surface. Perhaps his face told the same story.

As they strolled across the railway station overpass, with the gentle wind tickling their legs and the acrid smell of the train's engines strong in their nostrils, he glanced down at the other re-unions taking place. Not all were as sterile as his. Some women wept with joy. Some men too, he suspected, although they quickly wiped the tears away. Some couples clung to each other, while others walked arm in arm.

Katie trained her eyes to the ground, her golden hair tucked neatly behind her ears. His hand itched to reach for hers, to find some kind of connection with her, some place to start. But he didn't. He was scared that she would snatch her hand away again.

Scared.

He huffed out a laugh. What a strange thing to be scared of after everything he'd gone through during the war.

His laugh caused her to finally look at him. "Do you think I passed your mother's test? Will she have me under her roof?"

She frowned. "There is nowhere else. As it is, half the houses in the street aren't fit to be lived in after Hitler pointed doodle-bugs directly at us." Annoyance colored her tone, making her next comment snippy. "An air force barracks is the height of lux-ury compared to Hackney at the moment."

He sighed. This was not how he wanted his first conversation with her to go. He reverted to chitchat in an attempt to close the gulf between them. He might as well have commented on the weather.

"Is your whole family still at home?"

She shook her head. "Will and George died last year. We got word just before Christmas. Two telegrams at once. I've never seen my mother weep like that."

He wished he hadn't asked, but at least he knew and wouldn't blunder about asking where her brothers were. Katie pushed the few golden strands of her hair that had fallen from their fastenings behind her ears.

A sudden memory of another set of golden strands, these ones caked with blood, made his heart rate pick up. His breathing quickened. He tried to fight against it. This moment might not have been going well, but he didn't want to ruin it completely.

He closed his eyes and gritted his teeth, concentrating on driving out the ghost of the dead girl who seemed to have followed him back to England.

"Are you all right, Jonty?"

His mother-in-law's voice drew him out of the memory. He must have stopped while Katie paced on ahead, so that her mother and brothers caught up to him.

Forcing his lips into an apologetic smile, he fell in step next to Martha. He suspected Martha Baines once had the same English-rose prettiness as Katie. They shared similar blue eyes, though Martha's had a weariness to them. He remembered the way she had looked at him in those days after Betty was born, as though she were continually assessing him, though for what he wasn't sure.

She gave him the same look now. "No one is the same after the war." She looked toward Katie, who was just now realizing Jonty wasn't at her side. "You'll be rebuilding . . . so get your foundations right this time."

Foundations? Did his marriage to Katie even have foundations? It was built on a lie. He didn't have time to ask what she meant.

Katie returned to his side, and Martha went ahead with the boys. He reached out and took her hand. She stiffened, so that it felt like grasping a cold set of sticks.

"We'll find a way to begin, Katie-my-love."

She nodded, but she didn't relax for the rest of the walk home.

CHAPTER TWO

"It's getting late. Do you think Dad will be here?"

Katie set the chipped plates on the dining table, leaning toward her sister to ask the question. Lucy set a mismatched knife, fork, and spoon next to each of the plates.

Lucy shrugged, gold hair tickling her shoulders. They were so similar in looks, but the four years of age might very well be four decades, as far as Katie was concerned. Lucy seemed so young. Too young to be getting married herself in a few weeks.

"Dad usually comes home when there's bacon to be had, doesn't he?"

Katie's mouth watered at the mention of bacon. Mum had begun holding it back as soon as she'd heard Jonty was returning, and the aroma now permeated the house. The savory smell of the warm air in the kitchen told them that even though their setting had seen better days, their meal would be worth waiting for. Liver and tripe were both so much nicer when bacon was involved.

"Did you tell Dad today was the day?"

"Yes." Katie nodded, adjusting the position of a plate to make sure nine settings would fit around the small table. "But he hasn't been around much lately."

She hadn't seen Dad for days. But no matter how meager the rations, they always cooked for him and never ate his portion, just in case he came home unexpectedly and demanded it. Tonight, dinner would go one of three ways. Her father might not come home. Then they would likely have a jolly dinner together. That had happened often enough in the past. Sometimes for days on end. She tried not to wonder where he was, since Mum was happiest when he was gone.

Her father might return home happy. He influenced the mood of every room he was in, and if he took it upon himself to be charismatic and charming, then the meal would be a delight.

But there was another possibility. Her father might come home in a mood. In that case, nothing would appease him. He might hold in his temper for Jonty's sake. But if he reined himself in tonight, things were bound to be worse in the week ahead. The longer he simmered, the louder he boiled.

"You've got guts, you know? To take Jonty back after all this time."

"Not really. I figure we all need a second chance now that the war is over."

"Just like Mum."

"What's that meant to mean?"

"She's always taking Dad back. No matter what he does."

Katie set down another plate and glanced through the doorway into the sitting room, where Jonty sat with her brothers. "Jonty's not like Dad."

Jonty was definitely not like Dad. Where Jonty sat on the sofa with her brothers, Dad mostly ignored his remaining sons. But there Jonty was admiring the Spitfire that twelve-year-old Dennis, the oldest of the four, had made. He and Charlie, two years younger, would disappear for hours on end to scavenge for good whittling wood in the rubble of bomb-damaged houses in the blocks around their little Hackney street.

As the oldest boy, Dennis took it upon himself to manage conversation with the scarred man who'd suddenly come to live with them. The younger two sat, terrified to speak. But she could see Jonty winning the others over with winks. Lucy's voice only barely distracted Katie from the scene in the next room.

"Well, you don't look happy that he's back."

"Of course I'm happy." Katie sounded snippy, even to her own ears. She didn't blame Lucy for raising her eyebrows in a look that said *I don't believe you.*

Lucy shook off the expression and stood back to admire the set table with a satisfied smile. "When Matthew and I are married, I am going to set the table for him like this every night."

"When you and Matthew are married, you'll be living in his mother's house same as me and Jonty live in this one," Katie snapped.

Lucy stuck out her tongue. The tone of their sisterly conversation could always turn quickly, as one got on the other's nerves. When they were little, two brothers had acted as a buffer between them. Not anymore. Lucy's carefree happiness reminded Katie too much of the silly girl she had once been. It niggled Katie even more since Lucy had become engaged to a boy from the same street.

"I'm just saying, you could always wait until there was a house for you to move into."

Despite giving over her evenings to sewing everything Lucy might need for her married life, Katie disapproved of Lucy's quick engagement. Katie had kept a close eye on Lucy's waist since the announcement but didn't see any signs that Lucy was marrying for the same reason Katie had.

"You've got no right to judge, Katie."

They stared at each other, but before either could say something they regretted, Mum announced her return from a neighbor's, struggling through the back door with an additional chair to complete the hodgepodge setting.

"I borrowed this from Mrs. G. I think it will do nicely."

They didn't have enough chairs of their own to seat that many people around the table at the same time and normally took shifts to eat. Younger children first, then adults. The other furnishings were as unpredictable as her father's personality. Not that Katie would dare say that aloud. Sometimes he bought Mum extravagant gifts—likely off the black market, although they didn't mention that. Sometimes he took things away out of spite.

Martha pushed the borrowed chair into its place and stood back to survey the table. She glanced at the back door and nodded to herself. "Well, we can't wait any longer. Tell the boys dinner is ready. And Jonty." Mum spoke Jonty's name like she was trying to work out where he would fit in the family.

"I'll get the cake," Lucy chimed. They'd pooled the family's sugar and butter coupons for the cake, and everyone was excited by the thought of eating it. Lucy placed it on the table as a centerpiece.

Katie poked her head into the next room and invited everyone to the table. The boys leaped up and ran for the kitchen. Jonty moved more slowly. His leg was noticeably stiff after sitting for so long.

"Your dad's not joining us?" Jonty asked as he passed her into the kitchen.

"We haven't seen him for a few days now. But I did tell him today was the day."

Jonty lingered in the nearness forced by the doorway, studying her face. She couldn't properly meet his eye but was all too aware of the rosemary-laced scent of his cologne. Her stomach twisted, so she glanced toward the table. Katie fumed when she saw pieces broken off from the rim of the cake.

"Which one of you boys has been nibbling at the cake?"

All four stared up from where they sat with guilty faces.

"Team effort, was it?"

With no icing to disguise the imperfections, they'd decorated the cake with flowers. Katie rearranged them now to cover the evidence of wrongdoing. "Why don't you sit opposite Mum, Jonty?"

They always kept the seat at the head of the table for her father, whether or not he was there. She took a seat on the opposite side of the table, next to her mother.

"Would you give thanks, Katie?"

Katie recited the standard prayer, forcing herself to feel the words. She added a sentence of thanks for bringing Jonty safely home. When she opened her eyes, she met Jonty's, which had brightened with a soft smile.

"So what will you do next, Jonty?" Mum piled a plate high with tripe and liver hot pot laced with bacon and topped with mashed potato. Honeyed carrots and parsnips, beans, bread, and more potatoes filled out the meal. Instead of handing the plate to the guest of honor, Mum stashed it in the still-warm oven before returning to the table to serve Jonty, then the boys, then Lucy and Katie. Mum always went last, even if it meant she only got scraps.

"Not sure. I go to the demobilization center next week, so perhaps I'll get a clearer idea then. I made furniture before the war, so there's always that. We have a great need for furniture makers in London right now, I think."

"Katie has a new job." Dennis blurted out the information. "She works with the toffs now. Soon she'll be too good for all of us."

She glared at her brother, then met Jonty's questioning gaze. "I haven't had a chance to tell you." Of course she hadn't. Their sparse exchanges in the last few hours had been nothing but practical and anything but private. "I was working at the hat factory, but last month I started with a seamstress in Mayfair."

"Mayfair? Really? That's impressive."

Her face warmed. It had been dreadfully hard to get Madame

Martin to take Katie seriously when she'd applied, and she was still unsure if her self-taught stitches were good enough to meet her employer's exacting demands.

"I didn't even know you could sew."

"I only learned recently. After Betty died." Every stitch she made in a garment, big or small, was an attempt to stitch life back together and mend the gaping tear in her heart.

"Ah. Well, you always had the fastest fingers in the armory, Katie-my-love. I'm not surprised you turned them to sewing."

"She's very good," Lucy added, perhaps to cover the awkwardness between Katie and Jonty. "You should see the things she makes at work—"

Katie elbowed her sister in the ribs before she could say more. Jonty did not need to be told about the delicate underthings she sewed each day for the rich women of Mayfair. Not at the dinner table with her brothers listening in.

"Well, maybe you won't have to work so hard, now that I am home."

Her face fell. Was he going to be one of those husbands who couldn't cope with the indignation of his wife earning money? She didn't mind that she sewed all day, then came home and sewed into the evening. Apart from the strain on her eyes, which sometimes gave her headaches, she loved any moment she could create beautiful things with a needle and thread.

"I like the work, Jonty."

The dinner table was not the time to explain just how much she enjoyed her work, but Jonty seemed to sense she had more to say. He'd always been good at knowing she had more going on under the surface than she let on. When he gave a single Scottish nod, she wished for the same powers to know what he was thinking.

The conversation slid through to safer topics. The complicated end of the war now that Germany was defeated, though Japan was still an enemy. Whether Mr. Clement Attlee would oust the beloved Mr. Churchill in today's election, and if he did, would his radical plans be fair for the whole country? Plates quickly emptied. Every plate except her own. Nerves prevented her from eating more than a nibble.

The creak of the back gate sounded, changing the mood in the room. The boys sat straighter in their chairs. Lucy paled. Mum scurried to the oven to retrieve the plate she'd left there to warm. Dad was home.

He'd always been on his best behavior during the handful of times Jonty had spent with him. Should she warn Jonty what he was really like? Too late now. Katie's stomach tightened in anticipation. The remaining bacon on her plate lost its appeal.

Dad appeared, framed in the doorway, reminding her that though he seemed like a giant of a man in her mind, he was actually only an inch or so taller than her. The family froze in place as Dad surveyed the scene.

"So you're home!"

Jonty's skin tingled with the collective hold of breath. He glanced at Katie, whose eyes were glued on the man in the doorway.

"Jonty's come home, Bill. Isn't it wonderful?" Martha opened the oven.

Jonty couldn't decide the exact tone in her voice. Was she warning her husband or placating him?

"Come and sit down at the table. We didn't know what time you'd be here, so I kept your dinner warm."

Bill rubbed the palms of his hand together before pulling out his chair and sitting down. Martha brought him his plate, carrying it carefully with a tea towel to protect her fingers from the heat.

"This looks like a week's worth of bacon. Have you been scrimping this week?"

"Saving it, Bill." Martha resumed her seat and took up her knife and fork. She didn't meet her husband's eyes.

"What's the occasion?" Bill jerked his head toward the cake.

"Jonty's homecoming, Dad. Remember?" Katie kept her tone light.

Bill shoved his fork into the food, lifted it to his mouth, and ate in silence.

"Jonty was just about to tell us about his plans, weren't you, Jonty?" Lucy skillfully moved the conversation along.

Was he? Jonty glanced around at Katie and her family, unable to recall exactly what he'd been saying before the mood around the table had shifted.

He'd met Bill before, of course. Jonty thought him amiable and easy to get along with. But the man at the head of the table seemed fixated on his food. Maybe he was just hungry.

Jonty saw Katie flick questioning eyes at her mother, who gave the smallest shrug in return. Their minuscule communication went unnoticed at the head of the table.

The sound of Bill's eating filled the room. "Are you not going to eat?" Bill eventually looked over his empty plate to Katie's half-full one.

She seemed to have lost her appetite.

"I'll get you some more bread, Bill." Martha rose to take Bill's plate.

"If she's not going to eat it, I'll have it." Without ceremony, Bill grabbed Katie's plate and began shoveling the food into his mouth.

His younger boys looked on enviously.

"Why don't you boys run along into the next room and turn on the wireless?" Martha said.

"But there's still cake to come."

"Go into the sitting room, boys! I'll call you when your father is ready for cake."

Martha's light tone held a sharp edge that was enough to send the younger boys scampering out of the room. Dennis lingered in the doorway, as though he wanted to stay with the grown-ups. Jonty sent him a wink, letting him know it was all right for him to go.

"So what are your plans, then?"

Was Bill speaking to him?

"Are you going to take Katie off my hands for good this time?"

Katie said nothing at the dig clearly intended for her. She simply reached for a glass, concentrating too hard on the stream of water from the jug as she poured.

The penny dropped. The women were treading carefully, waiting to determine Bill's mood. If Katie had warned Jonty, he would have been able to identify what was going on. The uncle who'd raised him was the worst kind of drunk. Oh yes, he knew all about shutting up and keeping still so as not to upset the master of the house. Jonty pulled a bland, inoffensive mask across his features.

"We won't be in your hair much longer, sir." Jonty offered Bill deference that he didn't deserve, knowing that if Bill felt important, it would help his mood. "Katie and I appreciate your kindness."

Katie smiled weakly at Jonty as a thank-you for keeping the peace, even if he spoke for her while doing it.

"I didn't think you'd come back for her."

Katie looked like she had been slapped as she stared at the place on the table where her plate had been. Her cheeks burned, but she didn't speak.

"Bill, you don't mean that! Of course he was always going to come back." Martha delivered her rebuke in a way that made the man's claim seem frivolous.

Since Katie wouldn't lift her eyes from the tablecloth, Jonty couldn't take his cue from her. He'd keep up the deferential play-acting. However, he needed Katie to know he was on her side in all this. No matter what. His eyes didn't leave her as he spoke.

"Of course, Katie's the love of my life, sir. I'll never leave her."

From this moment on, he meant to make good on those vows they'd made. Her father obviously didn't cherish her, but Jonty most certainly would.

An urgent knock sounded from the front door, cutting through the tension at the table, making all the women jump.

"Goodness me." Martha made light of the fright by laying a hand on her chest. "Who could that be at this time? Katie, you're closest. Would you mind seeing who it is?"

Katie hurried to the door, no doubt happy to have a chance to compose herself after her father's humiliation. Bill, Jonty noticed, didn't move a muscle. While Jonty couldn't see Katie at the front door, he heard the excitement in her voice.

"Jan! It's been so long since we've seen you! Come in."

A stark contrast to the greeting he'd received at the station earlier in the day. He also noticed how Bill's frown inverted when he heard who the guest was. The boys in the sitting room all scurried to the door to greet the visitor with happy cheers.

"Come through. Let me introduce you to my husband," Katie said.

"Husband?"

A male voice followed Katie into the kitchen, and before long its owner did too. A handsome man with blond coloring and pale-blue eyes, in an air force uniform. Jonty immediately sized him up from the insignia he wore. Officer stripes on the sleeve and "Poland" badged on his right shoulder.

Jonty knew half his story. The men of the Polish Air Force had flown valiantly over Britain in 1940 when the RAF had been exhausted by the German attacks. Their skill and the passion with which they'd fought had played a decisive role in England's victory in those early years of battle. The other half of his story—and why Katie was lit up like a Christmas tree—was still a mystery to him.

After a chorus of hellos, Katie introduced the newcomer.

"Jonty, this is our friend Jan Delovski. Jan, this is my husband, Jonty Ables. Jan is the nephew of Mrs. Grabowski next door, but we've sort of adopted him as our brother."

He couldn't help the stern, Scottish frown that took over his features. This Jan had brought a very different color to his wife's cheeks than she'd had moments ago. An excited flush, he'd call it, if forced to be poetic. And the rest of the family seemed overjoyed to see him too. The spark of jealousy was unreasonable, but he failed to quash it.

Jonty stood and held out his hand, unable to shake the frown. "Jan, is it?"

Jan took Jonty's hand and shook it with an eager smile. The kind of eager smile that Jonty usually had but couldn't manage right at the moment.

"I'm very glad to meet you," Jan replied with a soft Polish accent. "I'm sorry to interrupt your celebration."

"Will you join us? We were about to have cake."

It shouldn't annoy Jonty so much that Katie asked the question. After all, he'd been about to offer the same.

Jan glanced between Katie, Jonty, and the cake on the table, then smiled apologetically. "I can't. But I would like a word with you privately, Katie." Jan turned to Jonty. "Is that all right with you?"

Jonty fought the frown rapidly becoming permanently affixed to his face. Who was this man? First he crashed Jonty's party, and now he wanted to take off with his wife! One glance at Katie told Jonty she wouldn't think kindly if he refused Jan's request. So Jonty forced a nod.

Jan took Katie into the sitting room by the elbow and spoke to her in a low voice that didn't travel back to the kitchen. But he could see well enough through the doorway. See the intimacy between the pair. The friendship. The trust. The closeness. The connection. All the things he'd had with his wife once. All things that had dissolved like dreams upon waking after Betty had died.

He told himself not to watch, but not before he saw Jan pass Katie a small packet. A gift? She certainly shook her head in the way women sometimes did if they were overwhelmed by the idea of a gift being bestowed. If it was a gift, she didn't unwrap it. She didn't even thank him. Instead he seemed to thank her. Jonty's insides sank as he watched Jan take Katie's hand and press it to his lips like some kind of knight of old.

And not brotherly at all.

He glanced down at his plate, only to look straight up again when he heard the door open and shut. Jan had gone, and Katie stood, clutching her package and looking bewildered. She hurried over to the basket that contained her sewing things and placed the package in the basket before covering it with her current project.

She didn't meet his eye when she returned to the table.

"He couldn't stay." She murmured the excuse.

"What did he want?" Bill asked.

"He just wanted to say goodbye. He's going away for a bit."

"That's what that was, was it?" The gruff suspicion in his own voice caught Jonty by surprise. He sounded like Bill. Katie obviously thought so too, because she met his eye with a wounded look.

Martha took it upon herself to distract everyone. "Let's have cake, shall we?"

CHAPTER THREE

"So."

Jonty closed the bedroom door but stayed beside the doorframe, surveying the distance between himself and his wife, despite the small bedroom. He'd washed his hands and face and changed into his RAF-issued pajamas. Katie perched on the bed, studying him like a wary cat ready to pounce out of harm's way.

Her gold hair was fixed in a braid over her shoulder. She'd tied her dressing gown tight around her waist. One hand, knuckles white, clamped it closed at the neck. She kept her eyes trained on the floor, as though preparing for the worst.

After they'd all listened to the disappointing news on the wireless that the results of today's election couldn't be called until votes from citizens overseas were counted, Martha had insisted they take the room she would normally share with Bill. So they could get reacquainted, she'd said. When Katie had declined with wide, fearful eyes, Jonty had said he wouldn't dream of kicking Martha out of her bed. Still, Martha had insisted. So here they were.

"So. What happens now?"

A look of horror and perhaps even terror crossed her face, as though she was having visions of him being some kind of brute.

He hurried to reassure her. "No, not that Katie. I mean, what happens with us? Do you still want to be married to me?"

She raised her chin a little higher. She'd always had a beautiful, defiant chin. "I turned up at the station, didn't I?"

True.

That was what he'd asked her to do in his letter. To show up at the platform to meet him if she still saw a future with him. It had seemed simple in his mind. They could go to a restaurant, have some tea, and discuss the future. An echo of his first proposal. If they resolved to call it quits, then he would simply find accommodation elsewhere. He hadn't expected her family to be there.

"I'm grateful you did, Katie-my-love." He frowned, knowing that now was the time to give the apology he'd practiced almost every day over the last two years. "I'm sorry for that night." Color rose in her cheeks, proving she knew exactly what he was talking about. "I will do just about anything to make it up to you."

She nodded. Despite the color in her face, she kept her eyes on his. "I'm sorry too. I didn't mean what I said that night. It was awful of me to say it."

His throat tightened. How much heartbreak would they have saved themselves from if they could have managed this conversation two years ago.

He took the few steps toward the bed and sat next to her, enough space between them that she wouldn't feel like he expected something. For want of words, he sighed. "Everything has turned out very differently to how I expected it would when we met at that café in Bottesford. Do you remember?"

She nodded, eyes trained on the floor now.

He was alive, for one. And there was no baby.

They'd been friends once. More than that, they'd been allies, conspiring to hide their secret from the world. In those precious months before Betty was born, he'd thought a fragile love had blossomed. It just wasn't strong enough to survive what had come next.

Now a gaping chasm sat between their hearts. Perhaps it was too poetic to describe it that way, but that was how it felt. So far away from where they were, who they were, in the beginning.

"But back then, we were friends. Do you think we can start that way again now?"

A deep frown line cut into her forehead as she took his words literally, giving them serious thought. Just as her silence was becoming too heavy, she gave her answer. "Yes, Jonty. I think we can start again as friends."

He sighed out the breath he must have been holding. She gave the smallest, most strained smile Jonty had ever seen. Katie had once smiled easily. The act transformed her face, lighting it up. The Polish man, Jan, had brought on a smile like that earlier this evening. Jonty determined then and there to make her smile like that at him. One day. Somehow.

He reached across, took her hand, and squeezed it, which had the opposite effect to the one he had been intending.

She stiffened and shrank away. "Just friends, Jonty." Her voice came out tight and small. And scared.

How he wished he could turn back time and do things differently in those days after Betty had died. That was impossible, so he just had to embrace the second chance she had given him.

He nodded. "Just friends. I promise that I willna ask for more." He couldn't help his Scottish brogue from slipping out. He wouldn't ask. He wouldn't press her. But he dearly hoped that in time the beautiful woman in front of him would one day want to give herself to him.

He cleared his throat and dropped her hand. "I'll sleep on the floor, shall I?"

She nodded and leaped up, pulling the blankets with her to make him a cot on the floor.

"You don't have to go to any trouble." He grimaced, remembering the place he had slept while hiding in France. Wooden floorboards would be luxury compared to the cramped dampness of a cellar. But she seemed to want to stay busy, so he let her.

"So who was the man who visited tonight? Jan, wasn't it?"

Her fussing movements slowed ever so slightly before picking up their pace. "Mrs. G's nephew. And he's become close to our family."

"Does he call in often?"

"Only when he's in London seeing his aunt. He's usually based in Norwich."

Jonty vaguely recalled hearing that the Polish squadrons were now based out there while they waited for news about whether or not they could return home. But Norwich wasn't that far away. Why did the man need to give Katie a special goodbye? Suspicion burned as he recalled the intimacy the man had with her. He fought internally to calm it.

"What did he give you?"

"What do you mean?"

Jonty frowned. The bed on the floor didn't need the focused attention she was giving it. Was she avoiding his eye?

"He gave you a package of some sort. I saw from the kitchen."

She finally met his eye, only to lie to his face. "It was nothing. Just something he asked me to keep safe for him."

"Keep safe? So are you two close?" He thought to ask the question delicately, but it probably came out as an accusation.

She understood his meaning well enough. "It's not like that."

"What's it like, then?" He sounded petulant, even to his own ears, but he couldn't stop himself.

"It's not 'like' anything!" She held his gaze as he waited for her explanation. "He's just a friend."

The color in her cheeks told him there was more to the story.

"Friend. Is he?"

They'd used that word too. But he didn't want to fight. In

fact, it had been a long day, and suddenly all he wanted was sleep. "Well, good night then, Katie."

As she slipped into the bed, he sank onto the floor, pulling the blanket up to his chin and facing away from her.

"Good night, Jonty."

Katie fidgeted with the blanket she had pulled up to her chin, despite it being a warm evening.

Alberta Beeson, at number six, had claimed she was more nervous when her husband returned from France than on her wedding night. It was a good comparison because, in the end, it was just like Katie's own wedding night. Jonty had said a gruff and awkward good night, then prepared his bed on the floor.

Only she didn't think that was what Alberta had meant. Sometimes married women spoke in a code Katie didn't completely comprehend, as though she only had some of the pages of the codebook. Of course, she laughed along with whatever knowing remarks her friends made. She understood some parts—she'd had a baby, after all—but it was so hard to know if she had a complete picture, when no one spoke directly about these things. She'd only known a handful of friends in the WAAF who'd willingly spoke plainly about what went on between a husband and wife. That had been her downfall. She'd let Jimmy Hardie fill in the gaps.

Jonty twitched when he finally fell asleep. It was a different kind of sleep than she'd seen before. She rolled on her side to watch him, struggling to recall that first night they'd slept in the same room. On their wedding, the pregnancy had made her so ill she could barely raise her head to notice him. By the end of the pregnancy, she had been too tired to care. And once Betty was born, she had been so consumed by the babe that she couldn't recall how Jonty had slept.

Katie pulled back the covers and tiptoed over him to the door. She turned the handle slowly and slipped through, concentrating on stepping in just the right place so the floorboards didn't creak. She padded down the stairs barefoot. In the kitchen, she ran herself a glass of water, hoping the pipes didn't wake Dad.

Staring at the glass in her hand, she examined her feelings with the kind of depth that only nighttime allowed. After they'd been married, Jonty had proved himself kind and good natured, not temperamental like Dad. He'd promised not to touch her until the baby was born, and kept his word, even as romance blossomed between them during her pregnancy. But Betty's death had turned the world upside down.

A few weeks after they'd buried Betty, Jonty had tried to make love to her. Not violently or forcefully. He'd probably just thought that if they got on with the business of being married, she'd have another baby soon enough. He couldn't know that was at the heart of her fear.

She'd exploded with what must have looked like rage and lambasted him with a tirade of the meanest, cruelest things a wife could say. It was grief talking, but it kept them apart for the best part of two years. He'd deserved none of it. She wanted to make amends, owed it to him. His letter had given her the second chance she didn't know how to ask for. But just because she'd slipped her wedding ring back on and shown up at the station didn't mean she had any idea how to begin again. She kept staring into the water, as though the answer were at the bottom of it.

"Couldn't sleep?"

Transfixed as she was with the bottom of her glass, Katie hadn't heard her mother enter the kitchen from the sitting room. She held a book in her hand, as she often did at this time of night. Mum loved her books and buried herself in them once her evening jobs were done. On nights when Dad wasn't home, she read aloud as the girls sewed. Mum was meant to be sleeping with Lucy tonight in the small bedroom, with Dad sleeping on the sofa. But Katie couldn't see him through the door that joined the rooms.

"I was just thirsty. Where's Dad?"

"Didn't like the idea of sleeping on the sofa, so he's gone out."

Katie nodded. She'd long since given up wondering where Dad went all night. His absence had made sense when he was an air raid precautions warden. But now there wasn't any reason for him to be gone. Still, his comings and goings, long and short, had characterized her childhood. Katie simply accepted the excuses Mum made for him, rather than ask the obvious question: Where did he go?

"Jonty's asleep."

Mum eyed her curiously. Since she didn't say more, Katie turned to leave. But Mum grabbed her arm. She caught Katie's eyes with her own to reinforce the squeeze of her hand. "Jonty is a good man, Katie. You could do much worse."

Katie saw all her mother's own bad choices in that penetrating gaze.

"I know, Mum."

Katie headed back upstairs and slipped into the bedroom. Jonty lay, still twitching, as he had when she'd left the room. She strategized exactly where she would step to get past him to the bed.

"Lily."

Jonty muttered the name just as her foot fell on the other side of him. She froze, unsure what she had heard. Realizing that it would be somewhat compromising—not to mention confusing—for Jonty to wake with her straddling him, she leaped to the bed. "Jonty?"

"Lily." He moaned again, guttural this time. The sound sent a chill through her.

Then the questions started. Questions with no answers bounced around her head in the darkness, stopping sleep even after Jonty resumed a more peaceful slumber.

And that biggest of them all . . . Who was Lily?

CHAPTER FOUR

Monday, 9 July 1945

"Excuse me."

Katie pushed through the rush-hour crowd. She was late for work. An unexploded bomb had needed defusing along the Central line, so she'd had to walk instead of catching the underground. Now, she ran down Regent Street, not caring about the stares from passersby.

"Watch where you're going!"

Katie threw an apology over her shoulder to the posh voice chastising her. She couldn't afford to slow down. Madame Martin had the strictest standards when it came to punctuality—when it came to just about everything, actually. Katie wouldn't disappoint her.

She slowed just before she reached her destination, straightening her hair in the window of a neighboring shop and heaving in some breaths. She wanted to look serene when she entered, not frazzled. Her run had made up time, and thankfully, she was only five minutes late. With another steadying breath, Katie pushed through the front entrance to the sound of the tinkling bell on the door.

Just breathing the air inside Chez Martin thrilled Katie. This wasn't the biggest or the oldest dressmaker in London. In fact, Madame had only relocated from Paris just ahead of the war, gradually growing her business under the most difficult of circumstances until she'd opened this shop a few months ago. But Madame knew how to make her shop seem like the most exclusive in Mayfair.

French perfume engulfed Katie's senses as she entered, and the cares of war-weary London disappeared. Behind the elegant window display—changed weekly to give an impression of decadence, even though they had as little to work with as anywhere else—sat the elegant showroom. The genteel blues and whites of the furnishings were crisp and fresh. Velvet chairs and a low ottoman created a space for customers to sit and enjoy tea while they discussed their needs.

A huge mirror dominated the room, making the small shop seem twice as large as it really was. Madame told customers that the mirror had once adorned a wall in Versailles and that a lover of hers had smuggled it out of France in an act of devotion. Katie doubted the truth of the story, but it certainly added to the glamour. As did the vases of fresh flowers sitting on every available surface. A heavy velvet curtain hid the changing room from the front.

It was the kind of place that a girl from Hackney had no right to be. Something which Madame reminded her about daily. Still, Katie loved her work. More than that, she loved being good at it.

"What time do you call this, Kat-reen?"

Madame Martin looked up from her appointment book, speaking Katie's full name in the French way. Even Madame's narrowed eyes didn't detract from her refined poise. She wore her hair pulled back, and she'd adorned her simple navy-blue dress with just a rose-shaped brooch. Maybe she was as old as Mum, yet she seemed agelessly elegant. Perhaps it was something about the way she stood and moved.

"I'm terribly sorry, Madame. They closed the Central line this morning to clear a bomb."

Katie dropped her usual glottal accent, giving her apology in the one Madame forced her to use. After seeing samples of Katie's work and giving her several tests to ensure that her self-taught skills met Madame's standards, Madame had only held reservations about Katie's background. She'd insisted that having someone in her boutique who sounded like she worked on the docks wouldn't do for the salon's reputation. Especially not when she was desperately aiming to snag the two princesses as customers.

"Can you at least try to be French?" Madame had said.

Katie's posh, born-with-a-silver-spoon-in-her-mouth tone was their compromise. She'd learned it by mimicking her superiors in the WAAF. She constantly reminded herself to use the French pronunciation of her employer's surname and not the English one.

"Well, get upstairs. It's nearly ten o'clock."

That was another of Madame's rules. Her workers must be upstairs before the doors opened for customers. She claimed it spoiled the ambiance to have workers traipsing through the room while she was trying to inspire women to buy her creations. Katie knew, almost by instinct, that Madame did it to maintain the illusion of exclusivity and discretion. While Madame made a show of everything being French downstairs, upstairs skill was all that mattered.

"Yes, Madame."

Katie hurried upstairs to the workrooms. Her three colleagues were already settled into the rhythms of their sewing. As the newest employee, Katie was still trying to find her place and her real friends among the other women.

"Hello, Collette, Françoise. Hello, Alice."

She greeted each by name but was met with silence, so she

murmured a brief apology and went straight to her corner by the window. Customers rarely saw the upstairs, so there was no reason to emulate the plush elegance of downstairs up here. Still, the windows overlooking the bustling street below lit the room well, especially in summer.

Instead of orchids and roses, it smelled like dust and cotton scraps. Not unpleasant—in fact, Katie loved the smell—but definitely not luxurious. This was where all the hard work of creating beautiful items happened. A large table for making patterns or cutting fabrics dominated the center, along with four sewing machines. Shelving, filled with bolts of fabrics and haberdashery supplies, lined the walls.

In front of the shelves sat two dummies displaying their works in progress. One was half-dressed in an elegant suit. The other was clad in the most luxurious nightie Katie had ever seen, made with an elaborate amount of fabric and intricate lace detailing around the scandalously low neck. Katie had been too embarrassed to speak when she'd first learned that almost half the commissions Madame took were for bespoke undergarments, especially when downstairs was completely respectable.

"'Ave you finished the embroidered collar for the French ambassador's wife?" Françoise demanded from her corner near the other window. She and Collette had once worked with Madame in Paris. They usually filled the space with their French chatter, snubbing the others unless they had to talk about work. "Madame was expecting this to be finished yesterday."

"Yes. I have them here."

Katie had stayed late last night to finish them. She scooped them up and carried them to her colleague with a smile, trying not to seem smug. She was just getting to know these girls, after all.

Françoise wiggled her shoulders in irritation but accepted the collar. "What about the neckline for the negligée?"

"Just about to start it."

"The suit is for the French ambassador's wife, but the nightgown is for his mistress," Collette claimed, with a sideways glance at Françoise. She tossed her blond curls over her shoulder. "It must be perfect."

Warmth rose into Katie's face. She wished she didn't blush so easily. Returning to her seat, she glanced at Alice, the quiet Polish girl sitting at the machines. Katie gave a shy smile. Alice might not say much, but she still understood what was going on.

Katie settled into her stitching near one of the windows. She needed the light for her hand sewing. She marveled again at the good fortune of being able to spend her days doing the thing she loved. Having impressed Madame with her embroidery, Katie now spent her days quietly stitching in the sunshine. It was like a dream.

Collette began bickering with Françoise—in English, not French, which meant she intended the other women to understand them. "Whom do you think Madame will ask to measure today? You or me?"

Over in the French corner of the room, as Katie called it in her mind, the women took pride in being the ones invited downstairs to take a client's measurements under Madame Martin's watchful gaze. They took pride in it because only they were ever asked.

"You did it yesterday, Françoise. It's my turn."

Of all the other jobs, Katie envied that one. The measurer got to see patrons enjoy the garments they made up here. They also got to study up close the dresses that clients wore. There were still so many shortages that they often remade old gowns into fashionable styles, and seeing the originals gave no end of inspiration. Katie rolled her eyes playfully at Alice, who grinned, standing up from the machine to do some hand sewing.

"Would you like to work over here? The light is better." Katie invited the softly spoken Alice to sit with her under the window so they could talk while they worked. Françoise and Collette went back to bickering in French as they laid out their work on the big table.

"Alice isn't your real name, is it?" Katie asked. The name belied the girl's thick accent.

"No. It's Alicja." She gave the Polish pronunciation, which wasn't so different, making Katie wonder why she bothered at all to change it.

"From Poland?"

"Yes. I am from the south. Krakow." She gave the Polish pronunciation.

"What is your home like?"

Perhaps they looked like sisters as they worked together. Alice had similar coloring to Katie, although her cheekbones were higher and her features finer. Her fingers, however, were just as fast. Katie had never even left England. In fact, moving north to an airfield in Lincolnshire was the farthest she'd been from Hackney. Even when Jan talked about it, Poland sounded so exotic in comparison.

"It is a beautiful city. But"—Alice's brow furrowed—"I don't know what is left of it now. I left just days before the Germans arrived."

That must have been six years ago, and Alice didn't look older than Lucy. "You must have been only a girl, then."

Alice nodded.

"So will you go home now?"

Katie thought about Jan and the way he talked about his home. He yearned for it deeply. She'd lost count of the number of times he'd mentioned how he worried for the people he'd left behind when the Polish Air Force had evacuated to France and then England ahead of the German advance.

Alice slumped in her seat. "No. It is under Soviet control now. The Germans were bad, but better than the Russians."

Katie had seen the newsreels about the camps being liberated in Germany and doubted what Alice was saying could possibly be true. But when she looked up, she saw the depth of hatred in Alice's young eyes. How could a girl who'd left Poland when she was barely—what, twelve?—feel such passionate hate? Perhaps it went back a generation to Alice's parents. Maybe back another to theirs?

"What? Never?"

Alice shook her head. The weight of her sadness made her seem much older than Katie had originally thought.

"Zat's a cheerful thought, Alice." Françoise's voice rang out across the room, silencing Alice for the rest of the morning.

The war wasn't officially over. But Jonty's war was. And with the joy came no small amount of trepidation.

"Jonathan Ables?"

A smartly dressed volunteer with a Navy, Army and Air Force Institutes badge called out his name, clipboard in hand. Jonty took a few moments to register the name. How long had it been since he'd been called anything other than "Jonty" or "Ables"?

He stood and met her broad smile.

"Come this, way."

He'd arrived at the army facility this morning, with dozens of men in various uniforms, ready for his official demobilization. Strictly speaking, he hadn't jumped the queue. He was Class A like most of the servicemen around him, but according to the *Release and Resettlement* guidebook, his group number, determined by age and length of service, wasn't due to be called until November. His discharge had, in the end, been medical.

He followed the NAAFI woman into the next room and was met with a wholly unexpected sight. Such places were usually characterized by bland efficiency and a whole lot of khaki. But this room had been decorated tastefully, with calming green and cream colors. It felt like a fancy market square, complete with the busyness and bustle that accompanied such places.

He took in a few of the scenes in front of him. Men at tables staffed by pretty girls were perusing leaflets. A display sat to one side with mannequins dressed in suits and trilbies. What looked like a shop counter stood at the far end, staffed with busy shopkeepers handing over essentials.

Still, the room couldn't completely escape its military service, and it held a resemblance to the room where he had enlisted. But that time he'd cycled through cubicles for medical appointments and interviews, not elegant storefronts. Back then, lured by the promise of food, board, and a ticket away from his alcoholic uncle, he'd been given a new identity as an RAF airman. He'd lived it to its fullest potential. Now that identity would be stripped away.

Who would he be once the uniform was gone? He was six years older than the boy who'd strode into the recruiting center, and a married man. He felt the age, even if he didn't feel like he was really married.

"Mr. Ables?"

The NAAFI woman with the clipboard and generous smile called his attention back to her. He noted the flicker of sympathy in her eyes as she took a closer look at his scars, but she was obviously practiced at this. She covered the disgust she likely felt with a smile.

He was grateful. Not everyone avoided gaping. Even if they kept their mouths closed, there was always something about the way they looked at him that reminded him of his disfigurement—a short breath in, a brief pause. In the worst cases, the person fumbled, so distracted by his appearance that they couldn't continue their train of thought.

"So this is where it ends?" he murmured, perhaps to the NAAFI woman, perhaps to himself.

"That's right. We won."

He nodded. But what happened next? Whatever it was, it would be the result of his decision, not because of an order from a superior. The thought of such freedom sent a wave of terror through him. Or was it delight? Sometimes it was hard to tell.

"Let me talk you through what happens today. First you'll get a whole new kit! See here?"

She had undoubtedly said that line hundreds of times, but

he appreciated the way the smile in her dark-brown eyes made it seem new and just for him. She guided him to the display of mannequins in front of several posters that explained his choices for new civilian clothing.

Choice! Now there was a strange concept for a man who had spent the last six years doing what he was told, when he was told, in the uniform he was told to wear.

"After we get the clothing sorted, I'll explain about ration books, identity cards, benefits, and the rest. Now, does anything here catch your eye?"

He'd never experienced such courtesy inside a military barracks, and the strange feeling tipped his mouth into a frown.

She hurried on in her explanation. "What kind of work do you do? As you can see from the display, you can choose a double-breasted suit or a single-breasted one with trousers, whatever is best for your work. They're made by the best tailors. Some of the men here also work on Savile Row! You also get two shirts and collars, a tie, shoes, a raincoat, and hat. Oh, and ninety clothing coupons."

"Ninety clothing coupons! My wife will be delighted."

Having spent a week in a house with three women planning a wedding, he was well aware of the outrage caused by the rumor that a new government might cut the clothes ration. Even Katie, a brilliant seamstress, claimed she could barely manage with thirty-six coupons a year. His chest expanded a little with the idea that he might bring something home to make her happy.

The NAAFI woman's brown eyes flashed her appreciation too. "I'm sure she will be. So you have some choices to make—what would you like?"

"Can I choose blue?"

That color had served him well for the last few years. Rumor had it that RAF uniforms were gray-blue because, at the end of the last war, some warehouse or another had stored a huge stock of material ordered for the tzar of Russia's cavalry before it was thrown over by the Bolsheviks. They'd offered it to the RAF at discount prices. Secretly, Jonty thought it had been designed by someone who knew the power of clothing to keep up morale during wartime. What man wouldn't feel courageous when women looked at him the way they did in the blue uniform?

"Of course. Come this way." She escorted him toward a side room but stopped at the door. "Mr. Hawkes will measure you for your fit in here."

He stepped into the room, where several mirrors stood in front of men in their underthings, attended to by men in civilian clothes, measuring tapes in hand.

Mr. Hawkes, he assumed, approached him. "Through here, sir." The man guided Jonty into a makeshift cubicle to remove his clothes.

How strange. Privacy and politeness weren't normally a consideration in the military.

While the tailor did his work, Jonty gave the skinny man in the mirror a rueful stare. The scars on his neck and shoulder were on full display, as well as the one on his leg. The tailor didn't mention anything about it. No doubt he'd seen worse things when once-wounded men were in their underwear.

He didn't often take the time to look at himself top to toe. He'd trained himself out of caring about his appearance, but he took in the full impact of it now. The whole left side of his face looked melted. When he smiled, the reconstructed skin pulled, making him look like a lopsided freak. The other side wasn't as bad, where his ear and neck were more damaged than his face. And that was to say nothing of the still-red scar wrapping around his left shin. And the ugly one on his hip. At least he could hide those two.

Jonty sighed as he dressed. There would be no more admiring glances for him, even with the blue. The war had torn away at him body and soul.

When he arrived in the main market space again, the NAAFI woman continued her practiced explanation. "So that's your suit done. There are a few other optional items if you need them. You can order them at the counter over here."

She pointed to the store-like setup. The shelves behind the counter stocked gloves, underwear, socks, vests, and scarves. He'd better take what he could. Other men might return to families who'd kept all their son's personal belongings safe, desperately hoping he'd be needing them again. But Jonty had nothing. And though Katie was more than capable, he didn't know if she would want to knit and sew anything for him.

"Do you smoke? Because we have cigarettes too."

Jonty said he did, but only because the cigarettes might help smooth things over with Bill when he returned to the house. He hadn't come home since Jonty's first night in Hackney.

"Now I have forms for you to sign, and when your clothes are ready, we exchange your uniform for civilian clothing. Nancy, over there"—she pointed to a young girl in a red cardigan behind a table stacked with leaflets—"will give you information on the job opportunities. And then there's tea over there." She indicated a petite girl with her back turned to them as she poured out amber liquid from an oversized pot. "My advice: Don't skip the tea. You never know who you'll meet. Now read this."

She handed him a document printed with an Air Ministry seal.

"Can you tell me where I sign?"

She pointed to the space marked with a line at the bottom of the page, and Jonty wrote his initials carefully.

"You forgot the date."

"Can you fill it in?" Jonty waved his hand over the paper. Better that she do it herself than he suffer the humiliation of her seeing just how hard he found the reading.

He headed toward the desk with the leaflets. The girl in the red cardigan, whose curly hair bobbed on her shoulders, greeted him. "We have plenty of information here about jobs and the like. Where would you like to start?" She held out both palms at the many stacks.

This would be tricky. There was nothing else apart from the

title to tell one from another. It wasn't that he couldn't read the titles—it was that it still took him such a long time to sound out the letters. He didn't want to do that right here.

"Where do you suggest I start?" He gave what he hoped was a winning smile, but it felt a little less persuasive without his blue uniform to back him up.

"Well, what did you do before you enlisted?"

"Carpentry."

"We certainly have a need for those! Why don't you take these and read them with a cup of tea?" She winked, gathered up three leaflets, and handed them to him.

He glanced in the direction she indicated. What was it with these ladies and tea? Still, he could do with a cup. It wouldn't be laced with rum, like the stuff they gave you at Bomber Command, but he was sure it would do the trick.

Leaflets in hand, he made his way over to the petite woman who had been struggling with the huge teapot when he arrived. Only a girl, no more than sixteen. As he caught sight of her features for the first time, a terrible flash of memory invaded his mind.

A young girl like this.

Same age. Same hair. Same delicate features.

But not pouring tea in a community hall.

This one was a farm girl.

He could almost hear her in his ears now.

Screaming in terror.

Begging for her life.

He blinked away the thought as his breath quickened.

But the blinking didn't help. He simply opened his eyes to a new, more horrifying vision of her with a red-rimmed bullet hole in her forehead.

He tried to get his breathing under control, knowing how stupid he would look hyperventilating here. But couldn't manage it.

The leaflets fluttered to the ground as he fled.

CHAPTER FIVE

After the debacle at the demobilization center, Jonty hoped for more at the employment office. He sat in a queue with several other men, all dressed in suits like his. All looking for a new purpose now that the war was done.

Not completely, the newspaper headlines reminded him. Japan seemed to want to drag things out to the bitter end.

When he had his turn at the desk, he ran the woman through his work experience.

"And you were conscripted?"

"Enlisted early."

Enlisting had meant he could choose his service, and the RAF had been the clear winner in his mind. He'd seen plenty of men broken by their time in the army during the last war. He never even considered the navy.

He still remembered the satisfaction of dropping the news on his uncle like it was yesterday.

"Traitor!" Uncle Hamish had roared. Of course he would

only think about himself, and his own loss, and not the greater problem of an imminent Nazi invasion of Europe.

"Any skills? Apart from"—she consulted the papers before her—"being an air gunner?"

"Carpentry." He'd been taken out of school and put to work as an apprentice from the age of twelve. *Apprentice* was the kind word for it. *Slave* was the other one. But at least he'd learned a trade. "We need a few of those at the moment, I think."

"Indeed we do."

"And the scars? Do they stop you from doing physical labor?"

"No."

He'd had good doctors and cutting-edge treatments to thank for that. They'd made him move the skin on his neck while it healed, gave him gentle exercises that allowed more movement and flexibility than some poor sods he knew. Painfully unwelcome at the time, but now he was thankful for them.

"Only beauty pageants. I can't do those."

The woman lifted her eyes off her form and flashed him a grin. The kind he used to receive a lot from women before the scars.

"I won't tick the box for Little Miss London, then."

It was his turn to grin. "Better not."

"And you're living in Hackney, you say?"

He nodded. Working close to home would be a good option. Half the houses in Hackney needed rebuilding, and though their domestic situation wasn't ideal, Katie loved it there. He'd prefer more privacy, but he figured if they lived with her family for the time being, they could at least save some money for the future. Whatever that might be.

"Do you have a family?" It was a reasonable question for a woman at the employment office. She couldn't know how complicated the answer was.

"Wife."

That was probably the simplest answer, even if it didn't really ring true. He'd arrived home to a sham marriage and to a family that wasn't his own. His answer dulled whatever flirtation was in the woman's eyes, but he left the office with a list of three places that were offering work as part of the rebuilding effort.

He glanced down at his new suit and sighed. Physical work required a whole new wardrobe. At least he knew a seamstress.

Jonty rounded the corner, balancing his boxes from the de-mob center in front of him, and almost got hit in the head with a cricket ball.

"Sorry!" Davy—who'd bowled the thing to his oldest broth-er—called out.

The boys had taken advantage of both the summer light and the fact that the street was still closed to all but foot traffic. Along with several others from the neighborhood, they'd made a cricket pitch down the center of the street. Jonty had to admit, the street was perfect for it, straight and long enough that even if the bats-man hit a six, no windows would be broken. He expected that they'd intended to aim for the two houses opposite Katie's. They broke the uniformity of the street by sitting in complete ruins.

Jonty set his boxes down and retrieved the ball, bringing it to where Davy stood at the end of the makeshift crease. Curious eyes traced his progress toward Davy, who stared up at Jonty, eyes wide and fearful. Jonty had the distinct feeling the children were trying to decide if they should run. The laughter that had escaped around the corner as he'd approached sat silent on their red lips.

"Looks like you need some lessons, Davy!"

Davy nodded silently, eyes still wide.

Jonty tried his best to smile in a way that would appear friendly to the watching children, working against his scarred and no-doubt-scary appearance. "Would you like me to teach you?"

Davy's face broke into smile. He nodded again.

"Does anyone else want a lesson?" he called to the other chil-dren.

Their curiosity overcame their fear. Soon he was instructing the whole street on the best way to hold the battered cricket ball, one finger on each side of the seam with the thumb underneath. Dennis and Charlie looked on, nodding sagely. Perhaps he was teaching them all something they already knew, but they still hung on his every word.

"You've got to get the arm right too." He demonstrated the action to Davy, who studied him seriously before attempting to mimic him.

"Straighter in the arm, ye ken? And make sure it brushes past your ear."

Some of the others practiced the motion. Jonty smiled to himself. He was not an expert, even though his game had come along considerably after playing with so many Australians during the war. But he figured he didn't need to be. This was a bunch of ragtag children, not the national team.

"Anyone else want to try?"

After a few furious nods, they all practiced their bowling technique as he tutored them.

"Shall we practice what we learned, then?"

They cheered and resumed their places about the street. Jonty took on the role of coach, standing next to the bowler and giving pointers. After all the children had taken their turn, Dennis tossed Jonty the ball.

"Your turn, Jonty." Jonty took the ball, tossed it up in the air, and caught it again. "Right then. Time to show you how it's done."

He should have known pride came before the fall. Maybe he was feeling too cocky. Maybe the surface of the street was uneven and made the ball bounce at an odd angle. Maybe he used too much force, considering the batsman was actually an eight-year-old girl. The result was that the ball went awry.

Smash!

The glass in Katie's neighbor's front window shattered. Jonty winced, while the children around him scattered back to their homes, deserting him. He sighed. Time to meet the neighbors.

Mrs. Grabowski met him at her door, returning his sheepish look with a stern one. She was older than Martha by a decade, perhaps more, but under the wrinkles sat an intelligent face with sharp blue eyes.

"You're Katie's husband?"

"Yes, Jonty. I'm sorry about your window."

Her eyes narrowed. "You drink tea, yes?"

Not words he was expecting, considering he'd just smashed her front window. "Um, yes."

"Well, come in. You clean up window and I fix tea."

He set to work cleaning up the shattered glass, wrapping the shards in newspaper to stop them from cutting anything. He covered the broken glass with the black fabric she'd handed him and promised to arrange a new pane of glass as soon as he could.

Before he knew it, she'd brought in a tea tray. He settled in Mrs. Grabowski's sitting room—a mirror image of Katie's own—drinking tea and hearing the entire history of Ivy Street and its residents. Mrs. Grabowski knew the neighbors' comings and goings and gave Jonty a complete briefing, as thorough as some of the ones he'd received in the RAF.

"Sarah Adams. Number ten. Husband is prisoner of Japanese. Imelda Parkin. Number eight. Sad business. So, so sad." She continued up the street, giving her assessment of each resident's life, including a colorful description of the day the V1 doodlebug blew up her neighbor's homes.

"Shook me to my bones and blew off my front door! But we are lucky, uh? No one was home in either of the houses!"

"Do you live alone, Mrs. Grabowski?"

"No, no. My husband died well before the war, leaving me with this place. It's too big for one old lady. So I take boarders. So many people needing a home."

He wondered if she gave this briefing to each of them.

As if to prove her point, the front door opened. A neatly attired man stepped through, removing his hat and hanging it on the peg by the door.

"Good evening, Mrs. Grabowski."

The man met his landlady with an easy smile, but she did not return it. Instead, she narrowed her eyes at him. "Your rent is late, Mr. Gregory."

"You'll have it tomorrow, as I said, Mrs. Grabowski."

He eyed the teapot, then Jonty. "Any chance of some tea?"

"In the kitchen at six p.m. as usual."

The shift in her mood took Jonty by surprise. He didn't know what he had done to gain Mrs. Grabowski's favor, but he was happy to have it. She was a dragon to her tenants.

The man caught Jonty's eye and rolled his own. "This is the way she lures you in, you know. Lovely cups of tea in the sitting room. It's all 'dinner at six' once you're a tenant. You'll see." He turned on his heel and headed up the stairs.

"Not if you pay your rent, Mr. Gregory. Not if you pay your rent," she called up the stairs after him.

Jonty hid his smile in his teacup as he took a sip. He picked up the conversation. "I met your nephew the other night."

"Nephew?" She didn't seem to know whom he was talking about.

"Jan."

"Ah, yes. Jan. He's a good boy." She effused over him for several minutes. How he'd flown in the Battle of Britain. How he now trained other pilots in Norwich. How he was so good to come and visit. How she hoped he could stay here now that the war was over.

"He's a good friend of my wife's, I believe." He tried to keep his tone light but ruined it by emphasizing *my wife*.

Mrs. Grabowski studied him, her eyes narrowed. He wondered if the dragon was about to turn on him too.

"I have known that family since they moved in here. All the boys were born in that house. Katie has been sleepwalking through these last years, since her baby died. I hope you wake her up."

What did that mean?

He didn't have a chance to ask before she continued. "Will you move?"

"Katie is keen to stay. She has her new job and enjoys being with her family, I think."

And truthfully, over the last week, he'd found he enjoyed the rhythms of a house with lots of people in it. Bill hadn't been around, so he could easily step into the role of big brother to the boys, which Martha appreciated. When she didn't have to occupy them, she could help Katie and Lucy with their sewing or read to them as they worked. If he wasn't sleeping on the floor and barely speaking with Katie, he would be able to say that the situation suited him too.

Mrs. Grabowski sighed. "She needs to wake up, Jonty. They all do."

Again, so cryptic. But movement and chatter on the street stole their attention away. He suddenly remembered he'd left his boxes from the demob center outside. He couldn't let anything happen to them, or he'd literally have nothing to wear.

"Thank you for the tea, Mrs. Grabowski."

"I like you, so you call me Mrs. G, like the others. Okay?"

Jonty grinned.

"You understand what I am saying, don't you? That whole family needs to wake up."

"Yes, Mrs. G. I do," Jonty lied, wondering if Mrs. Grabowski was actually a little senile, then hurried to retrieve his boxes.

Katie opened and closed her fist, stretching her aching fingers as she sidestepped the rubble on the street she had called home for most of her life. The warmth and light of summer meant that many people weren't happy to hide in their homes. Instead, they emptied into the street, enjoying impromptu gatherings and cheerful conversations that gave gentle meaning to the humdrum. A football hit her ankles, no doubt belonging to Charlie, who never seemed to be without one.

"Careful, Charlie!" She kicked it back to him, and he resumed playing with Dennis and two others. Davy and Tim raced about like wild things, ducking and weaving between the adults walking home, as part of their game of chase.

Still, she smiled inside. She loved coming home on a summer evening when everyone was out and about to welcome her. She timed her exit every morning in the hope of having as few delays as possible, but summer evenings were different. They were a time to linger and to chat before everyone disappeared behind the doors of their too-small terrace homes.

"Katie, come here."

Always bossy, Alberta Beeson from number two met Katie as she passed the front door. Plump and jolly, Alberta's hair was as dark as Katie's was fair.

"Evening, Bertie."

Katie had spent a lot of evenings with Alberta last winter. She was a newcomer to the street, and her husband was in the army. Since Katie was happy to listen and Alberta couldn't stop talking, it was a perfect arrangement.

"I have something for you." Alberta beckoned Katie into her home.

Katie enjoyed lingering, but once Alberta started talking, she was hard to stop. "I can't stay long tonight, Bertie."

"I'm sure you want to get home to Jonty." Alberta winked in that way Katie only half understood. "But you are going to love this!"

Katie followed Alberta into the sitting room and waited while she rummaged through a basket by the mantel. She took out a tightly wrapped package and pressed it into Katie's hands. Whatever was inside was soft and flexible.

"Is it fabric?"

Alberta nodded eagerly. Katie peeked at the contents, then slipped her hand in. The soft material meeting her fingertips confirmed her suspicions. "Silk!"

She pulled out one of the pieces, and it unfolded like a giant silk handkerchief in her hand. She recognized it immediately. The autumnal colors on the soft fabric weren't random patterns. They made a map of Europe. She'd seen plenty of these working at RAF Bottesford, where they were supplied for airmen to stash in their pockets in case they went down over Europe.

"Where did you get it?

"The Air Ministry is selling them off for two shillings and sixpence. I bought nine. I wondered if you'd be able to make me a slip or two. You're so much better at underthings than I am, and it's been so long since I felt anything but butter muslin against my skin."

Katie suspected that Alberta had another reason for wanting silk underwear, even if it was only the make-do-and-mend kind. She didn't need any married-women code to understand the grin Alberta wore. Maybe that was what the winking was all about. A naturally happy person assuming everyone else was blessed in the same way.

"If you whip five of them into a few slips for me, you can have the others to make something for yourself. That would be a good thing right now, wouldn't it?"

Katie could tell from her friend's raised eyebrows that she was fishing for information about Jonty's return. Her stomach tangled up in knots. "All right. I am busy with making things for the wedding, but a few slips shouldn't take too much time."

"Three. You must make one for yourself, remember. Jonty will love it!"

"Three slips." To avoid the onset of an awkward conversation with Alberta, she glanced at the clock on the mantel. "Goodness! Is that the time?"

She made it back onto the street, greeting Mr. Gregory one of Mrs. G's boarders as he came out on the street. He was muttering something under his breath about having to go out to get a decent meal.

"Good evening, Mr. Gregory."

"Evening."

He obviously wasn't in any mood to chat. So she hurried on, ignoring the rubble that had once been two homes, to where she saw Mum chatting with neighbors in front of number ten.

"Hello, Mrs. Parkin. Hello, Sarah."

She greeted her neighbors with a smile. Mrs. Parkin, however, maintained her sour expression, like she was secretly sucking on a lemon wedge. Katie didn't think that expression ever changed. But Mum had always told her to tread kindly around Mrs. Parkin.

"She buried every babe she ever had, and she deserves all the kindness she can get. Even if she doesn't hand it out to others."

Katie had only learned that kindness after Betty died, and she recalled going to Mr. Parkin's funeral soon after she had moved to Ivy Street. As the minister had read the rites, Katie's eyes had wandered to the three small headstones nearby. All the Parkin children, all boys, had died as infants. Laying one child in a grave was bad enough, but three? Even as a girl Katie had understood the immense grief, not knowing she would grow up to share in it as an adult.

"I see you're wearing your ring again?" Mrs. Parkin said. "I saw that Jan came to call the other night. I hope your husband set him straight."

Mrs. Parkin's miserable eyes missed nothing. Katie gritted her teeth, trying to choose kindness in response. How many times did she have to tell people Jan was just a friend? Probably as often as she had to remind herself when she was with him. The ring was part of that, reminding her as often as she saw it that Jonty was her husband.

"That Jonty of yours is lovely, Katie." Sarah Adams joined the conversation, smoothing over Mrs. Parkin's sideways insult. "A fine man. I saw him out on the street with the boys this afternoon."

"Really? He's home?"

"Well, someone had to set things right after they broke Mrs. G's window."

"Oh dear."

Sarah lived with her father and her adolescent son and ran herself ragged looking after them. She always looked haggard and worn out. But then, didn't they all after six years of war.

"Any word about Tom?"

Sarah shook her head. Her husband was stationed in the Far East and was a prisoner of the Japanese. Mrs. Parkin harrumphed, but not at the thought of Tom in prison. Katie followed the older woman's gaze to see the new object of her disapproval. Lucy and Matthew stood talking outside his home at number eleven. Her sister's back was against the doorframe, and Matthew leaned close opposite her, his arm outstretched so that his hand rested on the frame next to her head. Oblivious to how obvious their young love was, they clearly thought the rest of the world couldn't see them in this intimacy of the doorway.

"Relax, Imelda. They are hardly going to get into any trouble with the whole street watching, are they?" Mum said.

Just as her mother spoke, Matthew leaned in to press a kiss to Lucy's lips. Short, timid, and sweet.

"Lucky they are headed to the altar sooner rather than later, I'd say." To Mrs. Parkin's eyes, they might as well have been flouting the laws of public decency and at risk of inciting the whole street into a lustful frenzy.

Katie turned to Mum. "I'll go have a word." She didn't want to head inside just yet, but she also didn't want to continue talking here if Mrs. Parkin was going to harp. "I'll be back to make dinner. Is Dad home?"

Mum shook her head. He hadn't been home since the night Jonty had arrived. Actually, it made the nights enjoyable. She and Lucy would sew while Mum read, and Jonty occupied the boys, relearning some of that vibrant puppy-dog energy he'd once had.

Katie stole Lucy away from Matthew, using the excuse she needed her help with dinner. Lucy pouted, unhappy at being torn away.

"You'll be in each other's pockets soon enough."

The last word died in Katie's throat as she looked toward her own front door. A man in a crisp navy-blue suit stood talking to the ladies she'd just left, along with Mrs. G. He wore a trilby and carried several boxes, which Mum was now helping him with.

"Look at you, Jonty!" Lucy called out, hurrying ahead.

To Katie's mortification, she realized she hadn't recognized her own husband. She stopped, placing a hand on her belly to quieten the strange feeling there. When had she ever seen him in civilian clothes? She couldn't think of a single time. And he looked good.

She picked up her steps, approaching the excited babble of neighbors raining compliments on Jonty.

"Oh, the blue suits your coloring."

"Such a smart cut! And a new hat?"

The rest of the street was drawn to the excitement, and soon a crowd gathered around the door of number six. She couldn't even get close. She listened in as Jonty explained the course of his day.

"I got work helping fix the bomb damage to Liverpool Street Station," he informed the neighbors.

"Dressed like that?" Imelda Parkin disapproved of general happiness and picked up a problem in his story.

"Well, I happen to know a very good seamstress who might help me with what I need."

Katie frowned, wondering if the seamstress was called Lily. When she saw that the whole street was looking at her, waiting for her response, she realized he meant her. That strange feeling flipped in her stomach again, and she put her hand there to still it, managing to smile for the rest of the street.

"Well, step into my boutique," she joked, following Mum and Lucy into the house.

CHAPTER SIX

As he expected, Katie lit up like a sunbeam when he showed her the ninety coupons from the demob center. He felt like he had handed her a treasure chest with some old pirate's hoard, not a booklet of stamps.

"You can have some for a dress for the wedding."

Her sunbeam shone brighter. Mental calculations, no doubt to do with sizes and styles, did themselves behind her eyes. With the way her sunbeam made him feel, he wished he could give her all the coupons, but a man had to be practical.

"But I do need some work trousers and probably a shirt and shoes. I can't exactly wear the suit that they gave me on a rebuilding crew."

Her eyes raised to his. So blue and so pretty, even though she bit her bottom lip. "I could make you some, if you like."

"I was hoping you would. Only if you want to. If you have time, I mean. I know you have plenty of other sewing to do ahead of the wedding."

He'd seen the love she was stitching into things for her sister and wouldn't mind if some of it went into a garment for him. He'd never had someone sew something for him before.

"It won't take long. I can do them on my machine—it will be cheaper to do it that way."

Right. Of course. Economy motivated her offer. He should have known. "Well then, we'd better do it that way."

"If I'm starting from scratch, I need a complete set of measurements. Do you want me to take them now?"

He glanced around at the others in the room. Privacy was at a premium in this house. Her mother and sister were in the kitchen, and the boys were in and out of the sitting room. He didn't much like the thought of stripping down to his smalls right here. Luckily, she had the same idea.

"Shall we go to the bedroom?"

He followed her upstairs and into the bedroom, with her sewing kit and measuring tape in hand. With the door closed, the room felt tiny.

"Umm, I need you to undress."

"You don't like the new suit then?" He tried not to give in to the smile tugging on his lips, keeping a straight face to deliver his deadpan joke. But he winked for good measure.

She huffed, but those beautiful, full lips tipped up just that little bit. "I can turn around."

"Do as you like." He shrugged and stripped to his undershirt and pants. She'd seen the scars before, so he figured he had nothing to hide now. As he laid his new suit on the bed, he caught her staring at the scars on his neck and shoulder, before her gaze dropped to the new one on his shin. He'd had plenty of people stare with less friendly intent, so he wasn't embarrassed. Katie, however, turned crimson.

Perhaps she was recalling the time, late in her pregnancy, when they'd spent two days of his home leave in a cheap hotel to give her some respite from her family. The baby had made her sick and tired for the most part, but there had been that one moment when she'd reached out and traced her fingers along the ridges and furrows of the scar on his neck and shoulders. It didn't matter that he didn't have nerve endings there, because he felt her touch zing through every other part of his body.

He cleared his throat. "Well, you're the seamstress . . ."

"Right. Well then. I need to . . ." She held up her measuring tape but couldn't finish the sentence.

Red blotches rose on the soft skin of her throat. Her complexion was a tell he could read like a practiced cardplayer. This only happened when she was embarrassed or upset. The last time he'd seen her skin color up in this way, she was screaming at him not to touch her, to leave the house for good, that she wished he was dead. The sting of those words had lasted a long time and kept him away even after they'd faded. He'd long since regretted what he had done to cause them.

"You don't have to do this if you don't want to."

"It's fine."

She started at his neck, wrapping the tape measure around it. Her fingers grazed the notched skin of his scar. But her face was close. So close. Kissing close, which he tried hard not to think about, especially given the way the blotches were taking their time to fade. From the look on her face, she was trying not to think about that too. She stepped away, jotting down the number with a pencil in a little notebook.

"Hold out your arms to the side."

He obeyed. To get the measuring tape around his chest, she had to wrap her arms around his torso and pass the tape between her hands. Her face came close again. He felt the brush of her breath on his cheek. She smelled soft like flowers and sweet like honey.

It was a good thing she did his arms next. It stopped them from dropping to her waist and pulling her close to him. This was much more pleasant than being measured for his demob suit.

Every brush of her fingertips against the soft skin on the underside of his arms tickled in the most wonderful way. He swallowed and held his breath when she knelt to measure his waist and legs, inside and out, willing his body not to betray him.

"I have what I need now." She gave him a weak smile as the blotches on her neck faded. "The coupons will get some good-quality corduroy for work trousers, and I might already have some fabric for a shirt."

"Will there be coupons left over for something for you?" He gathered his clothes from where he'd left them on the bed and began dressing again. He had no idea what she'd need or how much such things cost.

"Yes." She sat on the bed, hunting through her sewing basket. "If I'm careful, I'll have enough for some trimmings for a work dress of mine that I'm remaking. Would that be all right? Madame insists we look the part when we are in the salon."

He didn't know what she meant, but from the way she smiled, he could tell she was excited about it. How could he say no when she lit up at the thought?

"I can't wait to see it. You have such a knack with needle and thread that I'm sure you could make something out of a potato sack and still look beautiful in it."

She glanced away.

"What kind of fabric are you making your dress from?" He didn't care about the dress, but he cared a great deal about keeping her talking and sharing what she cared about with him. Even if it was haberdashery. And keeping her talking would prolong the rare private moment.

"It's blue. It's actually the same fabric the RAF made their uniform shirt from. They were selling bolts off cheaply a few months ago."

"Well, I always thought you looked bonny in your uniform, so I'm sure it will suit you. You wore blue to our wedding too. Do you remember?"

No matter how fraught the circumstances became, he remembered his wedding as a happy day. A hopeful one. Several of his crew mates had attended the service in the registry office to balance out her large family. They'd had lunch at a café afterward.

He sat next to her on the bed, not too close but enough to feel her stiffen.

"Do you still have the dress? I would love to see you wear it again as a reminder of that happy day." He got the feeling that she was trying to smile for his sake, but it rang false. "Was it not a happy day for you? Do you regret marrying me?"

She looked at her hands, avoiding his eyes for far too long.

"I don't have the dress anymore. I cut it up, remember?"

Her eyes told the story he should have remembered. Katie had used scraps of fabric from her wedding dress to make a tiny gown for Betty to be buried in. He could picture, just as Katie was no doubt doing, the baby's tiny form in the blue-and-white fabric. She'd looked peaceful, like she was sleeping. He supposed she was . . . just not an earthly kind of slumber.

"I didn't mean to upset you, Katie-my-love."

He ignored the tug in his chest that told him to wrap his arms around her. He reached into his shirt pocket, pulled out his handkerchief, and offered it to her. Their fingers brushed as she took it. "That memory will fade one day."

Horror wrote itself across her face, as well as something close to betrayal.

"I don't want the memory to fade! It's all I have."

She ran from the room, leaving her sewing things in her wake, as well as Jonty, wishing desperately he'd spoken differently.

CHAPTER SEVEN

Friday, 13 July 1945

Madame appeared almost flustered when Katie arrived at work the following week. Almost flustered. She was too genteel to get completely flustered.

She looked up from where she sat studying her appointment book, her forehead pressed down into a frown that made Katie check the time. It was a quarter to ten—she wasn't late. But Madame Martin was particular about the way she arranged her appointment book. She didn't have appointments before ten and took care to have reasonable space in between clients. Katie knew this maintained an illusion of exclusivity, as though the shop existed solely for the pleasure of the customers there at the time. Of course, sometimes Madame had a reason for wanting to show one client off to the one coming in afterward. Those appointments were always underlined in the book.

"Françoise will not be here today, Kat-reen. I need your help measuring. Put your bag upstairs, then come straight back down."

"Really?"

Madame nodded. "Be quick about it. We have a very important client coming. And they'll be here before ten."

Katie took the steps two at a time, arriving upstairs to expectant looks from Alice and Collette. "I'm going to do the measuring today. Françoise isn't here!" Katie blurted out the honor as she stashed her handbag in the corner where she routinely worked. Her excitement met with a stone-cold stare from Collette, who returned to her cutting with forceful snips. Alice sent Katie an excited grin, eyebrows raised. Katie decided not to mention the client was an underlined one.

Voices floated up from the store, and Katie hurried back down the stairs, wondering whom she would meet. It must be someone important to almost fluster Madame. Perhaps a member of the royal family? Perhaps an American film star was visiting London from Hollywood? Katie paused on the bottom stair to compose herself, then slipped into the store. Only to come face to face with someone she knew.

Grace Deroy, formerly Katie's superior in the WAAF, and one of the most fashionable women in London, stood in the showroom. Her family went back as far as the Battle of Hastings, which Katie didn't know a lot about, other than it was a long time ago. They owned a huge estate in Lincolnshire. Grace wasn't royalty or a movie star, but she looked as though she could be.

Tall and statuesque, with a swanlike neck and a smile like Rita Heyworth, Grace cast her glance around the room. "Katie!"

Katie's chest seized. Her worlds rarely collided like this, so she had no idea what to do. Madame told her through narrowed eyes that now was not the time to drop the accent Katie usually adopted in front of clients.

"Miss Deroy. Hullo. It's so lovely to see you again." Katie cringed inwardly, knowing that Grace's accent was one of the very ones she mimicked when she put on this voice.

Grace's brow furrowed for the slightest moment before she

covered her confusion with a polite smile. "Indeed it is!"

Thankfully, Grace's mother plunged herself into conversation with Madame, covering the awkwardness.

"Burton and Co. have been with our family for as long as Henry and I have been married." Lady Deroy had a French accent not unlike Madame's. "To discover that they had betrayed Grace in such a way is simply reprehensible." Her accent became stronger with the heightened emotion in her voice. "We have closed our account with them. They will never have business with us again! But it is highly inconvenient with the wedding coming up. I had intended for them to make her entire trousseau."

Madame Martin cooed and tsked her sympathy, but Katie saw the delight in her face. To win a high-profile customer from a competitor like Burton & Co. was a business goldmine.

"Of course, Elaine." Madame's voice was a soothing purr. "I cannot comprehend such a betrayal. We will fix this. Anything for my old friend."

Katie assumed that the betrayal had something to do with the court case that had put Grace in the newspaper a few years ago. Her eyes flicked to Grace as Lady Deroy captivated all of Madame's attention. Grace was looking directly at Katie, a smile tugging at her lips.

Lady Deroy's wail stole Katie's attention back.

"But they had already begun cutting up my own wedding gown to remake it for Grace." Lady Deroy waved her hand, and a man in a chauffeur's uniform, whom Katie hadn't noticed, stepped forward to place a box on the ottoman. He removed the lid. "It's like I told you on the telephone. The gown is in pieces."

All the women peered into the box to see a jumble of material. The pale color and delicate lace told how this had once been a fine wedding gown. Lady Deroy glanced away, tears in her eyes, as though it was physically painful to look at.

"This will not be a problem for us." Madame assured her new clients with confidence Katie didn't feel. "We will remake this dress into one of the most stylish in London. But first we have to take Miss Deroy's measurements. Kat-reen?"

On her cue, Katie stepped forward and extended her hand toward the changing room, concealed by an elegant blue velvet curtain that hung from the ceiling and pooled extravagantly on the floor. "This way, please."

She avoided wincing as she spoke, but Grace looked thoroughly amused as she passed Katie and headed toward the changing room with a wink. Katie untied the curtain that would screen Grace from view. "Call me in when you are down to your slip, and I'll measure you."

In a few moments, she heard Grace call out that she was ready. Katie slipped through the curtain and narrowly avoided fawning. Grace Deroy was the most stylish woman Katie had ever known. She had even managed to make the clunky WAAF uniform look attractive. Seeing Grace in her underthings did nothing to change Katie's perception. In fact, it almost inspired envy. Even though the garments were unlikely ever to be appreciated by anyone other than her husband-to-be, they were made from the finest-quality silk, with elegant embellishments and delicate lace. Katie had to try hard not to reach out and touch the fine fabrics.

"What's going on, *Kat-reen*?" Grace said, mimicking Madame, but she didn't look angry. Instead, amusement lit her features. "Spill."

Katie dropped her accent but kept her voice low. She didn't think Madame would overhear her, considering the animated conversation she was having with Lady Deroy about how terrible Burton & Co. were. Madame was no doubt lapping the whole thing up.

"The accent wasn't my idea, but Madam Martin insisted. At least she isn't making me put on a French one."

Grace's face cracked into a smile. "You always were a good mimic!"

Katie began her measuring, working her way down Grace's

body, alternating between using the tape measure and writing Grace's elegant proportions on the chart attached to the clipboard.

Grace seemed unfazed at conducting polite chitchat wearing just her slip. "How have you been? I'm so sorry about the baby."

Katie's pencil stopped on the page where it was writing Grace's bust measurements. She had forgotten she'd once written to Grace about Betty while helping Grace find some missing relatives. She rarely thought about Betty in this luxurious space. Having Grace mention her now jarred.

Katie covered the confusion by smoothing the measuring tape around Grace's arms. "Jonty's home. Demobbed last week."

Grace smiled fondly as Katie measured Grace's perfectly proportioned waist and hips. "How is he?"

"He's well. We're living with my parents, and he's got work fixing Liverpool Street Station."

"I'm glad to hear it. I'll have to tell Maggie. Those two have a special connection, you know."

"I know. How is she?" Maggie and Grace were best friends. Maggie had been her commanding officer at Bottesford. Maggie had also been the first one to find out about Katie's pregnancy. She'd been kind, even though she had every reason not to be. She'd also worked with Jonty before and was the one who'd pulled him from the burning wreck that had left him scarred. Jonty called her his guardian angel.

"She's well. Alec is stationed at Metheringham now. The Australians are converting all their aircraft to fight the Japanese."

"Oh." All her worlds really were colliding. Katie hurried with the measurements for Grace's inner and outer legs. She would rather end this conversation without thinking about Maggie's husband. She had been in love with him once, but he'd never seen her. At least, not once Maggie was in the picture.

"Did you know Maggie's first baby was stillborn?"

Crouched near Grace's ankle, Katie strained to look up at

Grace, sorrow washing through her.

"I thought you'd want to know. But she just recently had another baby, and she's the most delicious little thing."

"Oh, I didn't realize."

"What is taking you so long in there?" Madame's call permeated through the changing room curtain and cut off their reminiscing.

"Nearly done." Katie adopted her accent and hurried to finish Grace's measurements. "Please give Maggie my best when you see her next."

A few moments later, Madame sat with Grace and Lady Deroy on the velvet chairs. The customers took tea and discussed their needs with Madame, while she drew in her giant sketchbook, giving form to the suggestions of each woman. Katie stood behind Madame, watching the designs spring to life with the skill of Madame's pencil.

Both Grace and Lady Deroy were fluent on the subject of fashion and clear about what they did and didn't like. Lady Deroy was insistent that Grace's wedding gown should eclipse anything that Burton & Co. made that season.

"But we understand economy is important, which is why we are reusing the fabrics and details from my mother's gown," Grace added.

Lady Deroy described the styles that she felt suited her daughter best, talking up ruffles and ruches, while Grace maintained she wanted something with cleaner lines. "More like Katherine Hepburn, you know?"

"You mean like this?" Madame clarified Grace's point with a quick sketch.

"Yes, but not long sleeves. It's summer, after all."

"I think I understand perfectly." Madame nodded. "Now you must have something special in mind for the evening, no? A negligée or peignoir perhaps."

The French words had once confused Katie. That was, until she'd seen Madame's sketches. Now, as she watched on, Madame's pencil brought forth designs of sheer, flowing nighties and dressing gowns to match.

"We can reuse a lot of the lace if we do it this way, and your new husband will approve of this style, I think?"

When Madame angled the sketchbook toward Grace, Katie peeked curiously at her friend.

Grace didn't seem embarrassed by the designs. She simply nodded in appreciation. "Oh, Madame, I'm sure he will."

As she pushed the fabric under the needle of her machine at home that evening, Katie thought through all the items she had made for Lucy's wedding. She'd made practical flannelette pajamas and a lovely cotton nightie with a hand-embroidered neckline. Katie had spent hours on the smocking. But Lucy had absolutely nothing like what Madame had in mind for Grace. Perhaps it was just a French thing. Or perhaps it was just another part of the married-woman code that everyone assumed Katie knew about.

"Ninety coupons! All for one man?" Lucy almost dropped her sewing when she heard about the coupons Jonty had brought home. "That's three times what I have. For a whole year."

They'd pulled the sewing machine out from its place by the wall and erected the ironing board in the sitting room. Together they worked between both, utilizing every surface, including the sofa and the two easy chairs opposite it. They could only sew this way when the rest of the family wasn't home. But Mum was visiting Mrs. G, and Jonty had taken the boys to get fish and chips. So they had the whole house to themselves.

"He is starting from scratch, you know. He's worn nothing but a uniform for five years."

Katie considered donating Alberta's maps to Lucy's trousseau—as Lady Deroy had called it—but decided not to mention anything. She hadn't had anything made from silk for as long as she could remember.

"But Matthew and I are starting our lives together!"

Lucy sighed and slipped into a happy hum, no doubt daydreaming about her life as a married woman. Katie pursed her lips. It wasn't fair of her to be irritated. A bride should be happy and optimistic. But Katie knew how easily carefree optimism could be beaten into submission by the hard realities of life. Katie reached for her sewing basket, searching through it for the right color thread. As she did, her fingers skimmed the package Jan had left.

She'd sneaked several peeks at the box when no one else was looking, but kept it concealed at the bottom of her sewing basket. She'd felt it thoroughly several times now, trying to make out what was inside. However, opening the brown paper that surrounded the contents seemed like too much of a violation. She thought it was a box of some kind. It rattled slightly when she shook it, so she thought maybe it contained cards, or photographs, or papers of some kind.

"Keep it safe for me while I am gone, will you? Keep it secret, but if my aunt ever asks for it, you can give it to her."

He'd been the one to suggest that she stash it with her sewing and try to forget she had it. But why had he given her this? Wouldn't it be more sensible to just give it directly to Mrs. G to keep it safe?

"Where are you going and when will you be back?" she'd asked, but he hadn't given clear answers. She wished the other questions running through her mind now had occurred to her when she'd been standing with him then.

Crash!

A clatter rang out from the kitchen, shooting alarm through Katie.

"Dad's home!" Lucy whispered.

Katie glanced at the half-complete seam in front of her. Dad was so unpredictable after he'd been gone a long while that she never knew exactly what he'd do. Once, when she'd left some of her sewing miscellany out, Dad had grabbed her basket and set it on fire in the backyard. They couldn't risk him doing that to any of the wedding items they were taking such pains over.

"Help me put away the machine, then go and get Mum."

The women shot into action, tidying their sewing things away faster than an industrial machine-made stitch. Lucy disappeared out the front door, while Katie scurried to collect the half-completed garments from the sitting room, steeling herself for what might come next.

"Dad. You're home!"

She greeted Dad as he was stomping around the kitchen, flinging open drawers and cupboards and rifling through the larder.

"Are you hungry, Dad?"

Frustration at not finding what he wanted caused him to rip the cutlery drawer completely out of its sliders, sending the contents clattering across the linoleum.

Katie flinched. But Dad stood still holding the drawer by the handle, looking forlornly around the kitchen. He swayed, and his eyes took time to focus on her. When they did, she saw a flicker of confusion and then recognition in them.

"Get me a sandwich."

She put her head down, stumbling on a stray spoon as she hurried to the bread bin. The boys had raided it after school. Thankfully, they'd left a crust or two. Dad wasn't in the mood to hear that she couldn't do as he ordered.

"Hurry up," he grumbled, sinking onto a seat at the kitchen table and slumping over it, one arm extended so his head could loll onto it. She managed a sandwich with thin scrapings of margarine and marmite. Nothing satisfying, but at least he couldn't complain about her disobedience.

Perhaps if she took long enough to make the sandwich, he

would fall asleep? She didn't want to risk it. She turned back to him with her meager offering and placed it in front of him.

When he saw the two crusts and their paltry contents, he swiped the whole plate off the table. The ceramic crashed against the floor, and the crusts ricocheted, joining the scattering of cutlery.

"I said I wanted a sandwich." His words erupted along with strings of spittle.

"There's no more bread." Where was Mum? She was so much better at dealing with him when he was like this.

"Well, make some."

Katie didn't know how to respond to this absurdity. Surely he knew that even if she started kneading this precise second, there would be no bread for another three hours at least. He wasn't pleased by her hesitation.

He grabbed her wrist and squeezed hard to make his point, pulling her toward him. "I said, make some." His words were hard and cold, as immovable as stone. He twisted her arm, coupling the pain in her wrist with pain in her elbow. She tempered her cry into a whimper, shrinking away from his smell. A body that hadn't bathed in days combined with a distillery floor.

"What's happening here?"

A cold, hard voice came from a figure in the back doorway. "Jonty!"

He stood in the doorway, holding the newspaper-wrapped bundle of fish and chips. She needed to warn him not to make a fuss. Dad let go of her wrist, and she sprang away to the other side of the kitchen. He slumped back down at the table.

"Your wife is making me a sandwich," Dad slurred.

Jonty's eyes flicked about the room, surveying the disarray Dad had created in just a few moments. Open drawers and cupboard doors. Cutlery strewn across the floor. Broken plate and sandwich lying discarded. Deep shame pooled in Katie's belly.

"My wife is doing no such thing." Jonty stepped into the

kitchen and put himself in between her and her father.

Protection. She instantly felt it.

But it would come at a cost. It always did. Her brothers used to try to stand up to Dad.

Dad rose to his feet, lurching to one side as he did. "This is my house."

Jonty didn't shrink or flinch. He stood his ground and let her hide behind him. "I think you should go to bed, Bill. You look like you need it."

She squeezed her eyes shut, waiting for the roar that would surely come and the fist that would land on poor Jonty after challenging her father's will.

None came.

She opened her eyes to see her father's stunned face, staring at Jonty. Rage simmered under confusion as Dad swayed on the spot.

Mum appeared in a flurry at the back door, Lucy behind her. Her eyes flicked between Bill, Jonty, and Katie.

"Bill! You're home. We weren't expecting you for dinner." Placation laced her voice. Mum's specialty. "Did I hear you wanted a sandwich?"

Dad simply grunted, his eyes still on Jonty, who still stood as Katie's immovable shield.

"There's no bread, Bill. Wouldn't you rather wait upstairs while we made it? The bed is much more comfortable than that chair, and you don't want to be bothered by all our kneading and nonsense, do you?"

Mum was quick to slide herself under his arm and guide him out of the kitchen and up the stairs. Katie stared after them.

Jonty turned to her, his eyes so full of feeling she couldn't look at them. "Are you all right, Katie-my-love? Did he hurt you?"

She shook her head. It was a lie, and Jonty knew it.

He held out his palm. "Let me see."

She extended her arm and laid her wrist into his gentle hand.

Taking her hand, he made a show of inspecting it with such impossible gentleness it made her breath catch in her throat. "Nothing broken, I think."

He kept hold of her eyes with his as he shut her fist and released her wrist from his care. His kindness and tenderness anchored her. She fought back tears, heat rising in her face.

She didn't want Jonty to see her cry and whirled away to join Lucy, kneeling down to pick up the mess from the kitchen floor.

CHAPTER EIGHT

Bill's appearance disrupted the routines across the whole house, throwing out the pattern they'd established after Jonty's first night here. After the fish and chips supper, he offered to sleep on the sofa so Katie could go back into the small room with her sister. Lucy declined the offer.

"You two take my room. I'll sleep with the boys tonight."

Katie retired first, washing her hands and face and using the lavatory before heading up to the bedroom. He then excused himself to do the same. When he entered the bedroom, she was already in bed with the covers pulled up to her neck. She faced the wall, but her hip stuck up in one appealing lump under the blanket.

"Katie?"

This room was smaller than Martha and Bill's, with barely room for anything but the bed. He glanced for a blanket to lay on the floor, but there wasn't one. His eyes traced back to the outline of her curves on the bed. She must know that a man who had shared a dormitory with twenty others knew when someone was pretending to sleep. Still, the pretense of sleep shouted clearer than any words: *Don't touch me.*

There was a little room on the bed for a skinny man, like the one he'd become. Perhaps he could slip in next to her. But he didn't want to do anything she might misinterpret. With more caution than a man defusing unexploded ordnance, he sat on the bed, taking up as little room as he could at the corner farthest from her head.

"Katie? I know you're awake. I just want to talk."

He yearned for a proper conversation with her. The face-to-face, heart-to-heart kind, where they weren't exchanging instructions. There was so much to say to each other, so much of the past to work through. Confessions to make, apologies to give. Though he was bone weary from the workday, he was impatient to start. Maybe if they started with tonight, they could work backward.

"So is he often like that then?"

The question hung in the dark space between them for so long that he almost gave up on her answering.

"Only when he drinks. Which isn't often. It's just, you never know when that's going to be." She rolled over and sat up in her far corner. Drawing her knees up to her body, she wrapped her arms around them. She wore pajamas, flannelette ones, which seemed unseasonal for summer. He mimicked her stance at the other end of the bed, happy that it fit neatly between the two walls so they could sit this way. "He'll try to make it up to Mum tomorrow—that much is predictable."

Without blackout curtains, light slipped into the room from the moon outside, highlighting her features. He welcomed being able to see her face. He really had received the better end of the deal when they'd married. She was a beautiful woman. Once, when he'd been trapped in a French cellar, he'd spent long hours trying to recall every intimate detail of Katie's face. In his mind, he'd run his fingers through her blond curls, reveling in the soft texture, the hint of fragrance. He'd drowned in the blue of her eyes, trying to picture their exact shape and the number of lashes framing them. He'd tasted the perfect shape of her lips.

Lingering too long on thoughts of her lips now was bound to cause him trouble, so he stayed on the topic at hand. "Has he hurt you before?"

She shrugged. "Not really." That wasn't a real answer, but the lack of certainty in it spoke volumes. "It's complicated. You know, I don't think he means to . . ." She let the sentence trail off.

But he knew how it ended. How many times had he made excuses like that where his uncle was concerned?

"Mum usually placates him."

Jonty's heart broke for Martha. She hadn't come down to share the chips he'd bought to treat them all.

"Where has he been all week?"

"I don't know. Mum says he's been extra busy at work, but I don't know why he hasn't been home at night. It's not like he has shifts with the home guard or as a warden the way he used to."

"I'm sorry if I made things worse tonight."

She pulled her mouth to the side in a grimace. "It's not your fault." He noticed she didn't allay his worry that he might have made things worse. "Something has been brewing since you got here. It used to be worse when the older boys were here. I think they joined up to get away from his unpredictability."

"I was the same. I just wanted to get away from my uncle." Had he shared with her about the man who'd raised him after his parents died? He couldn't remember, but it was a commonality between them, and he wanted to draw that out. "Was your father angry when they left?"

Katie took her time to think about the question. "Not at first. He was kinder to the younger boys in the first few weeks after they left. Maybe it was his guilty conscience."

"How did he take the news of their passing?"

"He disappeared for three weeks straight. I still don't know where. Mum said it was for the best he wasn't here. Which I still don't understand."

Her eyes focused on the pattern of the blanket between them, and a frown line deepened on her forehead. Perhaps she was trying not to cry . . . He couldn't quite see in the moonlight. His heart tugged toward her, wanting to clamber over and wrap his arms around her. His head told him that wouldn't be helpful.

"I haven't spoken to my uncle since I enlisted." His jaw tightened at the memory of the night he'd told his uncle he was joining the RAF, and the curses the man had thrown. "I don't think he knows, much less cares, whether I am dead or alive."

She sniffed and tapped her nose with the back of her hand. "Well, he knows. I can tell you that much. I went to Edinburgh to tell him that you were missing."

When he went missing? That was just in February. His heart expanded with the hope that she had been thinking of him at a time when he'd thought all hope for them was lost. He bent his head, trying to scoop her gaze toward his. "That was good of you. Thank you. I'm grateful that you went out of your way like that. Why did you not just write?"

Her shoulders lifted and fell. "I tried, but the letter was returned. I thought it was a mistake. So I went to find the shop you'd told me about."

If the letter was returned, it wasn't a mistake. His uncle wanted nothing to do with him. The feeling was mutual, but Jonty was intrigued enough to want to know what Katie saw.

"The shop was shut up, but a passerby told me that the man who owned it lived in the flat upstairs."

A picture of that flat where he had lived seven wretched years before joining the RAF appeared in his mind. He could almost smell the misery in the memory.

"Did you see him?"

She nodded. "He looked frail, but he was feisty."

"Frail?" It was not a word he'd ever heard associated with

Hamish Munro. The man towered over his teenage years. "Perhaps the drinking has caught up with him."

Sympathy flashed in Katie's eyes when they met his. And gentle curiosity. "Was he always like that?"

"As long as I lived with him. He's my mother's brother, but he was as different from her and my father as night from day. My parents both died within a few days of each other, and he was my only living relative. He kept a roof over my head and—occasionally, if I was lucky—food on the table." Jonty swallowed. "I think he looked after me for show, so the good churchgoing folk he kept company with on Sundays didn't know how he drank himself into a stupor on the other six nights of the week."

Jonty didn't think about those years much anymore. He couldn't recall mentioning his uncle to the blokes in the RAF. Once out from under the man's thumb, he didn't want to think about him anymore. But even though his throat suddenly tightened and the words must sound forced, he wanted to tell Katie. After what he'd seen tonight, he knew she would understand.

"But he was never kind to me. Ever. On Sundays he put on a show so he could go to church, but those were the nights he was the meanest." He clasped his hands tighter around his knees, almost wringing them as he tried to find the right words. "When I was a wee lad, my father gave me one of those tin-plate locomotives. Shiny green, with a key that wound it up and set it going. It was my pride and joy."

He laughed at the simple memory of playing with it with his father, his mother watching on. How old had he been then? Five? Six? Physical warmth bloomed through him as he relived the love they'd shared as a tight little family. His father's ginger coloring. His mother's golden smile.

"After I moved in with Hamish, I was probably too old for toy trains, but it was dear to me because it reminded me of them. I'd lost the key by then, but I worked out how to wind it up without one. I set it going up on the kitchen floor. That set him off."

He'd been nothing more than a child having fun, but Hamish wouldn't have it. Even though Jonty was not bothering him, he'd swiped up the train and told him that it was time to grow up. "He threw it into the fire."

A gentle gasp escaped Katie. Her hand flew to her throat in sympathy for the little boy he'd been. She understood. "Oh, Jonty."

As their eyes met in the moonlight, he felt the chasm between them narrow. Maybe just an inch, but it was something. "Katie, I think we need to move out of here and find a place of our own. Start afresh."

She sighed. "Where to? There isn't anywhere."

Nothing in London maybe, but there were other places where they could both find work. "Would you move out of London?"

She shook her head. "I don't want to, Jonty. I've only just got this job. I can't leave now."

"We don't have to move out of London, but we need to move on, Katie-my-love. You know we do."

"Move on from what?"

He sighed. There were so many things. Move on from the war. From the situation with her family. From the grief of losing a child. From him sleeping on the floor.

She slid down, rolled onto her side, and addressed the window. "I don't think I know how." She glanced at him.

Weariness from the day brought on a sudden yawn, which he tried to stifle since he preferred conversation with Katie to sleep.

It drew out Katie's pity. "You can stay on the bed, Jonty."

"Are you sure?" The softness of the bed was so much more appealing than the floor. Katie's softness was more appealing still.

"At that end," she added.

He gave a tired smile, happy that the gulf between them was smaller after this evening. "I don't have any ideas, I promise. But do you really want my smelly feet up next to your head? You're a brave woman, Katie-my-love."

He slid down. The bed was so wonderfully comfortable that

he barely heard her response as sleep rushed in.

It could have been minutes or hours later when Lily's face appeared in his vision. She knew few English words and he knew no French, but he understood the urgency of her tone.

"*Reste ici! Reste ici!*"

He knew she meant for him to stay put.

And he did.

While tanks rumbled and the gunshots rang out, he stayed put in the underground prison.

He tried calling her name, warning her about the danger of going out.

But in his dream, his voice didn't work no matter how loud he tried to be or how clear.

He couldn't make a sound. Over and over he tried to get the words out.

"Lily!"

He woke, jolting to a sitting position. Eyes darting about frantically, he oriented himself. He wasn't in France. He wasn't in the ground. He was sitting up in a soft bed. He closed his eyes, trying to steady his breathing. When he opened them again, Katie was sitting up, nursing her face and staring at him as though he were some kind of monster.

CHAPTER NINE

Saturday, 14 July 1945

"How is the dress coming, Lucy?"

Sarah poured tea for Alberta and Mrs. G, who had come to plan the final details of next week's wedding. Since the romance had blossomed between two of the children from Ivy Street, it seemed right that the street would host the wedding breakfast. Almost every house from numbers one to sixteen was going to be involved in some way, just like when they'd held a street party on Victory Day.

"Almost finished. Katie just needs to do the hem and fix the veil." Lucy beamed, loving being the center of attention. "But she's been so busy making other things lately."

"It will be done for the day, and that's what matters." Katie defended herself, massaging her wrist that still ached from Dad's grip the previous evening. She expected to have to wear long sleeves this week to cover the bruise. Thankfully, there was no mark from where Jonty's foot had connected with her face. She didn't like the idea of having to explain a black eye or to purchase the makeup to cover it. The dull ache would be gone by Monday. Unlike her questions.

"And Katie's so good at making the things you'll need to go under it." Alberta sent Katie a wink, no doubt referring to the slips that Katie had fashioned for her from the silk maps. Katie met her wink with a warning glance. She didn't want to get into a conversation about underwear with her neighbors around the kitchen table.

"Ah, it's an exciting time, Lucy. I remember the week I became a married woman. The anticipation. The wonderment—is that the English?—about what it would be like to be a wife."

Sarah and Alberta nodded, smiling kindly at Lucy in that too-knowing way.

"So what's left on our list of things to do?" Katie tried to move the conversation forward, worried it was about to slip into a code she didn't understand. She'd spent the week before her own wedding with her head over the latrine, after all. No anticipation or wonderment, just a desperate yearning not to vomit up everything she'd eaten.

"Music?"

Thankfully, Mum was on her side. She made sure that the talk centered on the logistics of the day, not whatever happened after.

"Maybe Jan can play," Mrs. G offered. "He is very good on the violin."

"Will he be able to come, then?" Lucy asked. "I thought he was away."

Katie tried not to be invested in Mrs. G's answer more than was fitting for a good friend.

"Ah . . ."

Katie's eyes lifted to Mrs. G after hearing her slight hesitation. "I hope so."

Mrs. G's brow furrowed. "But perhaps we need another plan, in case he can't be here."

"Dad has a gramophone we can use if we need to," Sarah offered, to the general agreement of the others.

"How's the planning going, ladies?"

Dad entered the kitchen through the back door with all the charisma and charm he'd been lacking last night. As she'd predicted to Jonty, he carried a huge bunch of flowers in his arms. "Is the wedding of the year going to go off without a hitch?"

The women around her, including Mum, laughed easily at his joke, but Katie didn't care to. After her conversation with Jonty last night—and a foot to the face that had kept her from falling back to sleep easily—she'd spent several hours thinking about the strange dynamic between her parents. How Dad was away more often than not. How Mum's reasons for his absences were feeling increasingly flimsy.

"Are these for me?" Mum said.

Dad nodded.

"Bill! They're beautiful!"

While Mum was fussing over a vase, Bill explained himself to the women at the table. "I'm afraid I came home three sheets to the wind last night and owe my wife an apology."

Alberta giggled, but Sarah and Mrs. G, who'd seen this behavior before, simply gave tight smiles. Mum set her vase of flowers in the sitting room and returned to the kitchen table.

"You don't want to be bothered with all our wedding planning, do you, Bill?" Mum was always placating him like that. Making it sound like they were the problem, not him. "Why don't you take the boys out? Jonty was going to help with them this morning, but he's been called away."

Katie almost scoffed. Dad rarely did anything with the boys. Perhaps that was why they'd taken so well to Jonty—he paid attention to them. Although, she had to admit that the rare times she'd seen Dad really talking with them as a father should, it had been part of an apology to Mum.

"Left you again already, has he?" Dad directed the barb to

Katie, disguised with a smile.

"He's just visiting his uncle in Edinburgh, that's all. It was a snap decision." No doubt brought on by the conversation they'd had last night. "He's coming back tomorrow."

She added the last bit so Dad would know that Jonty wasn't anything like him.

"Whatever you say." She wasn't sure if he was talking to her or to Mum, whose cheek he leaned over to kiss. Dad summoned the boys, and they followed him outside like little ducklings, happy to have his attention while it lasted.

"How long do you expect Bill to stay this time?"

Mrs. G's muttered question caught Katie's attention, dragging it back to the table. For the first time, she thought about what bound the women together more than simply living a few doors away from each other. Until recently, they were all alone in their marriages, abandoned in some way by their husbands.

Not intentionally, always. Mr. Grabowski had died before Katie knew him, and Alberta was now joyfully—if Katie judged by her winks and coded remarks—reunited with her Maxwell. Sarah's husband hadn't intended to be captured by the Japanese either. In May, when the street had celebrated the end of the war with Germany, Sarah had confided to Katie that she had been married for fourteen years but hadn't seen her husband in almost half that time. Sarah had tried to share a grim camaraderie with Katie.

"Happily ever afters are actually a lot of hard work, aren't they?"

They certainly were. Especially when your husband refused to answer questions about the woman who occupied his sleeping mind. Katie supposed she only had herself to blame if he'd had some kind of affair while they were separated. But was it that? She didn't know, and that made it so much harder to trust him like she was trying to.

Katie wondered if Mum confided in Sarah or Mrs. G about

what went on with Dad, or if they just stood by in solidarity because of the little bits they saw. She glanced at Lucy, who still radiated hope and innocence.

She prayed silently that her sister's marriage would be spared the strains placed on the others around the table, including hers.

The journey north on the shuddering passenger express, pulled by a steam locomotive, had seemed so straightforward when the woman at King's Cross Station had announced the route.

Stopping at Peterborough, York, Newcastle, and Edinburgh.

She'd clearly articulated towns and times as though the journey was simply geographical. For Jonty, the seven-hour ride up the Iron Road was anything but. He needed each one of those hours to prepare him to address the specter from his past.

He directed his attention to the countryside through the window as he mentally sifted through his memories and tried to think through every possible alternative that might greet him at the flat. He hadn't been back to Edinburgh since the air force had shipped him out.

He studied the scenery keenly as the train chugged across the Bridge at Berwick, then over the border into Scotland. Waverly Station appeared mostly spared from the wrath of the German Luftwaffe, unlike Liverpool Street, where he worked. Of course, the people of Edinburgh had suffered and sacrificed the same way they'd done in London, but there was much less physical evidence for it.

People about him jostled for their luggage, anxious to alight after the long trip. Jonty held back, happy to be one of the last to step off. When he did, he found his feet had memorized the walk to the shop.

As Katie had said, a handwritten "Closed" sign hung in the door, and he saw no sign of activity in the workshop beyond.

Instead, he saw ghosts as he peered through the frosted glass. Or at least, he imagined he did when his gaze landed on the spot he'd been standing when he'd told his uncle he'd enlisted. Sure enough, the crack in the glass that Jonty had made when he'd slammed the door on his way out hadn't been fixed.

He made his way to the back of the building and climbed the rickety stairs. Jonty raised his hand to knock at the door of his uncle's flat, pausing just before his knuckles hit the wood. Once he knocked, once he summoned his uncle to the door, there was no turning back. He'd have to face him.

He could leave now. Return to the station and then to London. No one need know that he'd come. But if he did, he'd miss his best chance to provide a home for Katie. A future they could share. He squeezed his fist, primed as it was to knock, trying to picture her face to anchor him in his purpose.

With a deep breath, he steeled himself and slammed his knuckles onto the wood. The shuffling on the other side ended with the door swinging open. There stood Hamish Munro, the man who had made his adolescence such a torment. The man who had taken him out of school with nothing but the most basic education and taught him enough about woodcraft to be his permanent apprentice. Or slave . . . *Punching bag* also came to mind.

But the man in front of him didn't look like he had the energy to punch anything. In fact, he looked feeble. His dark hair was mussed and gray. The once-bulky arms, strengthened by years of heaving planks of wood—and swinging punches at his nephew—had wasted. The pallor of his skin was decidedly yellow. The whites of his eyes too. Their wide surprise emphasized their color. However, his pupils were still as shrewd as they had always been.

"You?" His uncle greeted him unceremoniously after surprise and confusion had done their dance across his features. "Thought you were dead!"

Jonty shook his head. "Afraid not. Wished it sometimes. Are you going to invite me in?"

Once his uncle would have given him a clip over the ear for being so rude, but Jonty wasn't afraid of that now. He'd been through much worse. Besides, he could take the man opposite him if he wanted to. Maybe he should give the man a taste of his fists. No. That wasn't who he was. But his directness—and sudden appearance, no doubt—surprised his uncle into stepping back to let him in.

Jonty fought against the unsettling feeling of being back in his childhood home. Nothing about the decor had changed. In fact, the man following behind him in the hallway was more physically different than the flat in which he lived. The walls were the same dirty green that Jonty remembered as a child. The floorboards creaked in all the same places.

And the smell. The same mixture of damp, burnt toast, and moonshine. It sent a shiver down his spine.

Wordlessly he pulled out a chair at the small kitchen table adorned with a teapot and a bottle of what looked like water but probably wasn't. Uncle Hamish didn't offer tea or go through any charade of politeness. Perhaps he couldn't. A shuffle had replaced his confident stride, and he held his hands in his lap. Jonty had seen men do that when they didn't want people to see their shakes and tremors.

Uncle Hamish didn't seem inclined to open up the conversation. As a child, that man's stare had made Jonty feel small and insignificant, but Jonty surprised himself now by feeling indifferent to it, even a little sorry for his uncle. Jonty sat under his canny gaze, waiting for what felt like an age.

"You told me once that you hoped never to see the inside of this place ever again. And yet here you are, back!"

Jonty swallowed, to wet his dry mouth. He had said that. On the night he'd enlisted. When he'd slammed the shop door so hard that the sign had fallen off. Jonty stayed silent, bracing for one of the vicious tirades that long childhood experience had taught him to expect. It didn't come.

"I see the shop downstairs is shut. Are you not working anymore?" Jonty finally asked.

Uncle Hamish grunted. A sound Jonty remembered well. "What of it?"

"Well, it's space that's going to waste when it could be making furniture."

"You came here out of the blue to tell me I'm not doing my part for the war?" His uncle's grip on the hands in his lap tightened.

"No." Jonty paused. Best get this over and done with and then he could be out of this rank-smelling place and away from its crabby owner. "I want you to let me use the shop."

"Use the shop? For what?"

"For what you trained me in, Uncle. Furniture making."

"So you have come to beg me to take you back?" Hamish's lip curled as he spoke, indicating just what he thought about Jonty. That he was small. But Jonty had thought this scenario might play out, so he launched into the argument he'd practiced on the train on the way north.

"Not begging, Uncle. More hoping you'll see reason. I'm guessing the shop is shut because you aren't able to manage it anymore."

Hamish grunted again. Jonty thought it meant yes.

"Well, I could take it over. I'm not saying I'll work for free, of course." He'd worked as his uncle's slave enough for one lifetime. "But I can give you a cut. You could have ten percent of the takings."

"Fifty!"

"More like fifteen!"

"Twenty, then."

"Twenty it is."

Jonty paused. His uncle must be very sick indeed if he negotiated so easily. But not so sick that he didn't look for an opportunity to insult Jonty.

"Things not going well with that pretty wife of yours?"

"Things are grand." A lie was preferable to giving his uncle details about Katie. "But London is not."

"So you need a place to live? Rent will be extra, you know."

"We won't be living with you, Uncle." Jonty had been expecting this. Their own flat in an overcrowded tenement building would be preferable to being back here. "We'll find our own place to live."

An expression he didn't think Uncle Hamish was capable of passed over his jaundiced face. It was only brief, and his uncle quickly concealed it. If Jonty hadn't had long experience with Hamish Munro, he might have thought it was disappointment.

"I'll think about it."

Jonty stood to leave. That was the best he could hope for.

"Goodbye, Uncle."

"Wait. Are you in Edinburgh tonight?"

Jonty paused at the urgency in Uncle Hamish's voice. He turned back. "At the hostel. I leave on the first train tomorrow."

Uncle Hamish frowned. "Well, fancy a drink?"

He indicated the bottle on the kitchen table. It really wasn't water, then.

Jonty almost laughed. The man's liver was obviously close to giving up the ghost, and yet here he was, still determined to poison it at every opportunity. He looked into those yellowed eyes, trying to read them. Uncle Hamish dropped his gaze to the table, realizing there was only one chipped and smudged glass. "You'll have to wash yourself a glass."

"No." For the first time in his life, the man in front of him looked small. "I don't drink. You taught me that."

Jonty hadn't meant his words as an insult, but they had that effect.

Hamish snarled. "Get out, then. And don't come asking me for anything else. My answer's no."

CHAPTER TEN

Sunday, 15 July 1945

"Keep your eyes closed."

In front of the small mirror in Mum's bedroom, Katie finished fixing Lucy's veil just as she would for one of the customers at Chez Martin. The veil was Mum's. She had stored it with care, so it only had a few moth holes. Katie had painstakingly mended the delicate fabric with tiny stitches. However, to conceal the darning, the veil had to sit just right.

"All right. Open them."

Lucy's beaming expression reflected in the mirror. Katie absorbed the glow with silent satisfaction.

"Oh, I love it." Lucy sighed, studying the workmanship. "You can barely see where the holes were."

"No one will ever know. Especially if we pin it this way." Katie adjusted the pins at the top. She would have liked to disguise the holes with tiny glass beads and trim it with lace, the way Madame was planning for Grace Deroy's gown. But they couldn't afford such frippery, especially as the veil draped all the way to the ground.

Lucy's brow furrowed in the mirror. "Do you think we should ask Mrs. G to keep it safe? From Dad, I mean?"

Katie considered the question. If the past was anything to go by, Dad's good mood would last another few days. But Jonty's presence added a variable she wasn't sure about. Happily, Dad and Jonty had been able to avoid each other, largely because Jonty was in Edinburgh. She was expecting him back any moment now, which filled her with a strange, restless anticipation.

"I think it will be safe with the other things." They'd devised a special place under the floorboards in Lucy's room to keep the wedding clothes they were making. It had been a long time since Dad had burned Katie's sewing in the back garden. But after the other night, they wouldn't take any chances. "But you'd better put it there now. There's just enough time to try on your dress so I can fix the hem."

Lucy took one more glance at herself in the mirror before her face fell. "Do you think he's going to turn out like Dad?"

"Who?" Katie helped her sister unpin the veil.

"Matthew."

Katie paused her unpinning and switched her gaze to Lucy's suddenly serious face in the mirror. Lucy's hazel eyes appealed to Katie. "What if . . . what if he turns out like Dad? Or what if . . . what if things go wrong like they did with you and Jonty?"

Katie's eyes locked on her sister's in the mirror. She couldn't do much but stare and gape. She wanted to offer reassurance. Calm Lucy's heart with her own observations about Matthew. Say that he was a man who was cut from a different cloth to Dad. That Matthew had only ever treated her well. And not just Lucy, but everyone else on the street who'd watched him grow said what a fine and caring young man he'd become.

"Matthew will see you right. He won't . . ." The sound of a knock at the door interrupted them, stealing away the words pressing through her throat. Jonty must have forgotten his key. Her heart lightened at the thought of seeing him, but his timing ruined their sisterly moment.

"It will be fine. I promise." She offered Lucy a sisterly hug as Jonty knocked again. "That will be Jonty. Can you unpin the veil yourself?"

Lucy nodded, though clearly disappointed the conversation wouldn't continue.

"Coming!" Katie flew down the stairs to the front door. She threw it open, expecting Jonty. Her smile drooped into confusion when she came face to face with her former commanding officer.

"Maggie! What are you doing here?"

Maggie Morrison—although she was Maggie Thomas now—was the last woman on earth Katie expected to see standing on her doorstep. How long had it been since she'd last seen her? Two years? Maybe more.

"I've come to see Jonty! Grace told me he was demobbed." Maggie peered into the house. "Is he here?"

"Jonty's not here." Katie glanced up the stairs to where Lucy had come to the landing, peering down curiously.

The hem! Lucy mouthed.

But Katie couldn't send her old friend away. "But I expect him back any minute. Do you want to come in and wait?" Katie held open the door. "He's on his way home from seeing his uncle."

Her final word faded when she saw the bundle Maggie carried in her arms. A baby. Not a newborn, but no older than two months, Katie guessed. A snuffling sound pierced Katie's heart as the bundle squirmed. She stepped back, recoiling from the child, but it must have looked like she was inviting Maggie inside, because she stepped into the house.

"His uncle?" Maggie's eyes widened, as though she understood the significance of the visit as much as Katie did.

Katie closed the door, catching a glimpse of Lucy's slumping shoulders. Katie turned back to point Maggie in the direction of the sitting room.

Katie could not take her eyes from the bundle strapped to Maggie as Katie waved her hand to the mess in the sitting room. "We're in the middle of making Lucy's wedding things, but find a seat where you can." She motioned to the sofa. "I'll make tea."

She hurried into the kitchen, only to realize that her heart was beating fast. Her breathing too. She struggled to compose herself. To be upset at seeing a baby was silly. She'd seen plenty of babies since Betty was born and hadn't had this reaction of . . . What was it? Panic? She took several breaths to compose herself. But her hands shook as she added the tea to the pot.

She heard a sniffily wail from the next room, followed by Maggie apologizing that the baby needed to eat. Why did that sound hurt Katie's heart so much?

It must be Maggie. Babies were just little bundles. Ones Katie could ignore. But Maggie, a living, breathing reminder of Katie's past, had just barged into her home without warning. Of course it made her skittish.

Katie's shaky hands meant making the tea took longer than it should. She forced calm onto her countenance, returning to the sitting room with a tea tray. She kept her eyes on Maggie, despite the feeding baby trying to steal Katie's attention.

Maggie looked the same as she did two years ago. Dark hair. A plain face. A bossy personality that had made her a perfect corporal. She was thicker about the waist maybe, after two babies.

Two.

Katie remembered Grace mentioning that Maggie's first baby had died before even taking a breath.

"So how have you been?" Katie asked.

While Katie poured the tea, Maggie gave a steady stream of details about her life since they had last seen each other. In any other circumstances, the details might be interesting, but Katie couldn't take them in. She fought to keep an interested expression and tried not to stare at the baby, despite the adorable, sleepy snuffles.

"Would you like to hold her?"

Katie's heart stopped. She shook her head. She never wanted to hold a baby ever again. Being the oldest of eight, she'd held many babies in her life, but not one since that day she'd laid hers in the ground. Her chest tightened. A lump constricted her throat so she could barely force out words. "I couldn't."

"Of course you can." The bossy commanding officer came out in Maggie. She wouldn't take no for an answer. "Someone has to while I drink my tea."

Katie couldn't do it, but she couldn't stop Maggie from forcing the baby onto her. Katie's arms worked without instruction, taking the babe and drawing her close.

"Her name is Edith. We call her Eadie."

Oblivious that she had left her mother's embrace, Eadie was perfect in every way. Angelic even. Swaddled in butter muslin, she had wriggled one little hand out of the wrappings and lay with it balled in a fist against her cheek. This pressed her adorable mouth open into a pout under a perfect button nose and long-lashed eyes. She let out a little sigh that sang straight into Katie's heart.

A tearless, trembling sob escaped Katie, as though this heedless child opened the part of her heart that she kept locked. Maggie should take her baby back right now, not entrust her to the arms of a sobbing woman. But instead, Maggie kneeled in front of Katie and put her hands on Katie's arms, embracing them both.

Katie tried to explain. "My Betty died."

"I know. I'm so sorry, Katie."

Katie tore her eyes from Eadie long enough to register the tears in Maggie's, as well as unspeakable understanding. Katie didn't need to explain herself to someone who had cradled their own unmoving child.

"Do you want to keep holding her? You don't have to if you don't want to."

"I do," Katie whispered, conscious of the trust that Maggie

showed by allowing her to hold her doubly-dear daughter. Katie's manners went out the window, and polite conversation abandoned her. All she was capable of in this moment was staring at the divine little face snuggled in her arms.

Eventually Maggie stood, returned to her seat on the sofa, and sipped her tea. They sat in silence, apart from Edith's occasional happy snuffle, until Jonty arrived. Maggie leaped up when she saw him, rushing to the door and flinging her arms around his neck. He almost fell over from the force of it. If Katie hadn't been so absorbed by the bundle in her arms, she might have been jealous at the closeness between the pair.

"It's so good to see you!" Maggie said.

Jonty stilled when he saw the baby. Katie raised her eyes, managing a small smile. She couldn't read his expression properly. Stern and serious, with that furrow that cut deeper when he was suppressing his emotions. He cleared his throat.

The moment dragged as each one looked to the other for a cue about how to act next.

Finally Maggie spoke. "You know, Jonty, I really feel like a walk. Katie, would you mind holding Eadie while Jonty takes me to get some air?"

With that, Maggie took Jonty by the arm and dragged him out of the house.

Jonty couldn't get the picture of Katie holding Maggie's baby out of his mind. So beautiful and yet so sad. The last time he had seen her like that, the little bundle had been in a heavenly sleep, not an earthly one. He'd been the one to kneel in front of her and encourage her to relinquish the bundle to the doctor.

"Katie-my-love, she's gone. You have to let her go."

He would never forget the look she gave him then. How her hollow, exhausted eyes had held all the despair in the world. She'd passed him Betty's body. So small. So still.

"So where are you working?"

Maggie's question drew him out of the memory. He'd already filled her in on what had happened to him in the last few months.

The crash.

Hiding in a farmer's cellar in France.

His rescue by the Americans.

Returning to England and being demobilized. Jonty gave her extra details that he thought her husband Alec, himself a pilot, would appreciate.

"I'm working at Liverpool Street, repairing the damage. As you can see, there's a lot of work going."

She glanced around at the destruction. "You must come to stay with us sometime. We have a tiny flat in Grantham now. It would be so much more sensible to live with my dad, but this way Alec can come home some nights."

He nodded, understanding just how much her husband would appreciate coming home to his own flat and not his father-in-law's house. "Sounds nice. The house here is very crowded."

"So how are things with Katie?"

He cleared his throat. It wasn't appropriate to discuss his marriage with another married woman, even if that woman was like a sister. But he had spent last Christmas with Alec and Maggie at her father's house, so she knew how bad things had been.

"Well, she still doesn't want a divorce, so that's something."

There wasn't much else promising that he felt comfortable reporting.

"She's still hurting about the baby, Jonty."

He cleared his throat again. He knew that. "But I don't know what to do about it."

"Have you two talked about it? Since you've been home, I mean."

He shook his head. She'd fled when he'd broached the topic the other day. He didn't even know how to begin raising it again. "Still trying to be my guardian angel, are you?"

He thought back to the night he'd met Maggie, although he couldn't remember that much. He certainly didn't remember the crash, which he counted as a blessing. But some things he remembered as clearly as yesterday.

The smell of gasoline and the taste of blood.

The heat of the flames as fire ate up the mangled front section of the aircraft. The grip of fear the moment he realized he sat surrounded by several magazines of unfired bullets.

The escape doors that should have allowed him to drop to safety had been jammed somehow, and he couldn't manage to open them, with his fingers so slippery with sweat and blood. Maggie had arrived as he was beating the Perspex of his pod with his fists, screaming and howling for help. He didn't know her name then, but her appearance was a miracle. So he called her his guardian angel.

The memories after that were a blur of images that he relied on others to knit together for him.

Intense heat.

Orange flame.

Searing skin.

Frantic fingers desperately working at the parachute harness that was stopping him from escaping the burning plane.

Being dragged along the grass to safety.

The long, long days in a hospital, where he lay utterly alone.

His guardian angel turned up again, next to his hospital bed, with a Bible under her arm. "One thing being a vicar's daughter has taught me is that the best thing to do when you feel helpless is to open your Bible."

Which she did. Every time. He'd done nothing but groan the first time she came. The pain wasn't as bad as he made out at first. He just thought she'd stop reading if he seemed like he was suffering. But his playacting strengthened her resolve. She managed to get through three of the four gospels from beginning to end over the course of a few weeks. The words were their own kind of pain relief. All that talk of being loved and saved. So different to his uncle's hypocritical sermonizing.

After months and months of skin grafts and saline baths and bandages and special exercises to keep his skin supple—not to mention lying on his stomach because it was the only way to get comfortable—he was offered a medical discharge. But it didn't seem right to quit while the war was still on. And low and behold, he ended up working at the same airfield as his guardian angel.

That was where he'd met Katie. She'd worked in the armory, packing the bullets into the belts of the ammunition he used in his guns. Her fingers were the fastest he had ever seen, and her face the prettiest. He'd spent a lot of spare time in the armory. So much so that her smile became his talisman each night he flew a mission. He would go to sign his ammunition out of the armory and not leave until he had seen it. She probably hadn't known how much she meant to him, until Jimmy Hardie did his worst.

Jonty realized Maggie was speaking as he relived the past in his mind. Not speaking. Lecturing.

"Do you know what I have to do when something goes wrong with my knitting and it's not turning out the way I thought it would?"

He frowned. What did knitting have to do with anything?

"I have to unravel everything and go back to the spot where I dropped the stitch and pick it up from there."

How could he tell Maggie that since things had never really gone right for him and Katie, he couldn't identify exactly one point in time to go back to?

No. That wasn't true. There were moments before Betty was born when he'd thought his crazy marriage scheme might result in lasting happiness. He'd been so optimistic about the future that he'd requested safer work in a training school so that he could be a real husband—and more importantly—a real father once the baby came. He'd proposed sure that he wouldn't live to see the end of the war, and yet there he'd been planning a future for them.

Betty had been born blue and sickly. Katie had shut him out, and any hope he'd had died with the child.

"I tried once. It didn't work. Just pushed her further away."

"Did you just say 'once'?" His guardian angel developed a touch of school headmistress. "You tried 'once'?"

His frown deepened, possibly into a scowl.

"Don't harrumph at me."

Had he? He hadn't realized.

"She is still caged in by grief, trapped there. Once won't cut it! If the nurses in the hospital changed your bandages once, would you have healed? They did it every day for months, and look at you now. Your skin has grown over and around. And yes, you have scars, and sometimes they hurt, but you can move on. Just because the wound is in her heart doesn't mean she doesn't need the same loving care. You're the only one who can do it, Jonty."

She must be right. Maggie usually was. But he still had no idea where to start. "I'm not good at romantic gestures."

"Don't forget how you two came to be married in the first place. That was the biggest romantic gesture I've ever seen."

CHAPTER ELEVEN

Friday, 20 July 1945

Katie rounded the corner to see Jan, leaning against the wall near the cemetery, finishing a cigarette. One leg was bent up, foot flat against the wall. She noticed him before he saw her. How could she not? He was terribly handsome in his blue uniform. Broad shoulders, even if he was a bit skinny, and such piercing-blue eyes.

"Jan! You're back! I didn't expect you today."

Jan hadn't been specific about how long he'd be away, but she had the impression he'd wanted her to mind that package in her sewing basket for months, not weeks. Jan was the only one who knew about her Friday afternoon visits to the cemetery. She hadn't even told Jonty. Over the last two years, Jan had often come, standing at a respectful distance while she tidied Betty's grave.

After Maggie's visit, Katie had been unable to ignore the urge to visit Betty's grave this evening. It wasn't a wise decision. She was needed at home to put the finishing touches on the wedding gown and do all the other things that needed doing ahead of the big day tomorrow. But she wanted to be here. How had Jan known?

"I came on the off chance you would be here. I didn't want you to be alone."

He pushed off the wall and presented her with a bouquet of flowers—for the grave, of course, not for her. But still, her heart leaped in her chest. What woman didn't enjoy being given flowers? The blooms engulfed her with the happy scent of summertime.

"They're perfect! Thank you."

Jan fell in step beside her. He must know the way to the grave as well as she did by now.

"Why didn't you come by the house, if you got back early?"

"I wasn't sure about coming to the house with flowers, what with your husband back. Perhaps I can accompany you after we visit the grave. I have something to give my aunt."

Of course, a man shouldn't be buying flowers for another man's wife, should he? Not that there was anything inappropriate about flowers intended for a grave, despite the way her heart clamored. Jonty might not think so. She downplayed any tension.

"It's not Jonty you have to worry about. It's Lucy. What with the wedding tomorrow, she doesn't appreciate anything that distracts us from our preparations."

Her comment extracted a smile from Jan's serious face. "I wanted to ask you something."

She glanced sideways at the urgency in his tone. "All right, but we'll have to hurry. I wasn't planning on staying long this evening. The wedding is tomorrow, and there's a lot to do."

"Has your father been home recently?"

She shook her head. "No. And I'm glad." She explained about the tension in the house since Jonty had returned.

"Will he show up for the wedding, do you think?"

She paused. She hadn't considered the possibility that he wouldn't turn up, although she should have. Mum could walk Lucy down the aisle if required, but since Lucy wasn't twenty-one yet, she would need Dad's signature on the papers. Surely he'd be there.

"I think so. I know that he's not always reliable, but I expect him to get his act together by the weekend. After all, he didn't miss mine, and there's been so much more fuss about this one."

"How are things at home now that your husband has returned? Are you and he happy after all your time apart?"

It didn't feel right for another man to ask in that way. So she didn't look at him when she answered. "Of course. Things are fine."

She edged ahead so she wouldn't have to say more. They entered the cemetery gates and meandered along the path toward Betty's grave. Although crowded with headstones, the burial terrain had once been the ground of a grand house. It still had plenty of trees providing a calm, garden-like feel. Jan hung back while Katie approached the tiny grave.

"I'm sorry I haven't been here for a while."

Katie laid the flowers to one side while she pulled out the long grass from around the grave. She read the words on the gravestone as she did, although she knew them by heart.

Elizabeth Martha Ables, 22 days old. Sleeping in the arms of the Savior.

The engraving had been costly, and she'd had to weigh every letter. She'd known she wanted Betty's full name. She had deliberated so hard over what to call her daughter, deciding on Elizabeth after Jonty's mother and Martha after hers. She asked Jonty if he thought his mother would mind if she knew the baby wasn't really his.

He'd been certain. "I think she would be very honored."

Elizabeth was a solid name with so many variations, just like Katie's own name. She'd meant for her daughter to get a lifetime of use out of all of them. But in the end, they barely even had time to use the name Betty.

Just twenty-two days. No one measured the age of their child like that unless every one of those days was counted dear.

Sleeping in the arms of the Savior was Jonty's touch. He'd said something like it when he'd taken Betty from her and given her over to the undertaker.

"She slept in your arms while she was alive, Katie-my-love. We can trust her to the Lord's arms now."

Katie hadn't been here since starting work at Chez Martin. When she'd admitted to Maggie it had been weeks since she had visited the grave, her friend had assured her it was meant to be that way. And Mum said women who spent too much time at the graveside of their children eventually went mad. But guilt still nagged when Katie saw how far the grass had grown.

"I don't want people to think I don't love you, sweet girl."

The flowers she had placed there last time had dried and turned brown in the summer sun. She removed them, took a jam jar full of water from her handbag, unscrewed the lid, and tipped the contents into the vase she kept there. After adding Jan's flowers to the vase, she took a moment to appreciate the cheerful display. "There you go."

She would like to stay longer, to take more time, to think more deeply. But her family would be wondering where she was while they were doing all the work for tomorrow.

Maggie had said not to focus on the earthly grave but the heavenly home. "You don't need to stay stuck in the sadness of death when you know there's life beyond it," she'd said. Maggie was always so certain about such things.

Katie stood and looked back at Jan. He gave a small, sad smile when she rejoined him. She slipped her arm through his and turned them toward the gate, taking more comfort in his presence than she should. He joined her on the bus for the short ride back to Ivy Street. Neither of them spoke. However, she couldn't help but notice that something about his demeanor had changed. He'd lost his easiness and glanced over his shoulder several times, as though someone were behind them. When she looked, Katie saw no one.

"Let's get off here."

He grabbed her hand and pulled her off the bus a stop before the usual one before she had a chance to object or ask why.

"What is it, Jan?" she asked as he guided her rather hastily down the street.

"I've just remembered a prior engagement. A meeting with some friends on the other side of town."

Something about what he was saying—and his sudden change of heart—didn't ring true. She narrowed her eyes. "Jan, is everything all right?"

"Of course. But I need you to give something to my aunt for me. Tonight. Can you do that?"

Jan reached inside his jacket and pulled out an envelope with Polish writing across the front. She waited for an explanation, but he handed it to her without one, standing close, eyes focused on the road ahead, as though trying to pass her the envelope without an onlooker noticing.

A tingle ran up her spine, and she lowered her voice. "You're not in any trouble, are you, Jan?"

"Of course not." He gave a too-charming smile designed, she was sure, to distract her. The thick envelope felt heavy in her hand. She had never felt a wad of banknotes before, but this was the size and shape she imagined them to be. She almost laughed at the ridiculous thought as she slipped it into her handbag. Imagine anyone on Ivy Street having that much money.

He tried to laugh off the question, but she thought it sounded affected. "No. No trouble. Do you still have the box?"

She nodded. *What's in it?* The question burned inside her, but she didn't ask it aloud. "Do you want me to give that to Mrs. G too?"

He paused before answering. "No. But I need it back."

"I'll give it to you at the wedding tomorrow, if you like." He grimaced, as though the wedding was an unwelcome prospect. Strange, considering how well he'd come to know both Lucy and Matthew. "Mrs. G was going to ask you to play for us."

He glanced around, as though checking that they weren't being watched. What was wrong with him? They rounded the corner, heads still close.

"You are a very sweet girl, Katie. A true friend. I'll collect the box tomorrow."

"Are you sure everything is all right, Jan?"

Abruptly, Jan took her hand and kissed it, just as he'd done the night he'd given her the box. It had given her tingles then. Now it felt wrong.

She snatched her hand away as though his kiss burned. "Why do you keep doing that?"

"That's what I'd like to know!"

"Jonty!"

She knew he'd jumped to all the wrong conclusions, from the expression on his face. She hadn't done anything wrong, had she? She hurried away from Jan and slipped her arm through Jonty's. He raised his eyebrows in question.

She didn't meet his eye. "I'm glad you are here."

Jonty's look went from strange to suspicious, like a thundercloud threatening to storm. She didn't want to make a scene on the street, so she launched into introductions. "Jonty, you remember our friend Jan?" Even in her own head, she sounded strained, despite trying to keep her voice light.

"I do." Jonty's words were dangerously precise. "To what does Katie owe the . . . pleasure?"

"I happily ran into her on the bus."

Well, that was a lie.

"Hmmph." Jonty nodded, his gaze slipping between her and Jan. "Katie said you were away."

Jan smiled that too-charming smile again. "I was. I just returned this evening."

Really, he was acting in such a strange way.

"Thank you, Katie." Those blue eyes gave her a meaningful warning not to tell Jonty about the envelope in her handbag. Or maybe that was her guilty conscience talking.

"See you tomorrow. At the wedding?" she said.

"Of course. I wouldn't miss it for the world."

Jan turned and left. Jonty was silent, studying her with a curious expression that made her suddenly annoyed.

"Are you going to tell me what that was about?"

"It was nothing."

She dropped her hand from Jonty's arm and walked ahead, trying to give herself some physical distance from him so she could think it through.

"Really? Because it looked very much like something to me."

She'd never known Jonty's voice to have such a hard, bitter edge.

"Have you been"—he cleared his throat—"seeing him?"

His suspicion punched her in the belly. She stopped in her tracks. "How could you ask that?"

Jonty sighed, looking like he regretted speaking. Then he grimaced. "Katie, we didn't have the most conventional courtship, so I understand if, while I was away, you—"

"I never! Jan was my friend when I had no one else. That's all."

She fought to keep her voice down, not wanting to attract the attention of others. She didn't want to have this discussion on the street. In fact, she wanted to be in her house, where the presence of half a dozen other people would stop them from having the discussion at all.

She quickened her pace, but he kept up with her. She walked faster.

"Katie, don't walk away!" He grabbed her elbow.

She shrugged it off. "Don't tell me what to do!" Hot tears stung her eyes. Her calves ached with the strain of hurrying to escape.

"Please, Katie."

The desperation in his voice slowed her, like a force she couldn't name. She faced him. "I didn't do anything wrong."

"Do you want to tell me what happened then?" His eyes pleaded.

She hardened her heart. "It depends, Jonty. Do you want to tell me who Lily is?"

He went white. A deep crease pressed into his brow.

"I thought not."

She hurried on ahead, eager to ensconce herself to the safety of other people.

CHAPTER TWELVE

Saturday, 21 July 1945

Katie made it clear that Jonty had one role on the morning of Lucy's wedding. Stay out of the way. He added a second one. Keep the younger boys from stealing the food meant for the wedding breakfast.

"Your mum worked into the wee hours to make those, using the whole street's sugar ration."

He addressed Tim and Davy with his meanest glare when he caught one of them red handed stealing a biscuit. "If she sees even one missing when we sit down, then I don't even want to think about how hard the beating will be afterward."

The little hand dropped the biscuit as though it were a hot potato.

Jonty couldn't distract them with cricket or football in the street since that was where neighbors were setting up for the wedding breakfast, so he took all four boys to Mrs. G's, where there was less temptation and plenty of hard labor. Together, they carried Mrs. G's dining table and chairs onto the street.

Bunting fluttered in the breeze as they placed the furniture underneath its cheerful cover. He'd stayed out late last night with two of Mrs. G's tenants to help string it between the houses. The cheerful zigzag helped distract from the rubble of the homes opposite Katie's front door.

"Jonty! I need your help." They were just covering the table with Mrs. G's lace tablecloth when Katie approached. The vision that greeted him when he looked up tightened his throat and made answering impossible.

She'd worn special rollers last night to make her hair curl, and now it bounced around her shoulders, like she was in a film. Her blue dress—not new, he noted; she said she didn't have time—complemented her eyes. More than ever, he wanted to find a way into her heart and tend to the broken pieces there, the way Maggie had said he should.

"You look beautiful, Katie-my-love," he murmured.

A deep frown cut a line into her porcelain forehead as she pulled him away from the boys and whispered low. "Dad's not here."

"Still?"

They hadn't seen hide nor hair of Bill since Jonty had returned from Edinburgh. All the women in the house seemed convinced that he would appear in time for the wedding. But Jonty had grown uneasy the closer it got to the day. "Is this usual for him?"

"He does go away sometimes—"

Jonty hissed through his teeth, shaking his head. His already low opinion of Katie's father fell to a new subterranean level. "You mean disappears completely on his daughter's wedding day?"

Mrs. G approached from behind Katie, wearing her finest floral dress. She'd overheard the gist of their conversation. "Is your father not here, Katie?"

Mortification washed over Katie's face. She shot Jonty a glare, as though her father disappearing was his fault.

"Yes, Mrs. G. We haven't seen him for a few days. It's almost time to leave, and I thought he would be back by now."

"Has your mother checked the usual places?"

Katie's brows came together in confusion as she nodded. "She said to say that yes, she has. I think he's under the table, probably at the pub."

"But which one?" Mrs. G seemed to speak under her breath. "How much time is there?"

"We are due at the registry office at quarter past eleven."

Jonty leaned over to Katie and asked in a low voice, "Shall I start checking the pubs to see if I can find him?"

"Would you?" She spun toward him, blue eyes shining with hope.

When she looked at him like he was her hero, how could he not? "As long as someone keeps the boys away from the food. Or they'll be nothing left for the party, ye ken?"

"Done." Her lips, coated with the prettiest shade of pink, stretched into a smile that lightened his heart, despite his father-in-law's shenanigans.

Fifteen minutes and three pubs later, he found Bill Baines nursing a beer. The moment felt eerily familiar—he'd hauled his uncle home from a few pubs in his day. He wanted to throttle the man who should be at home waiting for his daughter to appear in all her finery. Finery that she and Katie had spent much of the last three weeks making perfect.

But he knew from experience he had to work out exactly how many sheets to the wind Bill was before he tried to get him out of the pub. That way he'd know if that man would come willingly or if Jonty would need to enlist extra help.

Bill sat scowling, his drink untouched in front of him. A good sign. Then Jonty noticed that Bill's eyes were glazed over. As though he were staring at the drink but not seeing it. Had the man been drinking since he'd left them all those days ago? No, this seemed different from one of his uncle's benders.

"Oi." The bartender called Jonty to the bar. "I've never seen Bill like this."

Jonty headed to the bar to get the lay of the land. "Is he a regular here?"

"On and off. But today he came in when I opened, sat down, and stared. I had to go over and put the pint in front of him, and he still hasn't touched it. Very strange."

So he wasn't drunk. Jonty cocked his head as he looked at Bill. The man's vacant stare hovered in the middle distance.

"Good thing. It's his daughter's wedding today."

"You better get him out of here then, although I don't know what use he'll be to you. Very strange."

Jonty offered the man coins for the pint. The barkeep took them and went back to his muttering. Jonty approached Bill's table warily. "Bill." He greeted his father-in-law and sat down at the wooden table opposite him.

Bill didn't even glance up in acknowledgment but kept his eyes fixed on a point just beyond his glass.

"The whole street is looking for you." *Not to mention your wife and daughters.* "Lucy is beside herself. She wants her father there for her wedding."

At the mention of his daughter's name, Bill's expressionless face dipped into a frown. His eyes focused on Jonty for the first time. "Lucy?"

Jonty bit back the sarcasm on the tip of his tongue, opting for something less inflammatory. "The wedding is today."

He certainly wouldn't have forgotten if he'd been anywhere near the house. The wedding dominated the place. Maybe that was why Bill stayed away.

Coward.

"Lucy's wedding. Right."

Even as Jonty let his uncharitable thoughts run rampant, he stayed in the seat opposite Bill. The man seemed to be registering his words but not his presence. One finger made a nervous tapping on the tabletop.

"Are you all right, Bill?"

If this had been an RAF mess and not a city pub, Jonty would say Bill was in shock. But as soon as Jonty had the thought, Bill's eyes fixed on him, transforming from vacant to shrewd in a second.

Bill glanced about the pub, as if trying to work out where he was, as though he were seeing his surroundings for the first time.

"I'm fine. What's this about Lucy?"

"She needs you at the registry office. She needs the signature of both parents."

Bill grunted in response and lifted his drink toward his mouth. Jonty intercepted it before it reached his lips.

"No time. You need to get cleaned up and your daughter wed."

Katie took a moment to rest her aching legs, propping her feet on a chair. She sipped champagne from a teacup to slake her thirst on the warm summer's afternoon. The wedding breakfast had become a luncheon as more and more neighbors had joined, bringing out food, tea, sherry, and enough merriment to keep everyone lingering. There might even be leftovers. She suspected the black market was responsible for the champagne Dad had brought with him when Jonty had hauled him home. But that didn't matter. Not when Dad's jovial mood rubbed off on everyone.

Lucy and Matthew sat in the center of it all, beaming happily. Young and in love and ready to start a new life without the shadow of war hanging over them.

"Jonty saved the day, you know." Mum had the same idea as Katie. She sat with legs raised, surveying the happiness around her. Mum was smiling, which made Katie smile too.

Someone had put the wireless in the window, and Jonty was in the middle of the jolly crowd serenading Mrs. G to the tune of "I'm Beginning to See the Light."

"He did," Katie acknowledged.

Jonty had arrived with Dad at the registry office with moments to spare. She was ready to declare Jonty a miracle worker for bringing Dad home in such a happy state.

"You two need to find a place of your own, you know."

What a thing to be bringing up at Lucy's wedding, of all places. How much champagne had Mum had?

"Trying to get rid of us both in one day, are you?"

"No. I like having you around. But it will be good for you to find a less crowded place. You two need it."

"There's not a lot in London, thanks to Gerry. And we can't move farther afield because our jobs are here."

"You're a seamstress, Katie. You'll find work wherever you go."

"But this is my home." Katie waved her hand at the lovely party, full of people she'd known since she was a girl. With everyone so happy, it was easy to ignore that the party took place in front of the rubble of a broken building.

"No, Katie. *He* is your home."

Katie laughed off the comment, taking another sip of champagne to ward off Mum's serious turn. *Is that what you tell yourself when Dad disappears for days on end? When he has to be hauled out of a pub to give his daughter away?*

She didn't speak the questions that had been bubbling under the surface since the night Dad had arrived home drunk. But they came out anyway, as a snort into her cup.

"Don't you take me for a fool, my girl. You and I might have been married under similar circumstances, but that man is as different to your father as chalk is to cheese."

The joy of the party dissolved as Mum's words hit her straight in the heart. "What do mean?"

"You know what I mean, Katie. At least you were his. Your father wouldn't have stayed if there was any doubt."

Katie felt like Mum had slapped her across the face right there in the middle of the party. She dropped her voice to a whisper.

"You knew? How?"

Mum kept her voice low, but it was still certain and direct. "I've had eight babies myself and seen many more born. If that child was his, it would've had red hair. That's just the way it goes when the mother has your pale coloring. But that child got her dark hair from her father—and there's no way it came from Jonty."

Katie couldn't stop her mind from picturing her darling daughter and the thick black hair she'd been born with. She had tried desperately to keep it tucked into a little hat.

"You are just lucky that the child was naturally small and no one suspected. Did he know the child wasn't his?"

Katie's heart ached inside her chest. Her mother was wrong: There was nothing lucky about Betty's short life. She nodded meekly. "The marriage was his idea."

"Oh, Katie. That man is pure gold. He is good at his heart, you hear me. Good. And being married to a good man can see you through a lot in this life."

Jonty led Mrs. G back to where Katie sat with her mother, then extended his hand to Katie. Mrs. G's eyes shone after being twirled around for a song or two, as they had done last night when Katie had handed her Jan's package.

"Jan had promised me a dance, but he's not here. Jonty did very well in his absence."

"Jan's not here?" She looked around to confirm it. Didn't he say he would collect his box from her today? He'd seemed so adamant yesterday.

"Will ye dance, Katie-my-love?"

Just as he asked, she saw Lucy signaling to her. Mum saw it too and hurried to her daughter, before beckoning Katie to join.

"I have to go to Lucy. Matron-of-honor business."

He drew back his hand, his smile showing his disappointment. With her mother's words fresh in her mind, rejecting him felt more significant. He was a good man who had done a good thing today.

He stepped back to give her room as she stood. But she closed the distance and, right there in front of Mrs. G, leaned in to kiss Jonty on the cheek, the rough skin of his scars under her lips. "Thank you for today, Jonty. You saved the day."

She'd caught him completely by surprise. The look on his face when she stepped back was all wonder and delight. A smile twitched on her lips. Then she felt her cheeks heat. Knowing she was under the curious gaze of half the women in the street, she hurried inside.

As Lucy said her final goodbye, Katie sensed she was hoping to glean some last-minute advice for her wedding night from her closest confidantes. Katie let Mum offer specifics since she had been so frank with Katie earlier. If only she'd been that frank before Katie had left to join the WAAF.

"He loves you, and he'll take care of you" was all Katie said, conscious that knowing how to interpret the married-woman code would be quite handy right now.

"And I'll just be down the street," Lucy added, tears spilling from her eyes after the emotions of the day.

"Yes." Katie nodded, blinking back tears that were silly, considering she'd likely see her sister every day. "Just down the street."

Martha kissed Lucy's cheek and tearfully reiterated how lovely she looked and how happy she would be, before the younger boys barreled in ahead of Dad.

He'd swaggered at the party, being congratulated by neighbors about having his daughter off his hands. Katie was still smarting from overhearing him respond "Hopefully, this one won't be back!" to the chuckle of the men around him.

"You've done well, Lucy. Matthew has grown into a fine young man."

Lucy beamed under Dad's kind words, wrapping her arms around his neck and squeezing him tight as a thank-you for being there. But Katie couldn't shake the feeling that Dad was playacting. He never did that when it was just the family. She resolved to ask Jonty exactly what had happened when he'd found Dad at the pub.

CHAPTER THIRTEEN

Thursday, 26 July 1945

"This is good work, Ables."

Jonty stepped back and admired the cabinetry in the new inquiries office. It wasn't all his work, but he'd done the finishing touches and enjoyed the satisfaction of seeing them done well. Colin, the foreman, stood next to him, equally appreciative.

Jonty nodded. "Aye."

Gerry had never managed a direct hit on Liverpool Street. Thank God. The deep tunnels underneath had been used as a air-raid shelter during the worst of the blitz. Had the Luftwaffe managed to find their target, the tragedy would have been overwhelming. Even without a direct hit, they'd hit near enough to cause structural damage.

"So what's next?"

Colin checked the list on his clipboard. The structural work involved several specialist craftsmen, including carpenters and stonemasons. In the scheme of things, Jonty's role was minor. But even though he was just doing odds and ends—carting materials from trucks to where they were needed or adding coats of paint—knowing he was restoring something satisfied him in a way that working in an office could not.

"I think I'll get you to work at the eastern entrance. It's mostly painting, but they're falling behind and can use an extra hand."

"Right then."

Jonty spotted a mark on the new cabinetry and reached out a finger to smooth it away.

But Colin lingered. "You don't say much, do you?"

Jonty paused, halting midway through his movement to look at Colin, who was studying him. Not him. His scars. Everyone always looked at the scars. "I figure I'll let my work do the talking, ye ken?"

Colin nodded. "Well, some of the boys and I go to the pub when we're done for the day, if you ever think, you know . . . you'd like to say more."

Jonty couldn't help but smile. "I'll keep it in mind."

What the foreman said was true. He spent most of his workdays in silence, which wasn't his natural state. But here, he found himself absorbed in the work and—considering how noisy things were with four boisterous boys in Martha's house—enjoyed its peace. Just him and a paintbrush all afternoon long.

"They told me I'd find you here."

Jonty's head shot up at the voice he recognized but never expected to hear at this worksite. "Alec Thomas? What are you doing here?"

Jonty abandoned his work to shake Alec's hand, wiping off the Lincoln-green smudges onto a rag first. Despite years as a pilot, as well as the strain of personal tragedy and new fatherhood, Alec hadn't lost his supernatural handsomeness. He could still fill in as Clark Gable's look-alike, should he ever need one. And though Alec didn't need any extra advantage, he still wore his Royal Australian Air Force uniform.

"Maggie told me you'd be here. She'd have my head if I'd been anywhere near Liverpool Street and didn't try to find you."

Jonty grinned. It was hard to say no to Maggie. Even more so when you were as smitten as Alec was, almost from the outset. "A wise man listens to his wife."

Several workmates eyed them strangely, probably wondering where Jonty's talkativeness came from. "It's good to see you. Are you in London long?"

"Just tonight. Want to join me for a drink after you knock off?"

An hour later they entered a nearby pub crowded with workers slaking their thirst after a long day. Jonty spotted Colin but sent him only a nod. This was a night for reminiscing with old friends, not making new ones.

"My shout." Alec headed for the bar without allowing Jonty to offer, so he found them a table. When Alec arrived with the drinks, he proposed a toast. "To old friends."

They tapped their glasses and took a sip, slipping easily into conversation. News from people they knew. Updates about friends who didn't make it through the war. When the war would finally end.

"We are converting the Lancs for the Pacific, but I'm praying the Japs just give up. They must know they are beaten, surely."

"You're a squadron leader now?" Jonty flicked his gaze to the extra stripes on Alec's sleeve. "Are you planning to stay in the air force once the war's done?"

"No. Bomber Command isn't the flavor of the month right now, but I'll see the war through to the end."

Jonty knew the criticism their war work faced as much as anyone. Earlier in the year, allied bombers had dropped more bombs on Berlin in one night than had fallen on London during the whole of 1940. It was right to question that strategy. But when he did, he always arrived at the same conclusion: How else were they going to defeat a tyrant?

"But as soon as it's done, I'm taking Mags back to a place that gets actual sunshine for more than two weeks of the year."

The perpetual gray of England was a bugbear for every Australian Jonty had ever met. He'd always loved the way Alec talked about the vastness of the sky in his homeland. "Sounds lovely."

"You could come. I heard the government wants to offer assisted passage to British migrants. Apparently, we have to populate or perish."

"What's *assisted passage?*"

Alec took another sip of beer. "Honestly, I don't know all the details, and it might just be a rumor. But it's something about migrants only having to pay ten pounds, and the government pays the rest."

"And you say it's always sunny?"

"Always." Alec spoke like a man who'd been away from his home too long.

Jonty grinned. "Where do I sign up?" They lapsed into silence for a moment. "So how's fatherhood?"

"Eadie smiled at me the other day." The joy in Alec's eyes was unmistakable.

Jonty only curbed his envy because he knew about the heartbreak that preceded it.

"I never would have thought that a bundle so small could make me feel something so big."

"That much I understand." It was just that Jonty's big feelings weren't the happy kind.

"Mags said you're living with Katie's family. How's that going?"

Jonty sighed, which he hoped was an answer in itself. "Quite frankly, I think I had more privacy when I was in the air force. It's complicated, but it's all we have for now."

He explained the situation with Bill and the trip to Edinburgh, which had failed to give them options as he'd hoped.

"You know you can come and stay with us anytime you like. Our flat is small, but you are always welcome."

"Quiet!" a voice called out from the other side of the pub, and a hush settled over the drinkers. "The BBC is announcing who won the election."

He and Alec listened to a somber Mr. Churchill concede defeat, acknowledging that Britain wanted to move on from the war and "face the future," as the Labor campaign had said. Jonty felt the man's words in his very soul.

"To the future?" Alec offered a toast.

"The future."

That night, Jonty sat on the bed, his military-issue Bible in his lap and Katie's pillow supporting his back. Seeing Alec and Maggie had inspired him to open the Good Book for the first time since . . . well, to his shame, he couldn't say. He was grappling with the verse in James about patience in suffering, when Katie opened the door, her cheeks pink with agitation.

"Jonty, I just found out that Jan is AWOL."

He'd come up here because Bill was home, acting like a dutiful father. The adults had listened to Mr. Attlee's first speech as the new prime minister together, but then Jonty had retired, sick of Bill's carry-on. He didn't blame Martha and Katie for enjoying it. Growing up with such an unpredictable man likely made them inclined to savor the happy moments when they arrived.

"Really?" He tried to keep his voice light and sound interested in her friend. After last Friday, when he'd come upon them arm in arm, heads leaning close—then seeing Jan kiss her hand again—he knew there must be more to the relationship that Katie was telling him. Since he wanted her to confide in him, he tried to remain neutral.

"He said he was coming to the wedding on Friday evening— do you remember?"

"I remember." They'd had a row straight after. "Is he usually so untrustworthy?"

"No." She shot him a look that said he was being petty, as he knew he was. "He was going to collect the package he'd left with me."

"Package?"

He shifted the pillow behind his back, enjoying the lavender scent wafting up from the sprig Katie kept inside the slip. Since the wedding, they had been back in the smaller room with the single bed, sleeping top and tail, instead of him on the floor.

"It's some sort of box, I think, wrapped in brown paper. But he was keen to get it back from me on Friday. I think it's strange he didn't come."

"What does Mrs. G say?"

"I don't know. She's not in. Mr. Gregory said she's gone to visit a friend for a few days."

"Are you worried for Jan?" They were verging on difficult territory. The last time he'd tried to press a conversation about Jan, she'd stormed off.

This time she stood, back pressed to the door, deep in thought. "I am. He was acting strangely on Friday. I've never seen him like that. I called RAF Coltishall. They said he had a leave pass for the weekend but should have been back by Monday morning. It's Thursday night now."

"Coltishall, you say?" He'd been there once. In fact, he knew of a quiet inn above a delightful pub. He rubbed his chin as he thought fast, hoping the inspiration he felt was due to the open Bible in his lap. Otherwise, it was likely to be nothing more than a foolhardy gamble. "You'll get more information in person, I think."

"What do you mean?"

"Well, you'll want to find his friends and ask them where he might have gone."

She stayed pressed up against the door, but the attention in those eager blue eyes was all his. "But I don't know his friends."

"That's why you need to be there in person. Go down to the

local pub, and I'm sure you'll find a few Polish men in uniform still celebrating that Hitler is dead. Ask them."

"Do you really think I could?" She left the safety of the door and stepped to the bed, taking a seat on her end. He reached behind his back and removed her pillow so she could have it for support. The scent of lavender lingered as he passed it over.

"I'd come with you, of course." He wasn't sending his wife into a strange pub full of unknown airmen by herself. Goodness no. "But men the world over will give a surprising amount of information when asked by a beautiful woman with a pretty smile."

She arranged the pillow behind her back. Did she even understand his weak attempt at flirtation?

"And your smile, Katie-my-love, is so bonny. I'm sure you'll get whatever information you need."

She looked at him directly then, and an altogether different kind of pink spread across her cheeks. Her small smile made him want to close the space between them. But he offered a bashful smile in return and went back to the Bible.

The only word he could work out on the page was *patience*.

CHAPTER FOURTEEN

Friday, 27 July 1945

Time was of the essence if they were going to find out what had happened to Jan. That was what he told himself when he'd planned to whisk Katie away that weekend. But if he was honest, he was more eager for time alone with his wife. No fickle father-in-law to contend with, no boisterous younger brothers, and no distractions. When he put his plan to Katie, she'd smiled at him in a way that made his heart squeeze.

Oh yes. The plan was a good one.

They'd have a full day to themselves, two if they left on Friday night, which meant over twenty-four hours of luxurious privacy, more if he counted the train rides to and from.

Suffering a migraine during the trip was not a part of the plan. He'd been so determined not to let anything ruin his scheme that he'd ignored the warning signs, including the stars in his field of vision, which told him one was coming on.

It only got worse from there. Katie had noticed something

was wrong at King's Cross Station. Of course, he'd denied it. He ignored the strange looks she gave him from where she sat opposite him. By Peterborough she'd asked him if he was feeling peculiar. At that point, denial was no longer an option. He had to keep his eyes closed, shielded from the light, and muttered from behind his hands.

"Why didn't you say something before?"

"I didn't want to spoil our plans. I was looking forward to having my beautiful wife all to myself."

His pitiful admission brought on a sympathetic smile from Katie. "Oh, Jonty."

"If we can just get to the inn, I can lie down for a bit. It might pass."

She raised a dubious eyebrow. "Close your eyes. I'll wake you when we are at Norwich."

Gratefully, he leaned against the window and let his eyelids slide closed. He supposed he slept. It felt as though barely any time had passed when he dragged his eyes open again, in response to Katie gently shaking him.

"We're here. And we have to walk to the inn."

He had to lean heavily on her shoulder for the mile-long walk from the station to the inn. The hammering in his temple intensified with every step, and the ground felt like it was moving under his feet. "I'm so sorry, Katie-my-love. This has only happened a couple of times before."

"Stop apologizing, Jonty. We just have to make the best of this."

By the time she checked them in at the inn, he didn't even have the energy to speak.

"Does he need a doctor?" The landlady eyed him suspiciously.

"He just needs to lie down, I'm afraid. A migraine."

The landlady tsked in sympathy as Katie slipped back under his arm and dragged him up the stairs to their room. She deposited him on the bed and removed his shoes while he groaned helplessly. Then she drew the curtains, which mercifully darkened the room.

"All part of my plan," he murmured.

At some point, the pain gave way to sleep. He woke to the smell of soup. It was dark outside the open window. He vaguely registered the gentle chatter of the patrons below, before opening his eyes to see Katie placing a bowl of soup on the bedside.

"The landlady insisted."

He pushed himself up, and his misguided hope that this would pass by tomorrow dissolved as the room swam around him. Katie arranged the pillows behind his back, but the physical closeness just taunted him. This was not part of the plan.

She handed him the bowl and spoon. "I've already had some."

So much for romancing her over dinner, then. He only managed half the bowl of broth before he had to lie down again. Katie must have thought he'd fallen back to sleep. And maybe he had. Even he was losing track of what was real life and what was dream. When he pried his eyelids open, Katie was opening her suitcase, untucking her blouse and unfastening her skirt.

His breath hitched in the back of his throat as she undressed down to her slip. Maybe this was a dream after all.

No, it was real.

For eyelids that had been so heavy earlier in the day, they were stubbornly wide open now. He told himself that if she started to remove the slip, he would find the strength to drag his eyelids down. From somewhere.

He'd promised not to touch her, but this was just looking. A husband shouldn't worry about gazing on his wife as she dressed, should he? Besides, shutting his eyes wouldn't make much difference. After what he'd already seen, his mind was quite capable of imagining her without his eyes doing their job.

The skin not covered by her slip was like the finest of porcelain. He hadn't noticed the slip at first, then his brain registered the familiarity of the colors—earthy tones with an occasional splash of light blue. She obligingly leaned over to retrieve something from her case, and he got a much closer look at the pattern.

He needed to reveal himself. "Katie, is that a map of France across your bottom?"

She yelped and jumped so high that she almost hit her head on the ceiling, snatching her skirt off the floor and holding it to her front. "I thought you were asleep."

That was clear. "Why is your underwear made out of maps?"

"They're silk. Alberta gave me the idea. The Air Ministry was selling them off for two and six, she bought some and offered them to me if I made some slips for her too. It's so much nicer than butter muslin."

She wouldn't look at him as she spoke, and her face had flamed into a color that matched his own red hair.

"You don't need to be ashamed. I think you're very clever to make something out of them."

He couldn't be too ill if he was contemplating leaping from the bed and tracing his escape route across the lines of her body, could he? His eyes must have revealed what he was thinking, because she shrank away and clutched the skirt to her more tightly.

"Katie-my-love, you're safe. I'm so sick I can barely stand, let alone try anything more energetic."

She relaxed, softening slightly in the dimly lit room, so he risked asking, "Can I see it properly?"

Slowly she lowered the dress she'd clutched to her front so he could see the garment. He mustered the last remnants of his energy to focus on the topographical features of the map, rather than those of her body. Turning his head to the side to account for the way she'd cut the fabric, he made out most of Italy as well as Croatia and Hungary in the details of the print. He wanted to linger on every detail. His eyes traced the garment from its hem at her thighs up to the alluring décolletage.

Not so alluring when he saw the red splotches on her chest. Even if she didn't mean to reveal how upset she was, her emotions wrote themselves on her skin unbidden. He'd learned that the hard way. One glance at her face now, stretched with humiliation that he was causing, made him repent for being so bold.

"Can I get dressed now?"

He nodded and made a show of rolling over to give her the privacy she needed. "But, Katie, one of those maps helped save my life, and even so, I think you've put them to a much better use."

Saturday, 28 July 1945

Katie didn't sleep well. She clung to her side of the double bed to stop Jonty from getting any more ideas than the ones her slip had already given him.

The migraine made his dreams worse. His calls for Lily became more desperate. Despite challenging him directly, she still had no explanation for who Lily was. Just the recollection of Jonty's fearful, guilty face when she'd asked him about her.

The pain must have eased sometime around dawn, because his sleep became peaceful just as the birds began their summertime song. At seven, Jonty was still sleeping soundly and silently, so Katie dressed and slipped downstairs to eat breakfast alone.

The publican's wife gave her a tray of tea and toast to take up to Jonty. "You've paid for bed and breakfast, after all."

Jonty was awake when she returned to the room, but so exhausted he was barely able to sit. She placed the tray on the bed and leaned over to feel his forehead, which was silly since he didn't have a fever. But his expression said he enjoyed the attention.

"Does your head still hurt?"

"I think the worst of it has passed."

"That's a good sign. Do you think you can eat some breakfast?"

"You have the toast. I'll have the tea."

She didn't need to be told twice to snatch up the jammy toast for herself. Popping the slice between her teeth before he changed his mind, she poured some tea and handed him the cup and saucer. He took a meager sip, then replaced the cup in the saucer.

"I'm so sorry, Katie-my-love, but I don't think I'll be well enough to go to the airfield with you today."

"I can see that."

The pallor of his skin made his scars much more apparent. He'd been too sick yesterday to change from his clothes. His disheveled, slept-in appearance made him look much less respectable than he was, like someone who'd been sleeping rough. She doubted he'd be much of an asset in the quest to find Jan looking like that.

"So what will you do?"

"We aren't too far from the aerodrome, so I should be able to walk. I thought I might just ask at the gate if I could speak to his commanding officer. Smile at him and see what I can find out."

She gave him a sly glance as she spoke, to test whether he understood the joke.

He did. A smile toyed at his lips behind another sip of tea. "Well, you do have such a bonny smile, my love."

His response gave her confidence that he could be left alone for the day. The full day in bed would probably be the restorative he needed. "You will be all right, won't you?"

He nodded. "I don't think I can do anything else other than sleep. But if I do that, I might be well enough to truly appreciate my lovely wife."

His words sent a thrill up her spine. Or perhaps a chill. She wasn't sure what he meant by *appreciating* her, but he hadn't disguised the longing in his eyes last night.

Her stomach did such an energetic flip that she launched off the bed. "I better be off then."

She searched for something in their suitcase, although she wasn't sure what. Willing herself not to be a coward, she sent him a shy goodbye smile as she was leaving, but he had already collapsed back down.

She fought the temptation to slow her pace as the Norfolk countryside surrounded her with summer bird calls. The smell of elderflowers and wild herbs hung in the air. The faint scent of the seaside taunted her. Jonty had said they were staying so close that they might be able to visit the sea while they were here, but she doubted that now. Anyway, it didn't matter, did it? They were here for one purpose alone. To get information about Jan.

RAF Coltishall sprawled across the green fields just like the one she had worked at in Bottesford had done. There were hundreds of other similar airfields in England. As she approached the gate, she wondered what would happen to all of them now that the Nazis had been defeated. Would they return to being farmland? Maybe the War Ministry was waiting for the Japanese to surrender to decide what to do. They couldn't close them too quickly, she supposed, since they were still home to American and Australian and, here, Polish air forces.

The familiarity of the guarded gate stopped her in her tracks. So similar to where she had worked at Bottesford. She straightened her shoulders at the reminder of her past self. How many times had she walked through gates like these?

Determined to find Jan, she plastered on her best smile and approached the guard box. The British army private inside looked more serious than she had expected. Jonty might have been overly optimistic if he thought she could get all the information she wanted with just a wave and a smile.

"Excuse me. I'm looking for a friend of mine, Jan Delovski. I wondered if you had any news about him?"

The man looked back at her with a stern, immovable expression. A scowl, really. "Why do you want to know?"

"He's my friend, and he's missing." She adjusted the smile that had slipped. "Is there anyone who knows anything? Anyone I can talk to?"

The guard turned to his telephone and made a call. Probably

finding someone to escort her off the property. She shook her head at her own foolishness in believing Jonty. Just because he was always saying she was pretty or bonny didn't mean it was true.

"Wing commander's office is up the path and to the left."

The smile that broke across her face was completely genuine. "Thank you."

She followed the path to an office that felt a little too much like her commanding officer's room at RAF Bottesford. The wing commander welcomed her in and offered her a seat opposite his desk. Katie fought off memories of conversations she'd had in a room just like this with Queen Bee, as they called the head WAAF at Bottesford. Admitting she was pregnant, being given the option to have the problem dealt with. Back then, she would have called the man in front of her WingCo. She took in a steadying breath. She didn't need any ghost from the past haunting her right now.

"Mrs. Ables? My sergeant tells me that you are asking about Jan Delovski."

"Yes. He's a friend. Well, a friend of my neighbor's really. Her nephew. And I heard he was AWOL. That doesn't seem very much like him."

The wing commander took out a pen and began writing down the details she was giving him. "How do you know him?"

"Mrs. Grabowski is my neighbor, and she's Polish. I met him through her. He was meant to be at my sister's wedding last weekend, but he didn't show up."

WingCo frowned. "I do remember him mentioning a wedding when he applied for his leave pass."

So it wasn't just her imagination. Despite how strange his behavior had been the night before Lucy's big day, he really had intended to be at the wedding. "It isn't like him not to show up. I'm worried about him. What's being done to look for him?"

The wing commander pursed his lips, pressing them together

as he considered her questions and the notes he'd written. "You think he might have met foul play?"

"Don't you?" Wasn't that the logical conclusion?

"Perhaps if you gave us a few more details about what he got up to in London, we might have a few more leads. When was the last time you saw him?"

WingCo scribed furiously as she gave all the details she could think of. "The last time I met him was the day before the wedding. He was very clear that he was going to turn up. He gave me something to give to my neighbor."

She decided not to mention the box. Just in case. Jan had told her to keep it secret, after all.

"Mrs. Grabowski, you say?"

"Yes."

"And what did he give you?"

"An envelope of some kind. Why?"

It dawned on her that WingCo was asking more questions than he was answering. So far she'd told him everything and learned nothing. "Don't you have any idea what might have happened to him?"

WingCo put down his pen and leaned back in his seat, his hands clasped across his stomach.

"If I may, Miss . . ."

His eyes traveled down to her hand, clutching the handbag in her lap.

"It's Mrs. . . . . Mrs. Ables."

She wished Jonty were here to back her up because the man in front of her looked doubtful and disapproving.

"The world has been upside down for the last six years. Many of us threw off the rules we'd been taught just to get through. But it's over now, mostly. I'd advise you to forget whatever you had with Jan and move on."

An indignant squeak escaped at his humiliating insinuation. "It's not like that . . . We're not . . . He's just my friend."

"Of course he is." WingCo made a show of glancing at his watch. "I'm afraid I have an appointment now, Mrs. Ables. Do you mind?"

"You're not doing anything to look for him?"

A tight, concluding smile stretched over the man's face. At least he had to be polite to her now. If she'd still been in the WAAF, he would have just dismissed her with a wave of his hand. If that.

She stood and forced herself to be polite. "Well, thank you for your time, Wing Commander."

Katie headed back to the hotel with more questions than answers.

CHAPTER FIFTEEN

Katie slipped back into their room, only to be met with the sound of a lightly snoring Scotsman. So she took out a book and spent the afternoon reading outdoors under the shade of a tree. He didn't stir before dinner, so she let him sleep, leaving a note in case he woke up.

As the pub hummed around her, she ordered a portion of fish pie with mushy peas.

"Is your husband still poorly?" The landlady appeared behind the bar.

"I'm afraid so."

"My husband gets them too. Has ever since he returned from France."

From the woman's age, Katie assumed that she meant the last war, not the one that had just finished. She saw in the woman's face the long road she had ahead of her as a wife. She longed to ask the landlady if time helped. If she would ever learn the full story of what had happened to her husband. But how could she ask such things of a stranger?

"Would you like me to make him a bowl of soup again, like last night? I can have it ready to take up when you've finished yours."

"Thank you."

As the surprisingly tasty gray-green dinner disappeared from her plate, she absorbed the atmosphere of the pub. The fireplace that would fill the room with a welcoming glow in winter sat unlit during summer. But the windows were thrown open to let the warm breeze in. Three airmen sat at a table near an open window, cradling beers and laughing. They wore Polish Air Force uniforms and, from the banter that drifted her way across the pub, spoke with light accents. Perhaps they knew Jan. Hadn't Jonty's original idea been for her to talk to Jan's friends? Perhaps this was her chance.

She eyed the men as she ate her pie, working up the courage to speak with them. A while back she had lived and breathed romance with airmen. Back then, she had been so lighthearted and carefree that she wouldn't have thought twice about approaching the men on her own.

But she was out of practice now. Besides, so much had changed since she was that silly, flirtatious girl in Bottesford. She ordered a glass of cider for good measure and channeled the Katie of two years ago. "Gentlemen, hello." She smiled her brightest to cover her nerves. "I'm looking for my friend Jan Delovski. I wonder if you know where he is?"

One of the airmen sprang to his feet. "Would you like to take a seat? My name is Pawel. This is Aleksander"—the dark man with the moustache nodded—"and Mikolaj." He pointed to a man with the brightest blue eyes Katie had ever seen. Bluer even than Jan's.

She accepted their offered seat but perched tensely and primly on the edge. "Katie. Ables. Mrs. Katie Ables." She dithered out of nervousness but finally gave her title so they wouldn't get any other ideas about why she was approaching them. "Did you know Jan Delovski?"

"Everyone is looking for Jan these days." Aleksander took a long draw on his cigarette and blew the smoke out his nostrils. "I don't know when he became so popular."

Who else is looking for him?

"Since he went AWOL." Mikolaj joined in with a grin. "The ladies love a bad boy."

"You would know, Miko," Pawel snapped.

"I wondered if he had someone in London he was meeting." Aleksander grinned wolfishly. Katie shifted in her seat under his look. "A very pretty someone."

He'd jumped to the same conclusion as the wing commander. Katie wondered what kind of character Jan had if his friends so easily talked this way about him. Maybe she didn't know Jan as well as she'd thought.

"It's nothing like that." She gave her primmest glare, but her face felt warm. "He's my friend. Do any of you know anything about where he's gone?"

They shook their heads in unison. Pawel, who seemed to be the politest of the three, spoke up. "We don't mean to offend you."

Miko snorted.

"But we did think he had a lover. He was always going to London on his days off. It wasn't in his character, but lately he'd become so secretive, that we did wonder."

"Secretive is putting it mildly. The man shut up like a closed book, after years of going on and on and on," Miko added.

Pawel rushed in to explain. "He left his wife in Poland, and we have had six long years of his pining, you see."

Katie stomach twisted. "Oh, I didn't know he had a wife."

"Just friends, huh?" Aleksander's stare penetrated through his curtain of smoke.

She felt herself blush furiously. "Yes. We were just friends. He's my neighbor's nephew and a friend of my family." That was true. She had done nothing wrong. "He just never told me this."

But then what did she really know about him apart from what Mrs. G had told her?

"Maybe his wife died," Mikolaj suggested. "He did get that telegram."

"What telegram?" Katie asked.

"It was a few months ago now, but that's when all the visits to London started," Pawel explained. "He didn't come home from this last one."

"Do you think . . ." She didn't want to speak the horrible thought that came to her. "Do you think that something has happened to him?"

Aleksander shook his head. "WingCo does. Says it's not Jan's character to disappear with no word."

Katie frowned. "That's not what he told me." She explained how she'd walked to the airfield and spoke directly with the wing commander. The men smirked at each other over some joke that she missed entirely.

"He probably thought you were a spy," Pawel said.

"A spy! But . . . I'm not . . . Why?"

"Because in his experience, when a pretty woman turns up out of the blue, smiling and asking questions, she is usually a spy." Aleksander smirked, as though he agreed with WingCo's assessment of her.

"I'm just worried about my friend. Why isn't everyone else?"

"Why? What do you know, Mrs. Ables?" Aleksander leaned on the word *Mrs.*, as though he also didn't believe her story.

"Just that he didn't turn up to my sister's wedding like he said he would."

She didn't want to mention the box to these men. She couldn't say why—maybe it had to do with the stare that Aleksander bored into her. A stare she suddenly wanted to get out from under.

"Well, it sounds like you three have just as little information as me. But thank you for sharing it. I'll leave you to it."

Before going back to Jonty, Katie let the full moon draw her outside. The air was fresher here than in London, the sky clearer. It wasn't cold, but she wrapped her bare arms around herself as she lifted her eyes to the sky. She didn't intend to stray far from the building, just cool her cheeks in the fresh air outside.

Once she might have called the silver shape up there a bomber's moon. During the war, weather like this would mean operations every night and days busy preparing for them. That felt like a lifetime ago. Now the moon simply looked beautiful, like a perfectly placed adornment on the shoulder of a gown.

The smell of a cigarette wafted over her shoulder, spoiling the memory and triggering a new one. She glanced back to see Aleksander slipping through the heavy door of the pub. Her heartbeat picked up pace.

"So you came all this way just to find Jan?" He held out a packet of cigarettes.

"I told you, he's my friend. My family's friend."

She glanced down at the cigarettes. Her fingers twitched. The Katie of two years ago wouldn't have hesitated to take one. She'd have giggled as he leaned close to light it. Flirting under the bomber's moon.

Now, she willed the tremble out of her voice. "I don't smoke."

"Are you alone?"

She lifted her gaze to his questioning eyes. Perhaps he thought she was a spy and wondered if she had backup. Perhaps he thought that if she was Jan's mistress, he might also be in with a chance. For a fleeting moment, she understood she could lie now and try on any of those identities like she was trying on a new dress to see if it fit. Wear it just for the night.

The thought dissolved as quickly as it came.

She glanced toward the door of the pub, behind him, conscious that she would have to push past Aleksander if she wanted to get back inside. "My husband is upstairs." *Oh, Jonty. Why couldn't you have been well enough to come for dinner this evening?*

"Of course he is." Sarcasm laced his words. He didn't believe her any more than the wing commander had. Aleksander extended his hand and ran the knuckle of his forefinger down the bare skin of her arm.

She shivered, suddenly ice cold in the summer evening. She couldn't seem to make her feet move, even though she drew back to escape his closeness.

"Why are you really here?"

"I'm not a spy, if that's what you mean."

"You're Jan's lover, then?"

She shook her head, willing her feet to move so she could put some distance between them. A memory played itself back inside her head amid the frantic beat of her pulse.

Another pub, another choice, another woman, another life.

Jimmy Hardie had been kind and attentive that night, but she'd only been interested in Alec Thomas. He looked like Clark Gable but sounded like Errol Flynn. He had kissed her once already at the hangar dance, and she had spent the previous week engineering a way to make it happen again. But his affection, if it had ever really been hers, had moved on. Well and truly stolen away by Maggie. Alec had barely spoken to Katie again.

Jimmy must have seen her desperation. He'd showered her with compliments and brought her drinks. He'd smelled good—weak cologne and strong cigarettes. She'd basked in the feeling of being wanted. She'd let him lead, and giggled when he'd found a private place behind the country pub.

Naive. Carefree. Lighthearted. All words that described her until that moment. But Jimmy Hardie had changed everything.

She'd been a fool then. But not now. A small voice, one that didn't sound like hers, protested. "I want to get back to my husband now."

Aleksander shifted closer. She wanted to move away, but her feet stuck to the ground. Why couldn't she move? Why couldn't she breathe?

"Is everything all right, Katie-my-love?"

Aleksander spun around, revealing Jonty standing in the pub doorway, face like thunder.

CHAPTER SIXTEEN

"Are you going to tell me what happened out there?"
Jonty risked the question when they were back in their room, the door closed safely behind them. His words no doubt sounded gruff and disapproving, not encouraging, as he'd meant them.

"Nothing."

It wasn't nothing. He'd seen her terrified expression in the moonlight, seen the salacious way the airman touched her. He'd also see the look of pure relief and gratitude she'd sent when she saw him.

Like he was her hero.

She hadn't looked him in the eye since she'd pushed past the airman, grabbed Jonty by the arm, and hauled him back inside. She sat on the edge of the bed that he'd made before he came down, arms wrapped about her body.

"Doesn't look like nothing to me, Katie. You're shaking like a leaf."

She was shivering as though it was the middle of winter, despite the pleasant summer evening. What on earth had happened? He perched next to her, sitting on the edge of the bed.

She sucked in a breath, then released it slowly, calming the trembles. "I mean, it really was nothing. He didn't hurt me. He barely even touched me. He had the wrong idea about me, that's for sure. But that wasn't what upset me. I just . . . remembered something. That's all."

"Jimmy?"

She looked him in the eye then. He saw the rest of her story in the blue depths. What he couldn't see, he guessed. Jonty hadn't been in the pub that night—if he had been, he might have been able to stop it—but Jimmy wouldn't shut up about it afterward. When the news of the deplorable betting pool called the Sweetheart Sweepstakes got out, Jimmy hadn't even faced disciplinary action. Women always seemed to suffer the consequences when it came to the bad behavior of men.

"I'm sorry ye were reminded of that tonight." Jonty should have thought that bringing her to a country pub full of airmen would dredge back those painful memories. But he hadn't planned on her being alone for most of the time, had he? "I'm so sorry I wasn't there."

"But you were." She held his eye. More than that, she reached over and squeezed his hand. "Thank you."

The contact was only brief, but it sent a zing straight to his heart. When she withdrew her hand, she didn't leap away. Instead, the blue in her eyes turned sympathetic, tracing over his face.

"Is the headache gone? Are you feeling better, now?"

"A little." He hoped the reprieve for his illness wasn't like the eye of a storm, giving him a brief respite before pummeling him again from the other side. "When I saw your note, I thought that dinner with my beautiful wife was the medicine I needed."

"Why do you always do that?" she whispered

"Do what?"

"Keep calling me 'beautiful'?"

"That's what you are to me. Didn't you know?"

"Oh." Not so much a word as a breathy sigh.

His compliment landed in a small flush across her pale cheeks. And not the blotchy kind that had crossed her skin last night. The encouraging kind that came with bright eyes and—he glanced down to be sure—the tiniest hint of a smile on her lips.

Directing his gaze to her lips might have been a mistake. They drew him in, like a banquet draws in a starving man. Despite the hitch in her breath, she didn't pull away or find something fascinating on the other side of the room to change the subject. Instead, she held perfectly still and let him lean closer, ever so slowly.

"I've got your soup, Mrs. Ables!" Accompanied by an awkward knock, the landlady's voice broke into the room through the door.

Katie jumped sky high, leaving Jonty in a delicate cloud of lavender.

Jonty pursed his lips together, looking at the well-worn carpet, while Katie opened the door. On the other side, the kind publican balanced a bowl of broth on a tray. She glanced past Katie at Jonty.

"Oh, you look better than the last time I saw you, if I do say so."

"Thank you so much for bringing dinner up, Mrs. Cartwright." Katie's voice sounded too enthusiastic, considering it was just soup and a slice of bread. She relieved the landlady of the tray. Maybe she was glad for the interruption.

"Yes, thank you." Jonty managed to be polite, even though he wanted to curse the woman for her poor timing.

When the landlady left, Katie placed the tray on the bed between them, like a barricade. He didn't feel hungry anymore. Not for food, anyway. Her kiss was an altogether different matter.

Still, he wasn't about to let scarce food go to waste. He took up the steaming bowl. "So what were you doing in the pub tonight anyway?"

"Smiling at airmen to see if I could find out any more information about Jan."

He sputtered, choking on soup that went down sideways. Those lips of hers gave a teasing smile this time, harking back to his clumsy attempt to tell her how beautiful she was. She did have the bonniest smile. But what was he doing suggesting she share it with other men, when he wanted those lips all for himself? He was a fool!

"It worked. I found out a few things."

"I'm not surprised." He'd do just about anything to see her smile. He was just about to tell her that when—

"Jan was, or is, married."

The skin on Jony's forearms stood on end. What kind of a scoundrel was Jan? Flirting with Katie when he had a wife! He tried to stay neutral, concealing his frown by shoving a spoonful of soup into his gob. "Married, and he never told you?"

"Jonty, I want you to know I'm not upset. The wing commander and the airmen I spoke to all jumped to the wrong conclusion, and I don't want you to. We really were just friends. I promise." She pulled those beautiful lips to the side as she thought. "He's never been as peculiar as he was that night before the wedding."

Jonty nodded. A heartache he had been holding dissolved with her reassurance. He mopped the dregs of soup with half the slice of bread resting on the tray next to the bowl.

"His friends said he received a telegram a few months ago, then started visiting London more frequently. So they all thought he was seeing someone. They said he was private about it. Which I suppose explains why they jumped to the wrong conclusion about me."

"Maybe he was seeing someone else." He hoped it was helpful

to chime in at that moment.

"Maybe." She nodded, chewing her lip as she considered the possibility. "But if that was the case, why didn't he give her the package?"

"What do you mean?"

"On the night you arrived home, he gave me something to look after."

Jonty remembered how he'd peered into the sitting room as Jan had handed the packet to her. "I thought it was a gift."

"Gift? No. He asked if I would keep it safe and secret and only give it to Mrs. G if she asked for it. When you met us on the street, he was adamant he would collect it at the wedding, but he never showed up."

"Do you want some?" He held out the remaining half slice of bread, but she shook her head. "So what's in the packet?"

"I don't know. I didn't look, I just put it in my sewing basket to keep it safe for him."

"Well, I think the time might have come to take a peek, don't you? When we get back home, we should definitely see if it helps us know if he is safe."

Katie leaped from the bed, collecting his dishes and setting them outside the door. Jonty stood too, then moved to a more comfortable position on the bed, sitting up against the headboard with legs outstretched. He patted the space next to him, hoping she might answer his unspoken question by sitting next to him. Maybe they could resume the moment before the landlady interrupted them.

Instead, Katie headed over to her suitcase. "We don't need to wait. I brought the box with us." She withdrew the package from her luggage and brought it to the bed, laying it between them. They both stared at the package, as though they could make it unwrap itself with their eyes. Katie gnawed on her lip.

"Well, go on. Unless you think it's got snakes and spiders inside."

She huffed a little nervous laugh. "I hope not." But gave the packet a gentle shake next to her ear. "Sounds like papers inside a tin."

"Not spiders then?"

"Jonty, be serious."

He wasn't sorry to lighten her mood, considering how heavy it had been. Or to see her smile. He was never sorry about that.

He watched on as she untied the string holding the outer layer of brown paper, to reveal a simple biscuit tin, blue with white Polish lettering. Katie laid it on the bed and went back to her staring.

"Well, it didn't sound like biscuits when you shook it, and I don't think it will bite. What are you waiting for?"

"What if I open it and it changes how I see him? I might find out something I can never unknow, you know?"

"Hmm. Do you want me to do it?"

"Yes." The word came out in a grateful rush, and she handed the tin to him. He made a show of peeking under the lid, putting on a shocked expression.

"Jonty!" Her eyes lit with laughter, combined with enough irritation for him to curb the clown that her earlier smiles had encouraged out of him.

"All right! All right." He laid the box between them again and lifted the lid. Inside lay pristine official documents for a man and a woman. Identity cards for each, as well as ration books and a marriage certificate.

Forgeries. There could be no doubt.

Katie picked up the documents and examined each one before handing them over to Jonty. He looked closely at the photograph on the woman's identity card. She had high Slavic cheekbones like Mrs. G, and light-colored hair. The name on the card was Emmaline, but that wouldn't be the truth.

"It's Jan." Katie showed him the photograph of the man's identity card. Except that the name on the documents wasn't Jan

Delovski. It was Adam Kent.

"What else is in there?"

Katie withdrew a typed document. But this wasn't official, like the other items in the box. This was several pages of writing, folded in half, then half again. Katie shrugged when she opened it. "I think it's in Polish." She handed it over.

Jonty flicked through the pages. Some had technical diagrams, breaking up the written text.

Then she sighed out the question on Jonty's mind. "Oh, Jan, what are you up to?"

Later that night, she lay on the bed with Jonty. It was fully made, and they were both fully dressed, illuminated only by moonlight. They had talked for hours about what they'd found in the box. Their speculations about Jan covered all sorts of ground. Most of Katie's absurd scenarios were from detective novels that Mum had read aloud while Katie had sewed each evening.

"Maybe he was planning to run off with his lover, but his wife caught up with him."

"Maybe he got hit over the head and has amnesia so doesn't remember the package."

"Maybe he's hiding in London somewhere, biding his time until he can collect the package."

But all the alternatives they tossed between them couldn't escape the weight of the forged documents in the box. People killed over documents like those. She'd heard, though she didn't know anything about such things, apart from her one or two forays into the black market.

When she saw Jonty yawn, fighting off tiredness, she suggested they retire. He used the facilities down the hall, and she expected he'd change back into his pajamas while she did the same. But when she returned to the room, she found him sound asleep on the bed. Lying on his back, still clothed, apart from his shoes. Without changing, she lay down next to him, mimicking his posture with her hand clasped over her front.

Listening to his gentle snore, she ran through the events of the day

Something had shifted for them tonight. Not in a way she had expected, and not in the way he wanted, she guessed, judging by the longing looks he'd directed at her lips during the evening. But whatever it was, it made her less inclined to cling to the edge of the bed. In fact, it made her disappointed that he was asleep.

Maybe that was safer. Tired from the sudden, unexpected bout of illness, he wouldn't want to try anything energetic. Which suited her fine. Or it didn't. She wasn't sure anymore.

"Katie?"

So he wasn't asleep. She froze.

"Yes?"

"Come here."

An invitation, not a demand. He unclasped his hands and held out his arm, meaning for her to slip under it and lay her head on his chest. Her body responded before her brain, drawn to the warmth and comfort he offered. As a pillow, he was hard, bony even. He smelled like vegetable soup and something masculine she couldn't quite describe.

Like home.

When his arm came around her, squeezing her gently, she felt a calm settle in her heart and radiate out to every part of her body.

He pressed his lips into her hair in a good-night kiss.

CHAPTER SEVENTEEN

Monday, 30 July 1945

Chez Martin was busier than Katie had ever known. When the newspapers got word that Madame was designing Grace Deroy's wedding gown—something Katie was sure Madame had told them somehow—the telephone barely stopped ringing. Madame now had a waiting list of clients, although as far as Katie knew, the princesses weren't among them.

Unfortunately, Madame also had one less worker. She'd unceremoniously sacked Françoise after the woman had arrived late three days running. Madame had begun advertising for another seamstress, but the process wasn't straightforward, since Madame had such high standards.

Even without Françoise, they'd done some of their best work on Grace's trousseau. Grace's wedding gown was the most elegant thing Katie had ever seen. The clean lines brought both elegance and simplicity to the gown. Grace would look almost regal when she walked down the aisle. They'd used the lace from her mother's gown as a subtle overlay and train. The result was incredibly fashionable without being extravagant. The same could not be said for Grace's nightgowns. They'd used almost all Madame's satin reserves to fashion a negligée worthy of a Hollywood movie star.

Without Françoise to gossip with, Collette sulked in her corner, occasionally mumbling to herself in French. Halfway through the week, her mood improved dramatically, and the mutterings became gentle humming.

"I think Collette is in love," Alice whispered as they put the finishing touches on Grace's nightgowns.

Katie glanced over, immediately recognizing the dreamy expression on Collette's face. "You seem happy, Collette."

"I am. I have a new—how do the Americans say it?—boyfriend."

"So tell us about him, then." Katie winked at Alice. "Where did you meet?"

With no Françoise to talk with, the gossip had clearly pent up inside Collette. It exploded out now. "At a party thrown by a friend. He was there by himself and seemed so lonely." Collette giggled, delighting in her memory.

"I'm sure you cheered him up."

Alice dipped her chin to hide her smile as Katie took the lead in the conversation.

"You could say that." Collette gave a sly smile.

"And is he handsome?" Alice asked.

"Very. Dark hair. Good dancer. I think his family is in politics. We've been out almost every night this week."

"Moustache?" Katie asked.

"No." Collette answered seriously, unaware Katie was pulling her leg.

"Tall?"

"Not as tall as I would like. But he makes up for it in other ways, if you know what I mean. He's a very creative lover."

"Collette!" Katie chided, while Alice concealed her shock at Collette's loose morals by concentrating on the sewing in her lap.

"What? He is taking me away next weekend, and I want to

make sure I have underthings just as nice as Grace Deroy's."

"They are beautiful." Katie sighed, redirecting the conversation to the mannequin she was working on. At the last minute, Madame had told Katie she'd pay extra if Katie worked late to make a second nightgown using the remaining lace and some pale-blue satin she'd acquired. Katie felt herself turn bright pink when Madame described the kind of plunging neckline she wanted Katie to create from the lace.

"But it will be almost see-through."

"That is quite the idea."

The result was truly exquisite and even more beautiful than the wedding gown itself. The lingerie adorned both the mannequins in the upstairs room now. The wedding dress was on a hanger downstairs, ready for Grace's final fitting.

"I don't even know the right English word for the nightgown we are making her." Alice made a flourish with her hand. "Most beautiful? More than beautiful?"

Katie adjusted the lace details along the neckline. She'd had just enough satin to make a matching dressing gown. She placed it over the mannequin's shoulders and stepped back to admire her work. It really was an extravagant amount of fabric, considering that no one but Grace's husband would see it.

But then maybe that was worth it. Jonty had quite liked the slip she'd worn at the hotel, and it was just made from the RAF maps. How much more would he like something like this? The heat rose in her face just thinking about how he'd run his eyes along her barely dressed body. She'd been upset about it at the time, but the memory wasn't painful. At all.

"These are certainly nicer than having two old maps sewn together!" Katie remarked.

"What do you mean?" Collette's curious voice cut across the room.

Katie explained how the silk maps were being sold off and how, if you cut them right, you could make two into a slip. "It's so much nicer to wear than muslin!"

Alice sighed and Collette grinned, twisting a blond lock around her finger. "But what did your husband think?" Collette raised her eyebrow.

Katie's cheeks warmed again. She glanced at Alice. The girl was so young it probably wasn't proper to say. But Alice's eyes looked back wide and eager.

"He said one of the maps had saved his life, but even so I put it to a much better use."

An almost wicked smile spread across Collette's face. "Will you show me how? This new boyfriend of mine was in the air force during the war too. He'll love it."

"Well, if there's any maps left—"

"Where can you get these maps?"

"I'll have to ask Alberta. I—"

Madame's bell cut her off, calling Collette down to Grace's fitting.

"That's for me." Collette straightened her hair but put her hand on Katie's arms just before she left. "Tell me later, yes?"

"All right."

Katie had no choice but to agree before Collette flounced down the stairs. This was Katie's cue. All morning she'd waited for a moment when Collette was out of the room to ask Alice about the document she had found in Jan's tin.

She had wanted to ask Mrs. G as soon as they'd returned from Norwich, but Mr. Gregory, her lodger, said she'd called to extend her time away. Apparently her friend was quite sick. Katie checked every evening to see whether Mrs. G had returned. An increasingly irritated Mr. Gregory met her at the door each day. By Friday she couldn't wait anymore. So she'd slipped the typed papers into her handbag, intending to show Alice today.

"Alice, can I ask you about something?"

Alice came over to Katie's workstation, no doubt expecting Katie to ask her opinion on her embroidery work. But Katie had laid the document out on the bench under the window.

"Do you know what this says?"

Alice picked up the top sheet and ran her eyes across it. Katie watched Alice's face as she read. The color drained from her features, and her blue eyes widened.

"What is it, Alice?"

When Alice's eyes lifted from the paper to meet Katie's, they were wide with fear. Tremulous, even. Which was a word that Katie had had to look up in a dictionary once after Mum had read it from a book. It felt fitting now.

"Where did you get this?" Alice asked.

She'd already decided to be honest but say as little as possible. "A friend left it with me, but now I can't find him. I'm hoping knowing what it says will help."

Alice shook her head. "This won't help him. And I won't get involved with it."

"What does it say, Alice?"

Quaking was another word that described Alice quite well right now. She dropped the paper onto the bench like it had burned her fingertips. What could it possibly say?

Katie didn't have the opportunity to ask more, because Collette came back up the stairs. Katie hastily grabbed a half-finished sewing project and plunked it on top of the papers. When she turned to face Collette, the dreamy romance had vanished from her colleague's eyes. She glared at Katie with cold, hard suspicion.

"Miss Deroy wants you."

"Me?" Katie squeaked.

"Apparently so." Collette flounced back to her workstation. "Well hurry up!"

Katie shot an excited grin at Alice. She still held her wide-eyed, fearful stare. Katie couldn't think more about Jan now, not with the Deroys waiting. She grabbed her measuring tape and headed downstairs, feeling Collette's glare as knives in her back as she went.

In the shop, Grace was already in her wedding dress and standing on the dais that Madame used to make the final alterations to a gown's hem. Lady Deroy looked on with fashion-critical eyes that had Madame fussing around, more flustered than Katie had ever seen her. Grace studied herself in the mirror. She wasn't smiling. Katie's heart sank. Maybe Madame—or even Grace herself—had called her down to insist she apologize for some fault in the gown. Maybe she would get fired, like Françoise.

She wanted to shrink away and hide. Just at that moment, Grace saw her at the bottom of the stairs. Her critical face dissolved into a wide smile. She winked at Katie as she approached.

"You have outdone yourself, Madame Martin. The details are exquisite."

Katie saw Madame's shoulders relax, which showed how tense she had been, waiting for Grace's verdict.

"This is a thousand times better than what Burton and Co. could have done for us!"

Madame beamed as Grace lavished praise on the dress. Pride washed over Katie too, as well as gratitude. Grace was kind to make sure she heard the compliments firsthand.

"Well, Kat-reen? The hem?"

Katie nodded, shooting a grin at Grace before kneeling to pin up the hem. Grace stood still, admiring her reflection as Katie worked. Madame liked them to be fast and efficient when pinning hems, so Katie tried to tune out the chatter and focus on making sure the fabric draped just so.

"How are the other preparations?" Madame asked Lady Deroy.

"There is still much work to do. The Air Ministry promised to get out of our house, but they are slow about it. We thought if we held the wedding in August, they would be gone. And are they? No."

"You know these things move slowly, Mother. Jack and I don't mind. Besides, we would have held a summer wedding outside anyway."

Lady Deroy did not sound like she was in the mood to be appeased. "You would think that Henry's position in the air force would get us some kind of special concession. But no!"

Katie pricked herself with a pin upon hearing that. She couldn't believe she had forgotten that, as well as owning half of Lincolnshire, Grace's father had some kind of high-up rank in the air force.

Katie scrambled to remember what else she could of Grace when they'd worked together. She had brothers in the air force too, didn't she? Perhaps Grace would be able to help her find out more about Jan.

She took her chance to ask Grace when she was helping her remove the gown.

"Thank you for asking for me today." She closed the blue curtain separating them from the shop.

Grace grinned. "I thought I might make Madame Martin sweat a bit since she's been telling everyone that we are now customers. But it really was sensational work. I love it!"

Glowing-white joy radiated around Katie's heart at such praise. "Thank you." She wanted to dwell in Grace's praise but had to get her question out before Madame called her back or became suspicious.

"Grace, your dad and brothers are in the RAF, aren't they?"

"Yes."

"It's only, I have a friend who might be in some trouble, and I don't know who to go to for help."

She gave the briefest explanation as she helped Grace shift the gown over her immaculately set hairdo, talking as fast as her lips allowed. When she finished, Grace frowned at her.

"I need to know more. Will you come for tea with me at The Savoy? When do you finish?"

"Four." Katie spoke before registering where Grace had invited her. "But I can't—"

"Of course you can. It's my shout. I'll send a car."

Katie didn't have time to protest, because Madame called her name.

At the end of the day, a car idled on the street outside, just as Grace had said. A gray-gold Bentley, complete with a chauffeur holding the door open. Katie stood, mouth agape, as he uttered her name like she was one of the shop's clients, not a humble seamstress.

"Mrs. Ables?"

Katie couldn't speak, she was so stunned to be addressed by the man.

He smiled, as if understanding her shock. "Miss Deroy insists."

Unable to say anything more, she slid into the backseat, imagining just for a fleeting moment she lived like this every day.

"What's this then?"

Standing at the door of the boutique, Collette raised impressed eyebrows at the car. Her jaw slackened when she saw Katie just as the driver shut the door. Something told Katie Collette was imagining a scandalous story for why Katie was being chauffeur-driven away.

The door closed with a click. As the driver walked around the front of the car, Katie's eyes followed Collette through the windscreen glass. Collette crossed the road and greeted a friend.

No, not a friend. Her new lover, judging by the kiss she gave him. A kiss that went on indecently long for the high street. Katie was about to look away, when the lovers' faces parted.

Collette whispered something in his ear that spread a devilish grin across his face. She pointed toward Katie, which made the man look at the car. Katie saw his face clearly for the first time.

Jimmy Hardie.

His eyes locked on hers. She knew he recognized her. Even at this distance, she saw the flicker of panic as his recognition sank in. But he was more practiced at covering than her. He looped his arm through Collette's and walked her in the opposite direction.

Katie slumped in the backseat so they couldn't see her as the car drove past. Only when the Bentley had disappeared into London traffic did Katie breathe again.

CHAPTER EIGHTEEN

Thursday, 2 August 1945

"You got a letter today, Katie."

Mum greeted her at the door when she arrived home from work. Tired and with sore fingers from so much sewing, Katie didn't feel like catching up on her correspondence right now. "Just leave it in the kitchen and I'll look at it later."

Mum didn't move from where she was blocking Katie's way.

"I think you want to look at it now."

She held out an envelope. Even without touching the paper, Katie could see that it was thicker and heavier than any other letter she had ever received.

"What is it?" Katie murmured.

"How would I know? I haven't opened it."

Katie took the letter and turned it over, curious to see who had sent her such a thing. An elegant embossed crest had been pressed into the top flap of the envelope, near where it opened.

The returned address read,
Sir and Lady Henry Deroy
Broughton House,
Grantham.

Katie's heartbeat kicked up. Was this what she thought it was? Trying not to damage the paper, she opened the envelope, excitement pulsing through her fingers. Sure enough, inside sat an embossed card. Katie's jaw hung open, and she squeaked at the back of her throat, too shocked to speak as she read the words.

Sir and Lady Henry Deroy invite Mr. and Mrs. Jonathon Ables to the ceremony of marriage of Miss Grace Deroy and Captain Jack Marsden, United States Army,

At eleven o'clock on Saturday 4 August.

And afterward to an outdoor reception in the grounds of Broughton House.

Dress: Civilians, Morning Dress (Ladies with hats). Serving Officers, Service Dress.

An answer is requested by 9 July.

The cards had been professionally printed with a blank line for their names to be filled in using elegant calligraphy. She read it several times, unable to believe her eyes. Judging by the RSVP date, they were a last-minute addition to the guest list, but that didn't diminish the honor.

"There's a note too," Mum said.

Glancing down, Katie saw a handwritten note, less formal than the invitation card, sticking out from the envelope. She plucked it out.

Sorry about the late invitation. There's someone I think you should meet. Please come. It will be lovely to have you there. Grace.

Her mother spoke first, raised eyebrows and an impressed smile. "You're moving up in the world, Katie! Tea at The Savoy and a car driving you home."

It was true. Those things had happened last week, but they didn't seem real. Grace had been waiting for her in the tearoom, looking ever so stylish. Katie had felt drab in her work clothes. She'd never been so happy that she had to dress each day to meet Madame's standards. Inside the hotel, Katie hadn't known whether to drop the posh accent she put on at work or keep it up. No one else in the room had come from anywhere near Hackney.

Over strong Darjeeling and pastries, with the ambiance of the finest hotel in London tinkling around her, she'd told Grace about Jan and what she had discovered.

"I know your dad is high up and thought he might be able to help. Or maybe one of your brothers, if you don't want to bother him."

Grace frowned. "Tell me more about the forged papers and the document you found."

"It's in Polish, so I can't read it. I asked a girl at work. She went white and said she wouldn't get involved." Alice wouldn't even look at Katie when she'd gone back upstairs and collected the papers.

"Right." Grace pursed her lips. Even with that expression, she looked sophisticated.

"Jan said not to tell anyone. I thought I might ask my neighbor Mrs. Grabowski, but she's away at the moment."

"This doesn't sound like something for my father," Grace said. "But there is someone who I think can help. And luckily for you, he owes me a favor."

Grace had promised she would sort things out, and then she'd put Katie in the car again with a box of chocolates—chocolates!—she'd insisted Katie take home to Jonty.

Now, here she was, being invited to Grace's high-society wedding. It felt like a dream.

"I don't know what to say."

Panic set in when she read the invitation again. The date was this weekend, and she had nothing to wear.

"I'm going to need a better hat."

Saturday, 4 August 1945

"You look prettier than everyone else here, Katie-my-love."

At least half of the people in this cramped church had been born with a silver spoon in their mouth. Wealth and fame worked as natural decoration. Yet somehow, his wife outshone them all. She had worked her fingers to the bone, making herself a dress in record time despite her long hours working in Mayfair. They'd used some of the demob coupons to procure a hat that was more style than practicality. It sat atop hair that had been professionally set. The hairdresser had been his idea, and he was pleased with himself for suggesting it. Not only did she look like the belle of the ball, she'd thanked him with a kiss.

"Keep your voice down," she whispered.

"Don't you know it's rude to outshine the bride on her wedding day?"

But she didn't look angry at his compliment. In fact, her eyes were shining. Her smile was as bonny as it had ever been.

The vicar invited them to stand and welcome the bride. Katie stood nearer the aisle, her back to him, as she waited for her glimpse of Grace.

He obeyed her command to keep his voice down, putting his lips close to her ear so only she could hear. "You will always be the most beautiful woman I know."

She stilled and didn't turn around. He saw the effect of his words in the goose bumps on her neck. It didn't help him concentrate on the procession.

Katie had told him all the technical terms for the bits and pieces on Grace's gown several times. Jonty still couldn't tell his appliqué from his overlay, but the dress was lovely. So was the way Katie shone with pride as wedding guests admired the gown as the bride passed.

Jonty turned his attention to the man in his US Army dress uniform waiting for Grace at the front of the church. Jack Marsden was a picture of pure wonder as his bride walked toward him.

At one point, he swiped at his face, and Jonty was sure the man was removing a tear.

Something about Jack's face felt familiar. Jonty couldn't quite put his finger on why. It had bothered him throughout the minister's introductory remarks about the sacred nature of marriage. He usually loved hearing wedding vows. Better or worse, sickness and health, richer or poorer. Such simple but all-encompassing pairs. But today all he could think of during the service was trying to place the groom's face.

After the service, Sir Henry Deroy had arranged for air force lorries to transport the hoi polloi—or at least those who didn't have chauffeur-driven cars—from the church back to his estate for the garden reception. Jonty had thought his days in the back of a troop lorry were over, but here he was in his demob suit, being jostled and bounced next to his elegantly dressed wife trying to keep her hat on straight. A giggly civilian girl, who gave his scars a fearful sideways glance, sat on his other side.

Across from him, Alec looked like he belonged, given that he was still in his Royal Australian Air Force uniform. But then, with the charm and good looks of a movie star, Alec usually did look like he belonged. Despite his summery tan and quick smile, the baby nestled in his arms made Alec look like a different man from the one he'd been when he was Jonty's captain. He held Maggie's hand with the one that wasn't grasping his child and gazed happily down at his wife, in her bridesmaid attire, like she was the only woman in the world.

"Do you know Jack well, Maggie?" Jonty asked.

Maggie grinned as the lorry pulled into the long driveway that led up to Broughton House. "He's such a sweetheart. They met working here, you know."

Jonty fished for more details that might help him place Jack's face. "What does he do with the army?"

Grace's family home had been turned into a mapmaking facility, and he'd heard mumblings about that being where they had met. Jonty figured Jack was an intelligence officer of some kind.

"He's a doctor."

"Doctor, you say?"

Jonty finally understood where he had seen Jack Marsden before. Hovering above him, in a US Army field hospital in France.

"This might hurt, but it's for the best," he'd said before attending to the wound in Jonty's leg.

Jonty had been too delirious with a fever, brought on by an infection, to understand exactly what the doctor was doing. But it hurt. The scar on Jonty's shin throbbed at the memory. His palms began to sweat.

Just then, the lorry pulled up in front of the house and released the wedding guests. Katie was so swept up in the beautiful setting that she didn't notice his clammy palms as he helped her out of the vehicle. Even Alec gave a delighted gasp at the scene set up in front of them.

Sir and Lady Deroy had spared no expense on the wedding of their only daughter. Katie had mentioned something about them needing to hold the wedding outside because the Air Ministry still had possession of the house. But even so, the garden setting was perfect. A string quartet played under a gazebo of roses as guests mingled and chatted among the blooms, served by waiters with silver platters. The scene made Lucy's cobbled-together wedding luncheon on Ivy Street look like dinner time in the poorhouse.

Farther along, on a flat section of the garden, stood a marquee guarding long tables decorated with summer flowers and silver candelabras. Jonty glanced at the sky—a clear day, as though the heavens were blessing the union. But the Deroys were wise to have tents as a precaution against the changeable summer weather.

"Say, aren't you the girl from Chez Martin?" A woman with a fluffy pink feather in her hat grabbed Katie's arm. "What are you doing here?"

Katie's face froze. He couldn't be sure, but he thought he saw panic wash over her. Katie gaped like a fish for a moment, then shot Jonty an apologetic glance. He thought she was apologizing for the interruption, until he heard her speak.

"Yes, I do work there. I know Grace Deroy from our time in the WAAF. This is my husband, Mr. Jonathon Ables. Jonathon, this is Lady Cavendish, the Countess of Thirl."

The look in Katie's eyes pleaded with him not to ask the questions that bubbled through him. First among them being, why was she speaking like she was some kind of duchess? She was putting on a voice. Perhaps even copying Maggie's musical timbre and crisp articulation. She probably sounded natural enough to people who didn't know she came from Hackney, but she sounded ridiculous to him.

He played along, putting on a voice that made him sound as though he was from the top of the heap in Edinburgh rather than its slums. "Lovely to meet you, Lady Cavendish."

He waited out several minutes of Lady Cavendish's praise for the salon where Katie worked, before asking Katie his burning question once the countess turned to leave. "What was that about?"

"She's a customer! I made a nightie for her last week." Katie made it sound like that should explain the put-on voice.

"You always talk that way to customers?"

"Madame insists."

Jonty frowned, which felt at odds with the party around him. "You shouldn't have to pretend. You are perfect the way you are."

He loved her as she was, glottal stops and all. Why would someone want her to change?

Katie responded to his compliment by slipping her hand into the crook of his elbow and pulling him along toward the marquee. "I don't mind. It just might make today a bit difficult, is all."

She stopped, dropping his arm and facing him. "I mean, it's not really lying when all you're doing is putting on a funny voice. You don't think less of me, do you?"

He couldn't help the smile that stretched across his lips at the idea that she cared so much what he thought. "No, I don't think less of you."

She bit her lip and leaned closer with a conspiratorial smile. "We could both pretend, you know."

"What do you mean?"

"Think about it, Jonty. We don't belong here. We only got this invitation so Grace could introduce us to her friend. Everyone else here is some kind of aristocrat. We could pretend to be posh. Just for today."

She smiled. And that was what did it. He was helpless against her smile. He glanced to make sure no one was watching, then gave a little bow. "Shall we, milady?" He held out his arm to her.

She grinned, and his heart almost exploded.

CHAPTER NINETEEN

Was she in a dream?

The tent was lined with an unrealistic amount of tulle, given the shortages, inspiring the feeling of dining inside a giant cloud. Food and wine flowed in such quantities that her belly felt as though it were bursting. So it must be a dream.

She was dressed for a dream. Her new hat was spectacular, thanks to Jonty's generosity with his coupons. And her hair had never been so beautifully done.

Characters from her past and present who didn't belong together spoke to each other in that out-of-place way they sometimes did in dreams. Alec Thomas—a man she had kissed once and was too mortified to say more than three words at a time to now—sat opposite her. The Countess of Thirl, whom Katie had measured for underwear just last week, danced with Jonty to "Dream When You're Feeling Blue." Surely that was a dream.

However, the thing that most made this day seem surreal was the bundle in her arms. Maggie had handed Eadie over to Katie's hungry embrace while Maggie attended to her duties as matron of honor. Real, tangible, filling Katie's heart with her healthy cries and contented snuffles.

Eadie, not Betty. Alec's occasional worried glance kept reminding her of that. But Katie didn't mind, not when she could live her dream.

"Would you care to dance, milady?" Jonty's voice brought her to reality, posh accent and all. A smile toyed on his lips as he held out his hand with an exaggerated flourish. Being caught in a happy little conspiracy with him, playing lord and lady of the manor, was another element that made today seem so unreal.

But she blinked at his question.

No. She didn't want to dance.

Dancing would mean relinquishing Eadie. Giving up the delightful scent of talcum powder. Waking from the dream.

Jonty insisted. A little chunk of her heart broke off when Alec reclaimed his daughter, but Jonty's gentle charm and crooked smile smoothed it over. Katie let Jonty lead her to the dance floor, which had been created by setting linoleum over the grass in front of a seven-piece band. The music had picked up pace considerably since Jonty's turn with the countess. Jack's American colleagues surrounded them, happy for the faster pace. But the tempo was too much for someone who hadn't danced for years.

"Jonty, I can't."

She tried to pull away, back to the safety of her seat. He wouldn't let go of her hand. In fact, he grabbed the other one and squeezed them both, stepping backward toward the other couples.

"Yes you can, Katie-my-love. Remember what fun we used to have dancing?"

The longing in his eyes reached over the lopsided smile on his lips. But longing for what? For a time when they'd danced without a care in the world? For happiness? For her?

"Don't you trust me?" He pulled on her hands, coaxing her onto the dance floor.

Snatching her hands away would be a declaration that she didn't trust him. She resisted just enough for him to know this wasn't simple. "Yes. I trust you."

Jonty stood close, engulfing her with the jasmine-tinted smell of his cologne. Her breath caught when he slipped his arm about her waist, letting his hand come to rest on her back. Then he took her other hand in his. The last time she'd held this stance had been . . . well, she didn't remember. Before Betty. Before she was even pregnant. Could she still do it?

"Then let's dance, my love." Jonty took a few moments to feel for the beat, then led her in basic foxtrot steps.

Her body recalled them perfectly, especially when guided by him. How could she have forgotten what a good dancer he was? It all came back to her now as he led her through more complex combinations.

"He's nothing to look at, but he makes you feel like you can fly!"

All the girls had said that after dancing with Jonty, during her short time at RAF Bottesford. His scars had meant he was usually the last to find a partner at the beginning of a night, especially among strangers. But by the end of an evening, word would spread and he'd be the last to leave.

Jonty grinned. "You ready?" Before she could answer, he swung her out.

Her feet remembered steps that her mind had forgotten. When they were face to face again, she grinned with him. The dance took over. Her body listened to his. A little press on her back telling her which way to go. A gentle tug of the hand indicating what was coming next. No words, just the carefree feeling of heading where he led. One move ran into another, just like the songs in the set. Neither of them noticed the time passing. Just like a dream.

"That wasn't so bad, was it, Katie-my-love?" Jonty asked when the band took a break and they returned giddily to their seats.

"It was wonderful." She felt the words in her bones, sure she was radiating joy as she smiled up at him.

But his face suddenly became intense. His gaze dropped to her lips, and for one moment she thought he might kiss her right here in front of all these posh wedding guests. Breathless, she spun on her heel and returned to their table places.

Mrs. Grace Marsden stood talking with Alec, cooing at Eadie in his arms. Another man Katie didn't recognize stood nearby.

"Katie and Jonty! I'm so glad you could come." Grace held out her arm, welcoming them over, making it seem as though they were long-lost friends. "I'd like you to meet a . . . friend of mine." The way Grace hesitated showed the relationship to be more complicated than that. "This is . . . well, Jack and I call him Wilson."

The man kept his face like a mask the whole time. Friendly, but with a lot more going on behind his eyes than most of the other wedding guests, she suspected. This was the man Grace had promised could help her find Jan. A wet blanket fell over her mood, putting her in her place. Jan was the real reason she was here.

"Pleased to meet you, Mr. Wilson."

"Tell him what you told me about your friend," Grace said.

Mr. Wilson glanced at Grace sideways, looking annoyed. "Perhaps we should speak in private?"

"I'll go find Mags." Alec made himself scarce.

Mr. Wilson eyed Jonty, who'd come up behind her.

"That's my husband," Katie said. "He knows all this already."

Katie repeated everything she'd told Grace about Jan going missing. "I spoke to his wing commander, but he wouldn't help me. And his friends thought he had run off with a woman. But I know something is not right. Jan was acting so strangely the night before he disappeared. And then there's the box he gave me."

She explained the false papers and Polish documents and how Alice had looked terrified when she'd read them. Mr. Wilson seemed bored by the whole story until she mentioned the papers. At which point, he looked directly at Grace, who sent him an "I told you so" look.

"And did you bring the box with you, Mrs. Ables?" Mr. Wilson asked.

"Sorry." Katie shook her head, feeling foolish, like a child who'd brought the wrong homework to class. "I was so excited to leave for the wedding this morning that I left it on my bed."

"Perhaps I'll come by and see it. Would sometime this week suit you?"

He spoke like he was arranging a social call. Katie sent a hopeful look to Grace, who smiled encouragingly. Then Katie remembered what Jan had said when he'd given her the package. "So I shouldn't show Mrs. Grabowski when she gets back?"

Mr. Wilson frowned, but a strange look passed over his face, almost as if he recognized the name. "I'm sorry . . . who is Mrs. Grabowski?"

"My neighbor. I thought she might be able to help translate the paper. But she's been away for over a week now."

"Grabowski, you say?"

Katie nodded.

"And she's missing too?"

"Not missing. At least, I don't think she is." Was she missing? Come to think of it, it was strange for Mrs. G to leave her lodgers so suddenly.

Wilson interrupted her thoughts. "Would you mind if I took a look first? Nothing to worry about, but I would like to see it. For now, don't worry about a thing. Enjoy the party." He smiled kindly, then his eyes fixed back on Grace. "Goodbye, Mrs. Marsden." He farewelled the bride with a meaningful look.

"She didn't give him the address." Jonty stared after Mr. Wilson.

"Don't worry about that," Grace said. "Wilson will find you. It's what he does."

Jonty worked hard to avoid the groom through the afternoon. Partly for his own sake—because the scar on his leg ached when he looked at him—and partly for Jack's. After all, the man didn't want a reminder of his gritty wartime work popping up at his otherwise lavish wedding. But now the bride and groom were making their way along the tables, farewelling their guests and laughing with a couple just a few seats away.

Jonty dreaded the moment they arrived where he sat. He hadn't explained to Katie everything that had happened in France yet. She was already suspicious of him calling out in his sleep. She might never forgive him if she knew just what a coward he'd been. He had no idea if Jack would recognize him, but he didn't want to risk it. He glanced at his watch, wondering if they could escape before the couple reached them. Maybe he could convince Katie to make excuses now and catch the train back to London tonight, rather than stay with Alec and Maggie as planned. As the bridal couple inched closer, radiating happiness, Jonty's palms began to sweat.

Katie must have noticed. "Are you all right?" She smiled, but he couldn't enjoy it. "You've gone green. It's not another migraine, is it?"

"I'm fine, my love." Maybe if he scooped her up and kissed her smile, the bride and groom would just leave them at it, pass them over. That would be his preferred way to avoid coming face to face with the doctor he'd rather forget.

Not going to happen. Katie would never allow it.

Maybe Jack wouldn't recognize him. Jonty deflated. His scars meant everyone always recognized him. In a desperate, last-ditch effort, he was about to excuse himself to find the lavatory. But it was too late—the pair arrived.

"Jack, these are my friends from my days at Bottesford. You know Alec and Maggie, of course. But this is Mr. and Mrs. Ables. Katie is responsible for my beautiful dress."

All right, then. Katie's radiance when she heard Grace's compliment was worth staying for.

"Pleased to meet you, Mrs. Ables. You have done a wonderful job. My wife is resplendent." Jack slid his arm about Grace's waist and squeezed her into his side, like he wanted to hold her there forever. "And it's good to meet you too, Mr. Ables."

Jack held out his hand for him to shake. His expression went from smiling to disbelief the moment recognition sank in. Jack's eyes went wide. "I know you." Jack smiled, incredulous. "You were my patient in France."

All eyes turned to Jonty. He knew what was coming next.

Jack turned to Katie. "You must be Lily. I'm so glad he found you!"

Katie's face went from summer sunshine to rain in winter.

"It's Katie. This is my wife, Katie."

Jack paused, a flicker of confusion in his eyes. He covered it with a polite excuse about having a terrible memory.

"Forgive me. Katie, of course."

To everyone else, it would have seemed like a slip in memory on Jack's part. Not to Katie. She stiffened next to him, her radiance gone. Likely replaced by angry curiosity.

He'd have questions to answer tonight.

CHAPTER TWENTY

The evening lost its dreamlike glow after Jack mentioned Lily. No one else noticed Jack's slip. Except Jonty. She saw the guilt in his eyes. When he reached for her next, she shrugged away. He never gave a straight answer to her questions about Lily, and she burned to know why. How could she not fear the worst when Jack thought Lily was Jonty's wife?

When Grace and Jack had moved on to speak with other guests, she wished she could run after Jack and ask him more. But the couple was about to leave. With all the soft caresses they were sharing—not to mention the special things Grace had packed in her suitcase—Katie suspected they wouldn't appreciate any delay.

Jonty was open about most things, but that name was the fastest way to get him to clam up. It could zip his lips, sew them shut with a thousand invisible stitches. Which left a terrible hole that her imagination tried not to fill.

They had been separated for two years. Who had this Lily been to him in that time? Jack Marsden seemed to think she was his wife. Katie needed that answer before there could be any more dancing, like tonight.

"I'm sorry. There's nowhere else for you to sleep but the sofa and the floor!" Maggie said after showing them into her small flat. There wasn't much more to it than a living area with a small kitchenette and a single bedroom.

"It's not a problem," Jonty answered. "We're just grateful we didn't have to catch the train back this evening."

Besides, Jonty won't be sleeping anywhere else but the floor until I find out who this Lily is. Of course, she didn't say that aloud. But she glimpsed Jonty's injured look. He understood what she was thinking.

The evening passed in relaxed chatter, punctuated by Maggie trying to put Eadie down in the bassinet beside her bed. Every time she tried, the baby would wake up after five minutes, protesting at the top of her lungs that she wanted to be picked up again. Maggie would sigh, collect the baby from the bassinet, and cradle her until she calmed down and fell back into a contented sleep.

"She gets like this at night, I'm afraid," Maggie apologized. "She sleeps like an angel during the day, but at night she's quite the opposite." Maggie looked exhausted from the cumulative effect of nights with the baby on top of a busy day at the wedding.

"You can leave the bassinet outside your door if you like. I don't mind going to her if she wakes. And if I can resettle her, you'll get a full night's sleep." Maggie, Alec, and Jonty all stared at her so intently that she felt she had to give references. "I'm the oldest of eight, so I've done it plenty of times before." Just not since Betty.

"A full night's sleep." Maggie's eyes lit up at the prospect. "Sounds wonderful."

"That's very kind, Katie. I'll get the bassinet out of our room." Alec jumped to his feet and positioned the baby's bed outside the bedroom. He seemed extra eager to get some sleep. "I have to get up early to return to my post tomorrow," he explained.

Maggie laid Eadie in the bassinet, listing off instructions. "She's well fed, so if she wakes, it's not because she's hungry. She just likes the company, I think."

"We'll be fine, I promise. You go and get some sleep."

"You're sure?" Maggie glanced at Jonty, who was hiding whatever he was thinking behind some kind of smirk.

"Of course."

As much as Katie wanted to interrogate Jonty, she also craved that feeling of a baby in her arms again. Besides, the baby might serve as a buffer between them. A distraction, if they needed it.

Before long Alec and Maggie retired. Jonty prepared his place on the floor. Soon enough, Katie heard Edith stir. Little cries. Not hungry ones, just a baby wondering why it was alone.

Katie stepped over Jonty and scooped Eadie out of the bassinet. As she did, she heard Maggie's breathless laughter on the other side of the bedroom door. It didn't sound sleepy at all. Katie hurried back to the other side of the room, trying not to think about the couple behind the door, who were obviously not sleeping.

The baby settled perfectly once Katie's arms were around her, so she snuggled down on the sofa, cradling the darling child. Eadie was, as Maggie had said, a perfect little angel. The telltale prickle of tears began in Katie's eyes and nose, and her throat tightened.

Maybe she shouldn't have made such a hasty offer. Could she really look after the baby through the night, if she started this way? She swallowed down the tightness in her throat.

Jonty watched her from the floor. "Are you all right, Katie-my-love?"

She nodded, gazing down at the angel in her arms. Then a question escaped her, unbidden and out of nowhere. "Do you think our Betty is in heaven?"

Jonty looked as surprised by the question as she was by the

fact that she had spoken it aloud. But he answered quickly, sure of his answer. "I have no doubt in my mind that she is, my love."

"How can you have no doubt?" Surely he must have some?

"Don't you remember from Sunday school? 'Let the little children come to me'?"

She nodded, eyes still fixed on Eadie. "I suppose."

"No suppose about it." His confidence usually reassured her, but tonight she wanted more than platitudes.

As a man who didn't read well, he'd learned to listen. He was always so much better at understanding the finer theological points even when a sermon droned on too long for her to concentrate.

"When God makes a promise, he keeps it, Katie."

He rose to sit close to her on the sofa. The position, with him peering over her shoulder at Eadie, felt familiar. It brought on a sad flood of memories. He'd sat with her like that when they'd had Betty too. Mostly because Katie wouldn't give up her hold on the precious child.

"He's promised us that we are his children, and so it follows that our children are his children too."

Maybe that was what troubled her so much. Her faith was shaky at best, and Betty wasn't really his child, was she?

"Ooch, your thoughts are very loud, Katie-my-love. But you've got to stop thinking that way. She was my child too. I adopted her. And I know the Lord understands adoption, because we are adopted as his beloved children. So do not doubt our little girl is sleeping peacefully now."

She chose to believe him. "Well, you always did listen in church better than me."

Jonty made light of the compliment. "That would be my uncle's fault. He was a Calvinist. Didn't like dancing but quite enjoyed beating children who fidgeted during sermons."

She glanced at him in time to see him wink, even though it was a terrible thing he was joking about.

He'd hinted at his unhappy childhood before, but getting details was like prying open an oyster. Difficult, and she often hurt herself in the process. But right now she felt just hungry enough to want to pry him open to see what secrets lay inside.

She had wondered if that was the case, after meeting his uncle. He didn't seem to have a compassionate bone in his body. "Did that happen often? The beating, I mean."

Jonty stiffened, but only for a moment. He met her gaze for the briefest moment before dropping his gaze to the baby. "Not necessarily often, but he made sure the memory of them lasted. The first time, I had only been with him a few months, so I was maybe ten. He quizzed me about the sermon, and I suppose I got an answer wrong. So he took off his belt and strapped me across my legs. I wore short trousers, so I was bleeding after a few strokes. But he kept going. Said it would teach me to listen next time."

"How terrible."

"My parents were not that long dead. And with every lash, they felt further and further away. Maybe that's what he intended. They'd only ever loved me. They had never beaten me, at least not like that. And certainly not with the stench of whiskey accompanying every blow."

"I guessed that he was a drinker when I saw him in Edinburgh."

Jonty nodded. "He's still at it, despite how ill it's making him. I cried myself to sleep that night—trying to remember my mother's love and kindness. But he'd beaten it out of me. Then he drank himself into a stupor. Perhaps he was remorseful about the beating, but I don't think so. Since it didn't stop him from doling them out."

"I'm so sorry, Jonty."

Jonty shrugged. "It's in the past now."

But it wasn't. The sadness of the little boy yearning for the love of the parents he'd lost hung thick in the air between them.

"So how did you become such a good dancer then, if you were raised as a Calvinist?"

"Took it up as soon as I was out of his house, as my act of rebellion." He grinned. "It was the quickest way to meet ladies."

She let the happy sound of his chuckle wrap around her sadness, cradling it with comfort, the way she was doing to Eadie.

"I bet you were popular. You are a wonderful partner." She meant as a dancer, but the intensity in his gaze told her his mind had caught on the other meanings in the word.

"Were there many? Ladies, I mean?" *And any named Lily?*

"Some. Believe it or not, I was quite good looking once." He looked almost bashful at the admission. "But once I had the accident, my prospects dried up."

She'd figured that was why he had so hastily married her. His scars meant that women didn't exactly throw themselves at him anymore. They sat in silence and admired Eadie, perfectly sleepy in her arms. Plump and pink, as a baby should be.

"Do you want another baby, Katie?"

It was merely a curious inquiry, but it may as well have been a proposition. His breath on her shoulder had caused such delightful tingles across her skin in the church today, but not now. She shrank away and stood, pretending she needed to bounce Eadie and wasn't trying to put as much distance between them as she could in the small room.

"Never." She never wanted to bear another child if God just ripped it away. Even if Betty was in heaven, as Jonty said. It just hurt too much.

Jonty's eyes never left her, as though she was a puzzle he was trying to work out. He didn't understand. How could he? He hadn't carried the baby, felt her grow day by day. He hadn't been the one to pray steadfastly as she did that God would help her love the baby, despite everything. He hadn't been the one God had punished.

Finally, he shrugged. "Well, I think you're a natural mother, Katie."

Her face warmed. The pricking in her eyes and nose began again, and she fought to hold back the tears. To ward off the blotches on the face and neck, she walked back to the bassinet and placed Eadie, tightly bundled, back in. All was silent on the other side of the door now.

"Good night, Katie-my-love."

Jonty had resumed his place on the floor, so she tried to make herself comfortable on the couch. She should try to sleep before Eadie woke her up again. She shifted, but the sofa was barely big enough for two people to sit on, let alone one to lie down.

But it wasn't just the physical discomfort preventing sleep or even the way her conversation with Jonty rolled about in her head—it was the question that had been bothering her since the end of the wedding reception.

"Jonty?" she murmured. "Who's Lily?"

Jonty heard her question loud and clear. But he pretended to be asleep. She would know he was ignoring her, because she said that he usually twitched in his sleep. Still, he lay frozen by the question.

He needed to tell her about Lily. He didn't doubt it.

But how could he? Surely she would send him away, never speak to him again if he told her the truth of the matter.

Just like she couldn't bear the thought of another child, he couldn't bear the thought of admitting his failure. Eventually Katie fell asleep, and even though Eadie woke her several times during the night, they both pretended she had never asked the question.

Through the night, he formulated a plan. When the gray light of dawn broke, he sneaked out of the flat and found the bicycle Alex said he could borrow. Then he cycled along the country road to the St. Mary the Virgin's church in Bottesford. The exercise helped clear his thoughts.

He and Katie had been married at this church. But that wasn't the reason he wanted to visit. No, he wanted good counsel, and the vicar here gave the best. Jonty had to wait an hour for the man to arrive and open the building for the first service of the morning. But when he did, he greeted Jonty with a smile.

"Jonty Ables! As I live and breathe. It's good to see you."

The reverend shook Jonty's hand, warmth and enthusiasm overflowing. The shine in his eyes was amplified by the thick glasses he wore.

As the vicar of a small parish that included an RAF Bomber Command air station, Oscar Williams had seen his congregation ebb and flow in recent years, according to the fortunes of the RAF in the skies over Europe.

He must have known that the man in the pew on Sunday might very well be dead by Tuesday. So his sermons weren't endless repetitions of platitudes or guilt-inducing rules. They were constant scriptural reminders that God tore himself apart out of love for poor, broken men. Men like himself. Oscar's years of ministering to war-weary congregants had taken a toll on his body. The gray in his hair made him look much older than Jonty remembered, but his eyes were unavoidable lights.

"But what are you doing here?"

"Grace Deroy's wedding was yesterday."

"Ah yes, the wedding of the year!" Oscar's eyes sparkled as he opened the door of the building. "I didn't realize you two were close."

"Katie knew her . . . and made the dress."

"Ah! The dress! She must be very proud. I've already heard the gossip about it. The most divine gown since the last coronation, if Mrs. Abington is to be believed."

Oscar grinned, reminding Jonty just why he liked the man so much. Wise counsel and good humor were a powerful combination. He knew everyone's secrets but never acted with any kind of piety.

"And how is Katie? The loss of a child is such a difficult thing to bear."

Oscar had known Katie was with child from another man when he'd married them. Probably from Maggie, who had no doubt gone to Oscar for advice. Jonty still remembered Oscar's words to him after their long conversation. Oscar had told him that if he was going to make a promise before God to love a woman he barely knew, he'd better make sure he knew what that meant.

"If you marry her, there's no turning back. Your job from now on is to love her and her child. Unconditionally, self-sacrificially, like Christ has loved you."

No matter whether she reciprocated.

No matter if his feelings changed.

No matter how the war ended.

"You have to put her first. No matter what."

Once Jonty said he was prepared for whatever God threw at him, Oscar had prayed. Not a prayer-book prayer but with words that begged God for direction, peace, and fortitude. He and Katie needed that kind of prayer again now.

"The last few years have been very difficult for her."

"And for you, I gather. Missing in France for a while, weren't you?"

Jonty sent Oscar a questioning look. "Yes, how did you . . ." He realized the answer before he'd finished the question. "Maggie?"

Oscar grinned. "Filled me in on everything when she moved back to Grantham."

"I was actually hoping to speak with you about my time in France. Do you have a moment, or should I come back?"

"Jonty, I always have time."

CHAPTER TWENTY-ONE

Sunday, 5 August 1945

"Alec, we have guests!"

Katie woke to Maggie's whispered chastisement. She'd only slept lightly, after Eadie eventually had decided to sleep in her crib. Massaging the crick in her neck, Katie opened her eyes to see Maggie saying goodbye to Alec from the front door.

Immediately she knew this was a private moment. She was intruding again, but she couldn't simply run away from the door, as she had done last night. All she could do was shut her eyes. But she found she couldn't do that either.

Alec was fully dressed, ready to return to his station on the first bus of the morning. She guessed Maggie had crept to the door for a final goodbye. A reluctant one, judging by how long the kiss was continuing. Barefoot and still in her nightdress, Maggie stood on tiptoe so she could press her lips to Alec's. Her arms surrounded his neck, and he snaked his around her waist, squeezing tightly. Eyes closed, and oblivious to her audience, Maggie stretched her neck, giving him plenty of room to nuzzle into the smooth skin of her jaw and run kisses down her neck. Katie could only hear the remnants of his murmurs. A good thing. His words were meant only for Maggie.

She should pretend to be asleep. Give them at least that much privacy in their own home. But she couldn't seem to do it. And she definitely couldn't stop the longing that swelled inside her when she compared the happiness of their marriage to her own broken one.

Katie forced her eyes shut, refusing to open them until she heard the door click, followed by Maggie's happy sigh. Then Eadie's wail.

"Good morning, darling girl."

Katie didn't need to have her eyes open to know that Maggie had picked up Eadie. She tracked them across the kitchen by Eadie's coos and Maggie's chatter. Once Maggie was done nursing, Katie made a show of waking, then noticed Jonty wasn't in his bed.

"Thank you for minding Eadie last night. I won't see Alec again for another two weeks now." Maggie did nothing to conceal her dreamy expression when Katie wished her good morning. "It was a lovely goodbye."

Katie tried to push the part of the goodbye she'd seen out of her mind. "Aren't the Australians demobilizing?"

"No." Maggie laid a baby quilt onto the rug and placed Eadie on her back to play. "They are converting the aircraft for the Pacific. Aren't they, Eadie-ba-deadie?" Maggie waved a rattle over the baby's face, eliciting a coo. "I don't want him to go, but he says he needs to finish what he started."

"When do they leave?"

Maggie shrugged. "I don't know, and honestly, I don't want to think about it. It's hard enough to see half my friends demobilizing."

Katie glanced at the blankets on the floor where Jonty had

slept, now neatly folded. "Have you seen Jonty?"

"No, but it looks like he left a note."

Maggie handed her the note from the kitchen table. Apparently he'd bicycled to Bottesford to see Oscar Williams.

"Keep your eye on Eadie while I make us some tea and toast, all right?" Maggie handed the toy to Katie.

"By the way, your work on Grace's dress was lovely," Maggie said once they'd finished eating. "And she showed me the nightgown! Grace has more French lingerie than she knows what to do with, but she said it's the nicest, most delicately made thing she has."

Katie beamed.

"Pity it wouldn't have stayed on long," Maggie added with a wink.

Katie's beam dissolved into a blush. She dipped her head, trying to disappear into her teacup.

But Maggie wasn't done. "So have you made yourself anything like that?"

The heat in her face intensified. She tried to explain the slip she'd made from maps but only managed halting half sentences in her embarrassment. Her mind raced to find some way to move the conversation on from such intimate things.

Maggie narrowed her eyes, as Katie spoke. "Katie, you and Jonty have been . . . intimate, haven't you?"

What a thing to ask at breakfast! Even though Maggie spoke gently, Katie knew from the heat in her cheeks that her face was covered in red blotches. She didn't want to talk about it. And yet she craved a friend who spoke plainly about these things.

Maybe she could be honest with Maggie. After all, she already knew all the particulars of Katie's past. She'd been the first to guess that Katie was pregnant. Maggie had helped her tell Queen Bee when Katie had been too sick to work. And Maggie had been at the wedding too.

Katie shook her head. "No." To her humiliation, tears came on without warning. No telltale prickling in the back of her eyes to give her warning. They came flooding out in a shuddering sob.

Maggie reached out, laying her hand on Katie's arm, as the tears subsided. "Katie, what is it? Has Jonty hurt you?"

"It's not that." Katie sniffed. "Jonty is a good man."

Maggie's face was awash with both relief and confusion.

"And it's not that we don't know what's meant to happen." At least, she supposed he knew what to do, and she'd had her encounter with Jimmy as education.

"Then what is it?" Maggie was a natural commanding officer. She wouldn't let Katie out of the kitchen until she'd confessed all. Maggie waited, eyes full of concern.

"I'm scared."

"Of Jonty? Katie, the man worships you."

"I'm so scared of having another baby, Maggie." Another swell of sobs rose up in her chest when she spoke the words that she'd hidden deep inside. Surely Maggie understood. Her experience had been different, but surely she had wrestled with similar feelings after the death of her son, hadn't she?

"There are things you can try to stop . . ."

Katie cut Maggie's tentative suggestion off with a reproachful glance. "You and I both know girls in the WAAF who tried those things and still ended up pregnant. And anyway, that's just how it is for women in my family. My mum's had eight. And . . . didn't you worry about it after what happened to you?"

"Well." Maggie seemed to weigh her words carefully. "Everybody's different, I suppose. I'm afraid it was a little bit of the opposite for me. I felt so empty and numb. And Alec made me feel alive. A husband's love can do that, you know."

From her experience with Jimmy, Katie doubted it. Her face must have said so.

"I don't know what happened to you with Jimmy, Katie. But I know it wasn't love. With love in the mix, it can be different."

For the first time since she'd known Maggie, pink bloomed over her friend's cheeks. Katie took comfort in the fact that as frank as Maggie was, she still found it difficult to discuss such personal matters.

"And I'm sure Jonty loves you. You can trust him."

"I don't think I can." The words came out in a whisper through her tight throat.

"Why not?"

Katie explained about Lily, the name that haunted his sleep. Intimate details about their marriage came pouring out in a way neither Katie nor Maggie were prepared for. How he sometimes cried out the name, sometimes moaned it. And she had no idea what it meant. How he hadn't done it before their separation. How she had no idea who this Lily was to him, but yesterday it was clear that Jack thought Lily was Jonty's wife.

"How can I trust him when she's always there?"

Eadie let out a little coo, and Maggie scooped her up from the floor. "Have you talked to Jonty about it?"

Katie shook her head. A stone settled in her stomach as she thought back to the half conversation they'd had last night. "He won't speak about it."

"That's unlike him," Maggie said. "Perhaps it has to do with whatever happened to him in France. I never heard anything when he stayed with us last Christmas."

A strange sense of relief crept through Katie at Maggie's puzzled look. She knew Jonty even better than Katie did. She could understand.

"Talk to him about it, Katie. It might not be what you fear."

Maggie brought Eadie along to send them off at the station. Katie seemed reluctant to let the bairn go, almost smothering the little thing with kisses. She couldn't be being truthful about not wanting another child when her every action said her heart longed for one.

His own heart, which had been in a vice since the wedding,

was soothed by his conversation with Oscar. He still wasn't completely at ease—not considering all the difficult conversations he had to have with Katie when they got back to London—but he felt like he could breathe again.

Maggie gave Eadie over to Katie so she could pull Jonty aside and hand him a pamphlet. "Alec told me to give you this before you went. He said he'd mentioned it to you?"

He looked down at the paper in his hands. *Assisted Passage to Australia.*

Jonty grinned. "Ten pounds, he said. The talk is you'll only have to pay ten pounds and the Australian government will pay the rest. Do you think it will happen?"

"I hope so. But I suppose it depends on the Japanese. Then everything has to settle down after the war. But I'll end up there eventually, and it would be lovely to have my friends there. How did your conversation with Oscar go?"

He ripped his eyes from the paper that was inspiring all sorts of runaway thoughts and focused on Maggie. "He's a wise man, you know."

"Of course. I just don't intend to tell him." A wink accompanied her grin. "He'll get a big head."

Maggie was probably the only person who could say such a thing about Oscar, since he was practically a brother to her.

"Seriously though. Do you feel better after talking with him?"

He nodded.

"Good. But I hope Oscar mentioned that any man who moans another woman's name in his sleep owes his wife an explanation."

Jonty's mouth hung open, and a strangled kind of sound he didn't recognize left his body. "He told you?"

Maggie raised her eyebrows. "No, he didn't. Katie did."

The train whistle blew, calling him back to Katie. He tucked the pamphlet into his breast pocket, keeping the whole idea close to his heart. But he had to clear this up with Maggie. "It's not what you think, Maggie."

"I know that. But she doesn't."

Maggie reclaimed Eadie from Katie's arms and waved them goodbye.

Katie yawned as the train pulled away from the platform. She had the window seat and leaned her head against the glass, her body angled away from him, giving him a cold shoulder.

"You can use my shoulder as a pillow if you like," he offered. "It's a bit bony, but warmer than the glass. You can't have slept well last night."

"I didn't." She murmured to the glass, eyelids heavy.

He sighed. So they were back to this. He'd hoped this weekend would bring them closer. Yesterday he thought it did. What grand fun they'd had, until Jack mentioned Lily.

He had to tell Katie about France. He knew that. Oscar and Maggie had both made it clear that was the key to the kind of closeness he longed for. But he still didn't know how to put what he'd seen—what he'd done—into words. So now it was just like after the weekend in Norwich when they'd caught a train back to a crowded house and went on with their separate lives.

Two steps closer together, one step further apart.

His thoughts trailed down to the pamphlet in his pocket. He itched to get it out and look over it now. He was such a slow reader that it would likely take him the full train ride back to London. But what would she say if he did? Australia was a long way away, and the idea was only half-formed. He didn't want her to dismiss it before he could properly think it through. So he fixed his gaze on the view outside the window, watching the green of the countryside slowly dissolve into the gray of the city.

As they passed through Biggleswade, Katie turned away from the window and wordlessly laid her head on his shoulder. His heart swelled in his chest, beating against the pamphlet.

In a cloud of Katie's soothing floral scent, he began to plan a future far away.

CHAPTER TWENTY-TWO

Tuesday, 7 August 1945

The summer weather put on a show just as Katie left work. Bright and warm, it was the kind of day that made her heart sing even though she had been inside for most of it. She took a brief detour to Green Park to enjoy some of the sunshine before descending into the crammed underground.

She watched the smartly dressed end of London go by—magnificent hats for the ladies and smart suits for the men—and marveled at the idea they were all here in this one place. Each had different reasons. Mulled over different problems. Strode confidently toward different dreams.

Settling on a bench under a tree, she turned her face toward the dappled light and breathed in the green kaleidoscope patterns of leaves against the sky. She sighed, closing her eyes at the peace in this pause.

Grace's wedding still felt like a dream. The phone at Chez Martin hadn't stopped ringing since the wedding. Madame had given them each a bonus for their work on the dress, since it was bringing in more business than she knew what to do with. She was planning to hire two more seamstresses now.

Katie had recounted every detail of the day to the girls on her first morning after the wedding, sharing the praise she had heard about the dress.

"I still can't believe you were there!" Alice's eyes opened wide with wonder.

"And I saw at least three other dresses that we had made."

She even told them what Maggie had said about Grace's nightgown, inspiring a sound from Collette that was one part delight, two parts jealousy. But together they all shone with pride.

A shadow fell over Katie's sun-warmed face. Her eyes flicked open, and her breath caught. Jimmy Hardie stood over her, blocking the sunlight and stealing all the air from her lungs. "Hello, Katie."

He wasn't wearing a uniform anymore. Without the sartorial splendor of air force blue, he looked unremarkable. Not handsome like Alec. And definitely not kind, like Jonty. Just stocky and brutish. And so much older than she remembered.

Her throat seized. How did he know where to find her? "Did you follow me?"

He nodded.

Katie's stomach churned. "What do you want, Jimmy?"

"May I sit?" He indicated the empty spot next to her on the bench.

She didn't answer, just stared unsmiling at him. But he sat anyway.

She glanced around, looking for the Collette. "Where's Collette? Does she know you're here?"

"I just want to talk," Jimmy insisted.

His eyes trailed across her, regarding her every inch. From her hair, tied neatly in one of the styles she'd seen at the wedding, to her low Coupon Buster heels. She couldn't escape it. To create space between them, she shifted over so far that the arm of the bench dug into her side. "I have nothing to say to you."

But Jimmy wouldn't let up. He eyes settled on her wedding ring.

"Are you still married to Jonty Ables, then?"

Her jaw clenched. What right did he ask to have such a question?

The afternoon light gave this all a dreamlike quality, like the light under the marquee at Grace's wedding had done then. But this wasn't the pleasant kind of dream, with dancing and happy chatter. This was a nightmare. And it was real.

Summoning courage, she fixed her eyes on him and glared. "Why wouldn't I be?"

"Well, you and Jonty . . ." He stopped speaking and shrank away from her ire. So he should. "And the child?"

Leave it to Jimmy Hardie to stick in the knife, then give it a twist. Her voice wavered in response. "Elizabeth. Her name was Elizabeth."

"Was?" Of course, he would be trying to find out whether there was some mini Jimmy running around the world. Still, he deserved to know. Perhaps he might even feel sorrow or regret.

"She died, Jimmy," she whispered. "Your daughter died."

"I'm sorry."

But he wasn't. The only thing she saw in the expression looking back at her was relief. Katie felt bile rise in her throat again. "Are you?" She stared straight at him, wanting him to know that she saw beyond his carefully styled appearance, wanting to make him squirm. But she couldn't keep it up. Couldn't keep staring into his unrepentant face. She tore her eyes away, gazing on the sun's shimmer across a single blade of grass. "I see you aren't in the air force anymore."

"Did my tour and got out. But I met someone and stayed over here. I'm a married man now."

How could Collette be so foolish? Katie already knew that if she were to say something, Collette would laugh off Katie's sensibilities, calling them old fashioned or simply "English."

"You're despicable, then. Carrying on with Collette." What if he'd told Collette about them? She wanted to know. She didn't want to grant him the power of making her worry about it. She looked at him again. "Have you told her about us?"

Jimmy's lip twitched, as though he didn't like such straight talk. But he answered simply enough. "No. But if you keep your mouth shut, so will I."

"I've done my best to forget about that night. I can't see why I would want to bring it up now."

"Good then." He stood.

Air rushed back into her lungs.

"And I am sorry about the kid."

She forced words out through a clenched jaw. "Shove off, Jimmy. I told you her name. The least you can do is use it."

But he didn't. He simply nodded, then strode off.

Leaving her all alone with her shuddering sob.

Despite returning to days of hard physical work and a house full of boisterous boys that allowed him and Katie no privacy, Jonty's heart hadn't left that moment of happiness on the train when Katie had laid her head on his shoulder. She'd stayed like that, asleep, until he'd gently roused her as the train pulled into the station.

This week, with every brick he carried, every plank he sawed, he thought about the logistics of starting a new life with Katie in Australia. His mind almost burst with the hope the idea inspired.

Today he'd worked a half day so he could investigate the possibilities. After returning home to wash and dress in his suit, he caught the bus and tube to the Australian High Commission building on The Strand. He'd been to Australia House several times during the war, thanks to the Australians he'd flown with. This was the first time he'd come to deal with the bureaucracy.

"How can I help you today, sir?"

"I'd like to talk about this." He pushed Alec's pamphlet across the counter to a bespectacled young clerk who sounded like he came from the City of London rather than one of the colonies. "How do I apply?"

He'd come prepared with questions about paperwork and passports. He even went so far as to sneak Katie's identity card from her handbag in case he needed it. But the visit was disappointing. The clerk's answers didn't even come close to scratching his itch for knowledge on this topic.

Yes, the Australian government was considering assisting migrants from England to immigrate.

No, they had no further details apart from the pamphlet he'd read.

No, they had no details about when the scheme might be in place.

Yes, he could register his interest. Fill out this form, please.

Jonty knitted his brows as he filled out the form. He was only halfway through when he heard the clerk clear his throat, and Jonty looked up. A queue had formed behind him. Three men in demob suits like his and a woman with a hat Katie would admire stood behind him, faces set in expressions of grim impatience.

"Perhaps you could bring the form back tomorrow, sir?"

Jonty nodded, defeated by the paperwork. He left Australia House, making a mental list of every Australian he'd met while in the RAF, determined to follow up on the details they'd shared in stories years earlier. He had some idea, thanks to Alec's description of endless sunshine. But he wanted a complete picture of what life might be like before he started a conversation with Katie. He would bide his time carefully so he could paint her a truly convincing portrait of a future she would want to be part of.

The newspaper stands near the underground snagged his attention by screaming at him. "IS THIS THE END?"

He bought a newspaper, which he read slowly once on the tube. After the terrible bomb that had been dropped in Hiroshima—

more fearful than anything Jonty had been part of—Japan was talking of surrender. The end was close.

Only halfway through the lead article, he tucked the newspaper under his arm, alighted the train, and climbed the stairs into the evening light.

The boys met Jonty at the door, eager to show him how far they had progressed in the carving and whittling he'd been teaching them.

"Dad helped me get the wings right!" Davey proclaimed proudly, with more than a little emphasis on *Dad*.

"He's home, is he?"

"Upstairs. Katie is in the kitchen."

Jonty groaned inwardly. Having Bill home would add an extra complication to the evening that he did not need, not when he'd been craving time with Katie. Still, he was washed and dressed already. Perhaps he could take her out to the restaurant on Mare Street, or maybe even to the pictures.

No, not the pictures. That would mean they'd sit in silence, when what they really needed was to have a proper conversation. Not about Australia—it was still too early for that. But he needed to tell her about France.

About Lily.

"This is good work, Davy. You've come along nicely."

He glanced upstairs, wondering what kind of man Bill Baines would be tonight. When he moved into the kitchen, Katie was peeling potatoes at the table. She'd surely mock him if he told her just how beautiful he found her simple domesticity.

Katie caught sight of him and smiled. His heart gave a little leap.

"Evening." He decided to try something he'd never done before and walked around the table to give Katie a peck on the cheek. Her small gasp of surprise was only audible to him, but when he drew back, the light in her eyes told him she wasn't upset. Which doubled the size of his grin.

"Don't you look all spruced up? I thought you were at work."

Now wasn't the time to mention his hopes and dreams about Australia, no matter how his heart burst to tell her. "I had the afternoon off, for some business in town to do with my demobilization."

Her eyes flickered with confusion, but thankfully she didn't ask for more information.

"Can I help with something?" He slung his jacket over the back of a kitchen chair, then rolled up his sleeves, intending to help Katie with the potatoes.

But Katie wouldn't let him. "Not when you're all fancy like that. You'll ruin your clothes."

"Actually, I was hoping that we might go out tonight. Would you like that, Katie-my-love?"

Her face lit up like Christmas, and at the sight, his heart danced a highland reel inside his chest.

"Really? Where?"

"The place on Mare Street. Then afterward I thought we could go dancing."

"Can't you see she's cooking my dinner?"

Bill's voice cut between them as he appeared in the doorway to the kitchen, his frown directed to Jonty. Katie shrank in her seat, attention firmly on the potatoes. A learned reaction, no doubt. Jonty's heart sank. Bill's belligerence could eat the happiness in any room.

"If she's still going to be living here, taking up space and eating my food, then she has to work to earn her keep."

Jonty studied his father-in-law in the same way a lion tamer studied the beast he wanted to subdue. His jaw was so tight that he could barely open his mouth to speak.

"Well, that's just it. She's not eating here tonight. I'm taking my wife out for dinner."

He stood, grabbed his jacket off the back of the chair, and held out his hand to Katie. She glanced at her dad, then at his hand, paralyzed with indecision. He knew from experience how hard this moment was. There would be consequences for whatever she did.

Please trust me.

He willed her to choose him, eyes pleading with her to take his lead. For her sake as well as for his. She made her choice, slipping her hand into his. Jonty let out his breath.

They could have left by the back door. It would have been simpler and easier not to pass by Bill, who blocked the door into the sitting area. But if they slunk out, the boys in the sitting room—no doubt attuned to everything going on in the kitchen—would never see someone stand up to their dad. They would never see a man treating their sister well. And he wanted that for them, wanted them to see there was another way.

Firmly clasping Katie's hand, for the sake of his own courage as well as hers, Jonty stalked past Bill, pulling Katie behind him. Bill muttered curses, calling Katie filthy names.

Jonty rounded on Bill, getting up in the man's face. Close enough to smell the gin on his breath. "Do not speak to my wife that way." He forced out every word into Bill's face, hoping one of them would land like a punch.

"While she's living in my house, I'll speak to her any way I want."

Anger bubbled in Jonty's belly. Righteous anger. Jonty's fingers flexed, but Katie squeezed tight on his arm.

"We're going to dinner, Jonty. Remember?"

She tugged him toward the door.

"That's right. Trot on after your wife."

Jonty's every muscle twitched, and Katie must have felt them all. Before he could spin to confront Bill, she leaned close to murmur in his ear.

"Don't let him spoil our night." She held his gaze, keeping

her plea strong in her eyes while he wrestled his rage back under control. "You promised to take me to dinner."

She ran her hand along his forearm and slipped it into his with one gentle movement.

"Let's go."

And such a smile. The kind that melted rage, that could soften a man's heart to almost anything—including the father-in-law who shouted after them as they left.

CHAPTER TWENTY-THREE

"Katie, I want us to find a place of our own."

They weren't even inside the restaurant when Jonty started the conversation.

"We've talked about this, Jonty. There is no other place. Not that we can afford."

Should he risk it? Sharing with her the dream while it was only half-formed. He couldn't see any other alternative right now.

"How would you feel about moving away from London?" He'd start with that, then build up to the idea of moving to the other side of the world. "There are plenty of other places that Hitler didn't try to destroy. They've barely been damaged. We could get a little flat like Alec and Maggie." *One where we aren't constantly at the mercy of your fickle father.*

Of course, he didn't say that exactly. "We can start a new life. Start a new family."

She stiffened, as she always did whenever he mentioned the prospect of a family. She stared resolutely at the ground for so long, it was almost offensive.

"Do I repulse you so much that you can't bear the thought of being alone in the same flat with me? Is that it?"

She looked at him then, eyes wide with surprise. "You don't repulse me, Jonty."

He huffed out a mocking laugh. "Right. That's why the moment I get near, you fly to the other side of the room."

Sarcasm dripped from his voice, making him sound more angry than sad. But he couldn't help it.

"I can't do anything about my looks, you know, but my heart is the same as the day you married me. I want to take care of you. But while we are living in a house with a man like your father, I can't do it properly. Not the way I want to, ye ken?"

He always sounded more Scottish when he was upset or feeling something deeply, like he couldn't stop the sounds of his soul escaping through his voice.

"I know I'm not a handsome man, but couldn't you just—"

"I'm not repulsed by you, Jonty," she repeated, resting her hand on his arm as though to prove that she had no aversion to his scars. "I don't even see the scars anymore."

Right. He didn't know if that was better or worse. If she wasn't repelled by the scars, then it must be something inside him. But what? He'd change just about anything if it meant she would love him and let him love her.

"I want to show you something."

Half an hour and a bus ride later, they were at the Abney cemetery. He thought she was taking him to see Betty's grave, but instead she pulled him wordlessly to a much older group of graves. Several of them. Jonty read the headstone of the largest.

Edward Parkin, aged 45 years.

He'd never heard of the man. "Who's this?"

"Mr. Parkin was my neighbor. He was married to Mrs. Parkin in number eight."

Jonty immediately placed the woman with a face devoid of

humor and heart. Perhaps this was why. She'd lost her husband so young. But why was Katie showing him this?

"I still remember his funeral. While we were all standing over the grave, I was looking at these." Katie stretched out her hand to the smaller headstones lined up next to the larger ones like morbid little ducklings.

Calvin Parkin, aged 1 month.
Matthew Parkin, aged 6 weeks.
John Parkin, aged 3 days.

"None of them survived, Jonty. None."

He raised his eyes to her face, trying to search out her meaning in eyes flooding with tears.

"What if I'm like her? What if I can't have babies that live?"

"Oh, Katie-my-love." He reached out and pulled her to him, relieved she didn't pull away. Instead, she let him fold his arms around her and hold her to his chest, where she sobbed. The warm, damp patches her tears created on his shirt testified to the depth of her pain. "I don't think it works that way."

But maybe it did. What did he really know about it? He said no more, choosing instead to stroke her golden head and press his lips into its lavender scent. Her sobbing eventually subsided, and she pulled away. She wiped away the tears from her face, which was once again unevenly red.

"It's not you. And it's not your scars . . . Mum's had eight. All my dad has to do is look at her with a twinkle in his eye, and she's having another baby. I think it's safe to say that it's the same for me. What if none of them live? I couldn't bear it!"

He cupped her blotchy face, resisting the urge to cover it in reassuring—but certainly unhelpful under the circumstances— kisses. "Whatever happens, Katie, I promise our home will be a happy one. Whether it's here or halfway around the world in Australia."

"Australia?" She pulled away. "What's Australia got to do with it?"

Had he really said that? He hadn't meant to breathe a word about it yet. But the word was out now, and the idea grew before his eyes.

"We could emigrate."

He hadn't meant the conversation to go like this. But the genie was out of the bottle now. He gave a halting explanation of the Assisted Passage opportunity, taking her hands as he did, trying to share his excitement and connect them inside it.

All she did in response was stare. For a full minute, maybe two. As though he'd cracked his head and she needed to make an expert judgment on his sanity.

"Australia?"

"Yes." The red patches on her skin intensified. He immediately regretted speaking without the right details to convince her. "I'm sorry. I shouldna have sprung it on you. But we can't continue to live like this."

"I can't, Jonty."

She withdrew her hands from his and fled.

She couldn't go to Australia. If she did, she'd never come home. And then how would she remember Betty? All she had was this little patch of earth. Katie stared at the words on the headstone, blurry through her tears.

Tears slipped down her cheeks, making damp splotches on the front of her mauve dress. This was the purpose of graves, after all. Having a place to go so you could remember, cry if you needed to, so you weren't carrying the sadness with you all the time.

"I thought I might find you here."

Jonty's gentle voice alerted her to his presence. Of course Jonty found her. This was the most obvious place for her to be. He walked up behind her and laid his hand on her shoulder. Strong and comforting. But kind as he was, Jonty simply couldn't understand that all her dreams for the future had died the day that Betty did.

"I always figured I'd have a big family. Because of Mum, you know. It's what I most wanted. Not with Jimmy, of course. But I didn't know anything about . . . well, anything. I can still hear Jimmy telling me that there wouldn't be a baby if I was standing up."

The small tightening of his hand on her shoulder must have mimicked the tightening of his jaw. She didn't want to dwell on that part of the story either. It was done. Over.

"On the day of Betty's funeral, Mrs. Parkin came over and gave me this awkward kind of hug. I've never known her to be kind in that way. She barely said anything, just something about how some women are cursed like us. Like we were the same. I don't know what she meant, really. But the words stuck inside me."

They'd grown too. Grown into a fear so strong that she shut herself off. From life. From Jonty.

"It hurts so much to lay one child in the ground, Jonty. How could I do it for more?"

He came alongside her now, holding her hand and gazing upon her with eyes so soft and gray. Overflowing with compassion and love.

"I'm sorry I told you to leave that night."

"No. Katie. We don't have to talk—"

"But we do. I pushed you away because I was scared, Jonty. Scared of this. Not scared of you. Your scars have never mattered to me. You have loved me since the very first day we were married. And I am sorry I haven't loved you back."

They stood for a long time, hand in hand. "Part of my heart is buried here . . . Maybe that's why I can't love you like you deserve. But it's definitely why I can't move any farther away than Hackney."

Her face crumpled, throat constricting as it tried to hold a sob down in her chest. He pulled her toward him again, murmuring her name. She didn't have the energy to draw back or resist.

She wrapped her own arms around him, burying her face into his neck while she sobbed. He shared each of her ragged breaths until she wore herself out.

When they stepped apart, he took her face in his hands again so that she couldn't avoid his eyes, bright with tears of his own. "You are right about one thing. I do love you. So much. We cannae change the past, but we can build a future. We don't know what it will hold, but we must begin. Aye?"

She closed her eyes, pressing her face against his hand, anchoring herself in the touch, wondering if he would lower his face to kiss her. Fearing he would. Hoping too. But he simply pressed his forehead to hers, and they stood that way until the light faded.

Arm in arm they walked back home, forgoing the bus so they could make the most of this fragile intimacy, established through shared tears. She clung to his side, partly because she was exhausted from crying and partly because being pressed against him felt so good.

Right.

Like she was home among his scent of jasmine and rosemary.

CHAPTER TWENTY-FOUR

Tuesday, 14 August 1945

"Katie, you must do the measuring today. No matter who Madame asks for!"

Collette met Katie with wide, urgent eyes when she arrived in the sewing room. She grabbed Katie's forearm and squeezed.

"Why?"

Katie didn't object to the privilege, but Collette's frantic face and her desperation to give the coveted job away struck Katie as odd.

"Because I've seen the book. It's his wife!"

"Whose wife? Oh." Jimmy Hardie's wife. "He's married?" She feigned ignorance.

Collette nodded.

"Did you know?" Katie asked.

"Not at first." Of course she didn't. This was Jimmy Hardie they were talking about.

"It's not that I care." Collette gave her shoulders a little shake, as though trying to shrug off the lie she was telling herself. "I just can't face her. If Madame calls me, please will you go?" Her fingernails dug into Katie's skin.

"All right! Don't cut off my circulation. I'll do it." Once released from Collette's grip, she grabbed her forearm and massaged the spot where Collette's nails had created crescent-moon shapes in her skin.

Half an hour later, Katie found herself opposite Mrs. Marina Hardie in her smalls. The stylish woman was one of the many new customers that Madame had attracted. The clothes she'd changed out of were beautifully tailored. She'd tamed her thick, dark hair under a fashionable snood. Her underthings were as fine as Grace's. The diamond on the woman's left hand was bigger than any Katie had ever seen.

"Raise your arms please."

The woman barely looked at Katie, who worked quickly. From the conversation Katie had overheard the woman having with Madame, she knew Marina Hardie was the daughter of an Australian diplomat. She'd briefed Madame on what she wanted as soon as she'd arrived.

"I have the High Commissioner's Ball coming up at Australia House. I read about Grace Deroy's wedding dress, and I need a gown as fine as that."

"But of course."

"My father is the High Commissioner, you know."

Suddenly Katie understood why Jimmy's career had taken a turn toward politics.

Madame had dropped into conversation hints about how busy they were in the boutique and how their prices had risen accordingly.

"Price is no object, Madame Martin."

The little bell over the door gave a polite tinkle. Katie only vaguely heard the sound, before the one voice she wished least to hear captured her ability to think.

"Madame Martin. So lovely to meet you. My wife has spoken of nothing but getting you to make her a dress for weeks now."

Jimmy Hardie.

Katie tried not to fumble with the tape as she wrapped it around Jimmy's wife, dressed only in her delicate slip, as Jimmy handed out charming compliments to Madame. She dithered as Jimmy spread his charm about the boutique.

"Is that all?" Marina Hardie snapped.

Katie pasted on a bright smile. "That's all." She went to pull back the curtain, when Marina spoke up.

"Before you go, are you the one who makes the undergarments?"

"Yes. I mean, we all do."

"Grace Deroy is saying that one of the girls here is particularly good at them. Finely cut, and, well, tantalizing without being vulgar. She's telling everyone to ask for that girl especially."

A smile teased Katie's lips, uncertain how else to respond to the compliment of being recommended personally by the woman of the hour. "Yes. I think she means me."

"Will you make me something?"

"Of course. Speak to Madame. She's got plenty of ideas we can—"

"Not Madame. I want you. I'll pay extra for some private work. Think about it."

The very last thing Katie wanted to think about was making undergarments for Jimmy Hardie's wife, no matter how much she paid. "All right."

She made a quick escape through the blue curtain, leaving Marina to dress. Katie contemplated running straight up the stairs, but Madame called out to her. Jimmy was quick to stand up from where he had been waiting for his wife, when she entered the front of the store. Suspiciously quick.

"Katie is one of my very best girls. She did all the detailing on Ms. Deroy's—no, I should say Mrs. Marsden's—gown."

Katie tried not to speak, worried her accent might slip. Anyway, she didn't want him to hear the plummy accent she put on. It would somehow give him a power she didn't want him to have.

"I do hope you'll work on my gown too?" Marina had caught the end of the conversation.

"Of course."

Katie probably overplayed the vowel sound, because Marina gave her a strange look.

"Have we met before?"

Katie scrambled for an answer. "I don't think so. But I was at Ms. Deroy's wedding. We knew each other when we worked in the WAAF together."

"Really?" She turned to her husband. "James, didn't you say you worked with the Deroy woman too? Do you know this girl?"

Katie thought she saw panic in his eyes, even as his wife waved him over.

"Yes . . . Katie, isn't it? Katie Baines. I almost didn't recognize you."

Liar.

"Actually, it's Katie Ables."

"So you did know James during the war?" Suspicion flared in Marina's eyes.

"Yes, I did." Katie willed herself not to turn red, even as heat rose in her face. "I'm married to another one of our friends from that time." She leaned into the word *married*.

"How lovely," Marina said through tight lips, looking like she'd eaten a sour lemon.

"Well, look at the time." Jimmy hurried to move his wife along, no doubt wanting to get Marina as far away from her, the unlikely keeper of his secret, as he could. "Sorry we can't talk longer, Katie. But I'm sure you ladies will create something beautiful for the party. Goodbye."

Marina latched on to Jimmy's arm as he hurried her out the door. The action said mine *more* clearly than the word ever could.

When Katie emerged from the underground, the whole of London seemed to be on the street. People blocked traffic. Swarms of them. More people than Katie had ever seen filled the footpaths and the streets. More people than on Victory Day.

Happy people. No, not just happy. Joyful.

They laughed, sang, cheered, and kissed, brandishing evening newspapers with headlines that proclaimed the good news as simply as they could.

"JAPAN SURRENDERS."

The war was over.

Really over.

Last week Katie had read aloud the terrible details of the final bombs dropped on Hiroshima and Nagasaki to her grim-faced family. Even Jonty, who had seen Hamburg set alight from the gun turret of a Lancaster bomber, looked horrified by the scale of the damage in Japan.

On Ivy Street she met Sarah happily embracing Alberta and practically dancing in the street.

"It's finally over, Katie. Tom will be coming home!" Happy tears rolled down Sarah's face, which inspired tears of Katie's own.

"And two days' holiday! Can you believe it?" Alberta grinned, glowing from within.

"Really, two full days?"

Alberta's smile only widened. "The prime minister announced it this morning."

Katie's aching fingers throbbed with delight at the thought of two unexpected days off. She waved goodbye to her neighbors, despite them urging her to stay, and hurried inside to make sure Mum had heard the good news.

She hadn't even taken off her hat when she heard a knock at the door. What had Alberta forgotten to tell her?

"Mr. Wilson?" The man from Grace's wedding waited on the stoop. "You found me!"

"May I come in, Mrs. Ables?"

Guilt sprang up within her. With all that had happened recently, she'd forgotten about the box. She hesitated, guessing the boys were out with Mum and Jonty hadn't returned from work yet. Who knew where Dad was.

Since Mr. Wilson was Grace's friend, she stepped back to allow him space to enter. "Good news, isn't it? The war is over!"

"This war, yes." Mr. Wilson glanced around at the small sitting room. "You live here with your parents, I believe?"

"Yes. And four little brothers. And my husband."

Mr. Wilson nodded, then moved on from the niceties. "You mentioned your friend Jan left a box with you, Mrs. Ables?"

"He did." She moved across the room to her sewing basket, expecting to reach in to feel the cool metal of the tin. But all she felt was the corduroy she was using to make another pair of trousers for Jonty. She peered into the basket, sure that it had been here the other night. But there was nothing.

Alarmed, she looked up at her guest, meeting his foxlike eyes through his glasses.

"I don't know how to tell you this, Mr. Wilson, but, well, it's gone missing. I'm sure it was here just the other night while I was working."

She scoured her memory. Yes, it was there. She remembered having to take it out to get to the work underneath. Lucy had commented on it.

Mr. Wilson's eyes lit up as though the fact it was missing was far more intriguing than what he'd expected to find. But he simply asked about the box as though he were making polite inquiries into the health of her family. "Who else knows about the box? Your family?"

"Just Jonty." She explained how they'd both opened it together. "Mum and Lucy might have seen it, but they would just think I keep my notions in it."

"What about your father?"

"I doubt it. He's barely home."

"Right."

Mr. Wilson glanced about the room. She felt terrible he had trekked all the way here at Grace's request and Katie was sending him home empty handed. "Would you like a cup of tea? Since I can't give you the box?"

"Perhaps you can just tell me more about what was in it."

She held out her hand, indicating that he should sit on the sofa, and took up a seat on the spot under the lamp she used at night. "Like I told you at the wedding, it had identity documents for my friend and another woman, but they weren't using his name. And another document in Polish that looked like it contained mathematics of some kind, but I couldn't read it. I took it to my friend at work who's Polish, but she wouldn't read it."

Mr. Wilson reached into his breast pocket and withdrew a photograph, which he handed to Katie. "Is this your friend?"

Katie took the photo. Jan in his air force uniform, looking dashing as ever. She nodded. "Where did you get it?"

Mr. Wilson answered her question with another question. "Did Mr. Delovski ever talk to you about his life in Poland? His friends and relatives there?"

"I thought he did. I mean, he told me a lot about Poland and when he was a child. But the other men in his squadron, who I went to talk to, said he was married. He never told me that. So I suppose he didn't tell me everything." She'd decided not to tell her family about that piece of news, although she couldn't quite say why.

"Did he ever mention being watched or followed?"

"Never. Although . . ."

She thought about how strange he had acted the last time she'd seen him. She tried to explain that to Mr. Wilson.

"When was this?" Mr. Wilson took out a pencil and notebook.

"Are you a policeman?"

Mr. Wilson's eyes flicked up. "No, but I do investigate things."

What did that mean? Uncertainty gripped her stomach, even as she gave him the date, trying to remember the details of the encounter. "He gave me something to give to my neighbor, but he never showed up to collect the box."

Mr. Wilson scratched her answer onto his notepad. "And what did he give you for the neighbors?"

"Just an envelope."

He lifted his eyes from the paper to study her over his spectacles.

"Did you look in it?"

"No." She answered too quickly. Mr. Wilson's raised eyebrow told her he thought she was lying. "I was scared to."

"Scared? Why?"

She chewed down on her lip. "Because I thought it might contain banknotes."

Mr. Wilson's second eyebrow met the first. "Banknotes?"

She nodded. "And if it contained banknotes, it was a lot. More than anyone around here has all at once."

"I see." He added a dramatic full stop to his page. "Did you look before you handed the envelope to your neighbor?"

"Of course I didn't look! I gave it to Mrs. Grabowski as soon as I got home. Mrs. Grabowski just said it was just some papers she was expecting from him."

"And you believed her?"

"Well, afterward I just thought I was being silly. Imagine anyone in Hackney having that much money. And I suppose I forgot, what with my sister's wedding and then Grace's."

Mr. Wilson sighed. She caught a hint of the frustration he was trying to hide. He removed his spectacles and pinched the bridge of his nose. "You didn't wonder about the money even after she disappeared for weeks on end?"

She hadn't. Not until now. "What do you think might have

happened to Jan, Mr. Wilson?"

"I don't know. But I'm beginning to wonder about Mrs. Grabowski." Mr. Wilson stood. "I might go and talk to some of her tenants. Thank you, Mrs. Ables."

"For what?"

"You've been quite helpful today."

"Have I? I lost the box."

"Yes. That might be a problem."

He handed her a card with a number to call if she remembered or saw or heard anything else about Jan. "If you find it again, or see anything else strange, like an envelope of banknotes"—he raised an eyebrow, as if to indicate that her not mentioning this earlier was a serious oversight—"would you let me know? Call anytime. Day or night. Someone will always answer."

He was out the door before she had time to ask more. She raced to the door and called after him. "You'll let me know if you find him, won't you?"

Mr. Wilson tipped his hat, climbed into the black car waiting for him on the curb, and drove off. Catching a glimpse of herself in the small mirror tacked to the entryway wall, she saw how ridiculous she looked, wearing her hat inside. Reaching up, she removed the pin holding it in place.

"Who was that?"

She jumped sky high at Dad's voice coming down to her from the top of the stairs. "Dad! I didn't know you were home!"

How much had he heard of her conversation with Mr. Wilson? An uneasy feeling stole into her belly. An envelope full of banknotes was definitely something Dad would be interested in. He came down the stairs, accompanied by the strong scent of gin.

"Who was that?"

"Just someone who is helping me look for Jan."

Dad scowled. "Police?"

"Apparently not. But he is an investigator of some kind. My friend recommended him." She tried to sound confident despite feeling small under his scrutiny. "Did you hear Japan surrendered? We have two days' holiday now."

"That's what the ruckus is on the street, then." Dad swayed a little and shrugged. But the news seemed to catch him by surprise. "Two days, you say?"

She nodded.

He grunted before thudding down the rest of the stairs, ripping open the front door, and slamming it behind him.

CHAPTER TWENTY-FIVE

Thursday, 16 August 1945

Even the sun celebrated the end of the war. There wasn't a cloud in the sky for the whole two days of their holiday. When a telegram had arrived from Maggie inviting them to spend a day of celebration at the seaside, Katie hadn't hesitated to take up the offer.

"It's good to be back." Grace flung open a bathing box containing all their beachside needs. Apparently she and Jack were honeymooning in this little pocket of coast, hastily cleared of barbed wire and anti-invasion defenses.

"My family holidayed here when I was a child," Grace said.

As the men set up the sun chairs from the bathing box and Grace cuddled with Eadie, Maggie pulled Katie aside. "I have something for you." She handed Katie a package not unlike the one Alberta had handed her a few weeks ago. Brown paper around supple fabric. "It's parachute silk. Promise not to ask me where I got it."

Katie grinned. "Do you want me to make you something?"

Maggie shook her head, glancing at where the men were setting up. "I want you to make *you* something."

"Me? Why?"

"Well, you never had a wedding dress, did you?" Katie shook her head. "And yet here you are making such beautiful things for other people. I think it's time you made something for yourself, don't you?"

Katie frowned. "But it's silk. Don't you want it?"

"Parachutes are big things, Katie. I've taken some for myself and some for Eadie, and there's still some left over for a nightie for you." Katie's face heated, and words escaped her, so Maggie continued. "And Grace gave me some of the lace left over from her mother's gown, to make a christening dress for Eadie, so I've put some of that in there too. Make something for yourself as delightful as you made for Grace."

"I don't know what to say."

"Don't say anything, then. Just make yourself something beautiful. All right?"

Katie slipped the packet into her bag before rejoining the others, stealing Eadie away from Grace and settling down on a chair of her own. She and Maggie both cast envious looks at Grace's modern two-piece bathing suit after she shimmied out of the sundress she wore over it. The green bathers showed off her athletic figure without looking immodest, like some of the new suits Katie had seen in the magazines at Chez Martin. Grace draped an effortlessly fashionable kaftan about her and put on her round-rimmed sunglasses before reclining on a chair to soak in the sunshine. Having Grace there was like having a day out with a movie star. Katie reveled in the secondhand glamour.

Jack appreciated Grace's good looks by leaning over and planting a happy kiss on his wife's lips. Katie glanced away from their bubble of happiness, only to meet Jonty's piercing stare.

She couldn't swim, so she didn't own bathers, glamorous or

otherwise. It didn't matter since she fully intended to stay planted on the seashore, minding Eadie. She wore a simple floral sundress in a light cotton, which she'd made herself from a design she'd found in one of Madame's magazines. It was a little shorter than normal and tied up behind her neck so that her back and shoulders were exposed to the delightfully warm sun.

"Shall we explore the ocean, Katie-my-love?"

She opened her mouth to object, but Maggie gave her no excuse. "You go. I'm sure Eadie's hungry."

Eadie was sleeping peacefully and not hungry at all, but Katie had no choice but to hand her back to her mother.

"But I can't swim."

"Neither can I. We'll only go up to our knees."

She clasped Jonty's extended hand and let him pull her to her feet. He wouldn't let her remove her hand from his until they reached the gentle waves. Low tides exposed more soft sand, which made her bare feet happy. Until they hit the chill of the water.

The day was one of the warmest they'd had this summer, as though even the weather wanted them to celebrate. In the heat, the shock of the cold water on her legs dissipated quickly, leaving her with cooling energy. Venturing in farther until the water came up to her knees, she took a deep breath, inviting the salty air into her lungs and marveling at the idea that the war was finally over.

A splash of water landed on her exposed back, simultaneously shocking and delighting her skin. "Jonty!" She reeled around to see Jonty grinning childishly at her, just before she suffered another handful of water to her face. She huffed indignantly, but his smile was full of mischief. Very much like he was challenging her to splash him back. A smile toyed with her own lips, but she wouldn't let it show.

Instead, she put on a stern face and waded toward him. "That's just so childish, Jonty."

She watched his face drop a little, putting him off guard.

Without warning, she bent, cupped a handful of water, and hit him square in the face with it. "Ha!"

He laughed at her feint, and she followed up with a bigger splash, this time using her leg to kick up the water.

"That's it!" Jonty wiped the water from his clearly delighted face. "You're in for it!"

She shrieked as she tried to dodge his splash, but her laughter rang out across the whole beach. They didn't need to know how to swim. They managed to get wet enough with their tit-for-tat splashing game.

Jonty borrowed a bucket from a child playing nearby, filled it with water, and dumped it over Katie's head. Her squeal as the water ran down her back and shoulders echoed out indignantly. She made a show of glaring at him, but she couldn't hold in her laughter.

At the game.

At herself.

At him.

At the sun on her skin.

At the war being over.

At how delightful it was to have fun.

Jonty closed the distance he'd put between them in case she retaliated and snaked his arms around her waist. Her breath hitched, but she didn't pull away. At that moment, despite the wonderful feeling of the sun on her skin, she didn't want to be on a beach full of people. She wanted to be alone, in private, with just him. She wanted him to do what his eyes, intent on her mouth, said he wanted to. Dip his head and let his lips linger on hers.

But they weren't in private, were they?

So she used his distraction to steal the bucket from his grasp, fill it with water, and dump it over him in one fell swoop.

"No." He grinned. "Not even a bucket of cold water can stop me from wanting to kiss you silly on this beach, Katie-my-love."

He kept his arms firmly around her waist as she laughed

heartily, trying, with playful squeals, to flee.

"Can I have my bucket back now?"

The freckle-faced boy waded over and looked at them severely. Katie stepped away and handed the little boy back his property. She thanked him for lending it.

"You got him good. I saw."

The boy inspired fits of giggles as he waded away.

As they retreated from the water to find towels, Katie's heart sang with happiness.

"So married life agrees with you, then?"

Jonty tried to withhold his sarcasm, but Jack was due some since the whole group had just witnessed Grace's fond farewell to her husband. Extremely fond, considering she was simply going to fetch ice cream with Katie. Alec and Maggie sat with Eadie under a sun umbrella, so it was just him and Jack left on the chairs.

"It certainly does." Jack grinned like the unrepentant honeymooner he was.

Jonty shook his head at Jack. Not that he was unhappy for the man—he just couldn't identify with the giddiness of a newlywed. He and Katie had never shared that. Jonty lifted his gaze and traced the crowd to find Katie in her sundress, blond locks tied in a braid that caressed her shoulder and bare back.

Lucky it.

How he managed to restrain himself from marching over and kissing her, he didn't know. But the muscles required to keep his hands to himself, even when they twitched to touch his wife, were well trained by now. Still, he should look at something other than her bare legs or the particular spot on her back where the flesh ended and dress began. He was a patient man, but even he had his limits.

"So what are your plans now that the war is over? Will you return to the US?" Jonty asked.

"Honestly, I don't know. I think I'll be in Europe for a while yet, as there are plenty of people who need doctors right now. But it's too soon to say where Grace and I will eventually settle. What about you?"

Jonty told him his hopes to eventually immigrate to Australia. "I think a fresh start will be good for the two of us."

If only he could work out where. He had no desire to rip her away from London after her confessions at Betty's grave. But the rent there was more than they could afford. And he had no idea where to begin with the other things she was worried about.

Except Lily. He knew he owed Katie an explanation about that. He shielded his eyes from the angle of the sun as he followed her progress in the ice cream queue.

As if Jack could read Jonty's thoughts, he mentioned his faux pas at the wedding. "I'm sorry if I put my foot in it at the wedding. I should have known better than to say anything. But I just remembered you as the man with the scars who called out 'Lily' all the time. I shouldn't have assumed it was your wife's name, but I must have had marriage on the mind." Jack shot him an apologetic look.

"Did I call out a lot?"

"It was all I remember you saying. But you were delirious with fever at first and with morphine at other times. And I only treated you for a short while before we handed you back to the Brits."

Jonty nodded slowly. "It's no matter. It's in the past."

Jack narrowed his eyes. "Is it?"

Jonty glanced up at where Katie and Grace were at the front of the line. Katie tossed her braid over her shoulder, unaware of just how beautiful she looked. They'd be back soon, so he and Jack didn't have time for a longer conversation.

Jonty shook off Jack's sudden seriousness with a joke. "I thought you were a surgeon, not a psychologist?" Searching for his wife's floral sundress, Jonty's eye caught on another figure pushing through a crowd. Though the people around her were clad for a day on the seashore, this woman stood out because she was dressed head to toe in farm clothes.

His breath caught in an audible gasp.

It couldn't be. His heart raced in his chest like a herd of elephants.

"Jonty, are you all right?"

He barely heard Jack, even though the man was just next to him. Jonty blinked and squinted against the sunlight.

The farm girl pushed through the crowd, away from him so he couldn't see her face properly. But the mousy hair tied in the braid down her back was the same as he remembered.

Jonty stood. "Lily?"

It couldn't be. But it was. He was so sure.

He half heard his friends' muttered conversation about him, and he stood, eyes shielded as he looked into the afternoon sun.

"Is he all right?" Maggie asked. "What were you talking about, Jack?"

"The time we met in France."

"Jonty, are you all right?"

Jonty only barely heard Alec's voice as he took off after Lily. He scrambled up toward where Katie and Grace waited for the vendor to serve their treats.

"Jonty? What's wrong?"

He pushed past Katie in the line, focusing on the braided girl. She disappeared among the bodies on the boardwalk. He pursued her, pushing through the crowd to find her again.

"How rude!"

He almost sent an older woman in a dark hat flying as he pushed past. When he turned back to apologize, the hat was gone. She wasn't as old as he'd thought. Her features were more gallic, and she stared at him in stern condemnation.

He stumbled back a few steps. His breath matched the pounding of his heart.

Something strange was happening. Maybe it was a peculiar

kind of migraine. But no, the girl looked so real in her farm clothes. He searched her out again, that flick of a braid slipping through the crowd away from him, closer now—or farther away.

His heart, his breathing, and the angle of the afternoon sun in his eyes conspired to confuse him.

"He's mad!" someone proclaimed in the distance.

Maybe.

Or maybe nearby?

Maybe it was about him.

Or maybe it wasn't.

Because nothing seemed real.

The braid flicked, capturing his attention again. He stumbled toward it, knocking into people on the promenade because, in the blinding glare, he didn't see them—he only saw an elusive farm girl out of reach ahead of him in the crowd.

"Lily!"

He called to her, but she wouldn't turn. Wouldn't look at him. She just pushed through the rest of the people. The braid flicked, suddenly within his reach. He lay his hand on her shoulder.

She screamed, whipping around when he touched her. But the braid didn't belong to a French farm girl. It belonged to a freckled English face.

Somehow, he'd chased a ghost right off the promenade and onto the grass behind. Turning away, he rubbed at his chest and tried to calm his breath.

"Jonty!"

He looked up to see Katie staring at him like he was a stranger. Melted ice cream ran off the cones and down the hands that held them.

"I think it's time you told me about Lily."

CHAPTER TWENTY-SIX

Jack prescribed water and shade for Jonty in the first instance. "It's been a hot day, and I haven't seen you drink a thing."

Katie sat with him, making sure he drank. The others disappeared for a walk along the beach, while Jonty leaned his back against one side of the bathing-box's doorframe. His forearms rested on his bent-up knees.

Katie poured more tea from a thermos into a cup. He accepted the tea, raising it to his lips as she settled back against the other side of the frame. She didn't speak but simply waited for him to begin in his own time.

He clearly didn't want to talk but he wasn't leaving this beach without giving her an explanation.

"I'll start with the night my aircraft came down over France. I thought for sure my time was up. Because why should I have so many lucky escapes when others get blown out of the sky the first time they fly? I could barely believe that parachute floated me to the ground safely."

"I'm glad it did." She smiled to encourage him, but he simply shook his head, heavy with sadness.

"You won't be when you hear this story."

She could taste the bitterness of his words in her own mouth. So she laid her hand on his arm. "Tell me."

"A crowd descended on me. I don't speak French and they didn't speak English, so I had no idea what was happening. At first I thought they were an angry mob tearing my parachute off me. Until one man managed to say in English, 'Don't be afraid.'"

"Like the angels always do?"

"Aye. That's what I think about those people now: They were angels. They hid the parachute and gave me new clothes so I didn't look like I was in the RAF. They combed boot polish through my hair."

"Boot polish?"

"There aren't many redheads in France, ye ken."

"I can't imagine you having dark hair." Her lighthearted remark was meant to encourage him, but she couldn't raise his mood.

He fell back into reflection. "Within five minutes of falling from the sky, I was disguised and given a rickety bicycle. I managed to understand, by then, that I needed to follow another man on a bike. I'd hurt my leg in the crash, so it was the longest bike ride of my life. At a farmhouse, he passed me to a family who at least spoke some English. They explained that I could trust them and they would help me, but first I had to hide. They ushered me to a compartment in the floor under their kitchen table, a cellar with just enough space for me to lie down. Me and several mice."

She shuddered in sympathy at being shoved into a hidden compartment with rodents. "Were you scared?"

"Then? No, because I understood they were trying to help. We'd all heard tell of the escape route by then. They wouldn't have shoved me into a hiding spot if they were intending to tell the Germans, would they?"

He took another sip of tea. "I figured I needed to stay hidden until the first danger passed, so I stayed put. Sure enough, the Gestapo came looking in the morning. I could see the hobnails on the officer's jackboots through a crack in the floor and hear his shouting. I didn't understand what he was saying, but he was furious. He stomped around, clearly suspecting something, but they kept silent. He never found my hiding spot.

"I know now that people on the escape routes would have usually tried to move me on quickly, but they couldn't because the Germans were retreating. I tried to ask for directions and showed them my silk map. But they said, in their halting, broken English, that it was too dangerous right now. I stayed in that hole for a week."

"Oh, Jonty." She regretted every night he'd slept on the floor instead of in her arms.

"They brought me food and tried to bandage my leg, but I had to stay hidden underground most of the time."

Jonty became still, as though his body was recalling how quietly he'd lain in his hiding spot. She resisted the urge to take his hand.

He lapsed into silence, as the memories must have become too difficult to project aloud.

But she'd coveted this story for too long to let him stop now. "What happened then?"

"Their daughter was probably the same age as you, same blond hair, but she wore it in a braid down her back."

"Lily?"

"Yes." His voice cracked on the word. "She had a little English and told me about how the Americans were coming."

So this was Lily, the woman who haunted his sleep.

"I could feel it, in the ground. Everything shook as tanks retreated along the road. I could hear the bombers up above. All I could do was lie there. I prayed night and day."

He sucked in a deep, trembling breath, and a tear ran down the right side of his face. She took his hand now, interlacing their fingers to anchor him with her in the present. He looked down at their hands as he spoke.

"I suppose they had hidey-holes like mine all over the village, and the SS knew it. So they showed no compassion as they left."

He paused as the memory played in his mind. Instinct told her this was what he dreamed each night. But during the day the words were physically difficult to get out.

"I heard them haul the family from their kitchen. They shot the farmer and his wife."

"Lily?"

"I don't want to tell you what they did to her, Katie. I don't want you to have that in your mind the way I have it in mine." He swallowed. "I . . . I stayed hidden in the ground the whole time. I wanted to save her. I tried to get out, but I was weak. The table above was too heavy to move from where I was. If I'd have called out, the SS would have found me and shot me through the floor. But I heard what was happening. All of it. Heard her beg for her life, and then the gunshot."

Her stomach twisted for the brave girl she never knew. Jonty dropped her hand and covered his face, sobbing into his calloused palms. "I should have revealed myself. But I was a coward."

The man she married, the one who had married her to save and protect her, didn't bear this shameful sin of omission lightly.

"I didn't even pray." He confessed another sin of omission that must have weighed so heavily on his heart. "At that moment, I abandoned her completely. I couldn't move that plank. I just lay there."

He slipped into silence. She took his hand again, partly to remind him she was there. Her heart ached with all the things she wanted to tell him.

That she didn't think any less of him.

That she was glad he didn't speak up, because they would have shot him where he lay.

That his survival was testimony to the extraordinary bravery of Lily and her family.

"How did you escape?"

"It must have been hours later, maybe even a day. I heard American accents and started shouting. They pried the floorboards open and got me out. As they took me away on a stretcher, I saw the brave people who helped me lying where they'd been shot. And Lily."

"Is that what you see in your dreams?"

His face crumpled as he nodded.

"They'd just left her there like she was a piece of clothing they'd torn off and discarded."

Tears flooded both their faces. Katie's heart hurt for this woman whose name she had resented for so long. But she ached for Jonty too, for the scar tissue on his soul that was as real as the marks on his face.

"My leg was well on the way to being infected. I also had a pressure sore on my hip because I couldn't move while I was underground in the cellar. I was delirious by the time I met Jack Marsden. But he says I called out Lily's name a lot."

His tears had stopped now, and he appeared exhausted. Depleted.

"I relive it every night, Katie. But it's always different. Sometimes I see her crumpled, dead, and still, the way he left her. Sometimes I see those scared eyes. Occasionally in my dreams, I get to save her and do what I should have been able to do in real life."

"Jonty, you said it yourself. You couldn't have done anything. Your wounds were infected, and you were weak. You'd have been shot if you revealed you were there."

He paused, lines etching themselves across his forehead, his mouth grim. Then he met her eyes. His eyes, deep gray and glistening with his tears, were pools of infinite sadness and shame. "I didn't think you would want to stay married if you knew."

"Oh, Jonty." Her heart flung her whole body at him, wrapping him in her arms so he would know that she forgave. "You and I won't be defined by what's in the past. Not anymore."

Her lips ached to find his, to kiss away the pain, but Maggie's voice stayed her.

"I'm so sorry to interrupt, but there's going to be a storm. We need to get going."

Maggie pressed her lips together in an apologetic grimace. Katie glanced at the darkening sky. They'd been talking so long, so wrapped up in his confession, that they hadn't realized how gray the sky had become.

Jonty jumped to his feet, breaking the spell of their conversation. "We'll help you pack up."

In the mad scramble that followed, Katie helped the others pick up shoes, baby bibs, lunchboxes, clothing, tea flasks, and everything else Maggie had so carefully packed earlier in the day. With everything bundled in their arms, they dashed for the cover of a nearby café. Most who had been on the beach just a moment before crowded into the café with them, marveling at the ferocious pace of the storm.

Katie set about packing the flotsam and jetsam of the beach day back into the bags.

"Is Jonty all right?"

Her head shot up at Maggie's question. She stood up from where she'd been kneeling, following her friend's gaze through the window.

A lone figure stood where the waves met the shore, looking out to sea. Knowing she looked foolish, Katie left the café, pushing through other beachgoers keen to take shelter.

As the rain hardened, she ran across the beach to Jonty, cool droplets soaking her clothes. His eyes were closed, his face raised to the sky. Raindrops replaced the tears that had been on his cheeks.

"Jonty Ables, after all you've been through, I won't let you get struck by lightning too."

His shoulders shook with a laugh—or a sob, she wasn't sure—but he opened his eyes and turned to her. She read a million different things on the scarred face in front of her, seeing for the first time the depth of the desperation and doubt he carried. The overwhelming shame. The fear that she would think less of him once she knew his secret.

"Can you ever forgive me, Katie-my-love?"

She gave the only answer that she thought he would believe, given their circumstances. She reached up and pulled his head down to hers so that their lips met in a long, deep kiss.

CHAPTER TWENTY-SEVEN

Tuesday, 21 August 1945

"Do you think that Madame will eventually get to dress the princesses?"

"If she does, I hope I can do the measuring,"

Katie chatted with Alice as they walked toward the tube station. The run of spectacular weather had continued, and it matched Katie's mood perfectly. Since returning from the seaside, Jonty had an energy that she hadn't seen since the early days of their marriage. Bouncy and optimistic.

Perhaps it was infectious, because she felt distinctly different too. Happier. Now that she knew who Lily was—both the role she had played in keeping Jonty alive and the terrible fate she'd met at the end—she couldn't resent the girl. Her nights weren't filled with wondering about her husband's secret. In fact, they only had one secret between them now. Hers.

But this secret was a delightful one. A parachute silk one.

Make yourself something as delightful as what you made for Grace.

Alice was the only one who knew her secret, because she'd helped with the design for the neckline that would look sumptuous but still be economical.

"How is your nightdress"—Alice paused to find the right English word—"progressing?"

"It's slow going. I can only work on it when he's asleep. And I don't have such good light at night as I do at Madame's. But I think in a week or two, it will be ready."

Katie's voice trickled away as she caught sight of an official black car pulling up on the street just ahead of where they walked on the footpath. Mr. Wilson stepped out of the car and into their path.

"Mr. Wilson, what are you doing here?"

The question slipped out in her Hackney voice, not her high-street one, inspiring a sideways glance from Alice. Deciding that Alice would understand the need for a posh accent at Madame Martin's, Katie kept her natural accent to speak with Mr. Wilson. She'd answer questions later.

"I have some rather sad news, Mrs. Ables. Would you like to discuss it with me in the car?"

Katie knew not to accept rides in cars from strangers, but Mr. Wilson was a friend—well, a friend of Grace Deroy's, at least—so she didn't think it would be a problem to hear what he had to say in the privacy of his car. She was about to follow his outstretched hand and slide into the backseat when she felt Alice's fingers squeeze into her arm. She turned to her friend. Alice shook her head in warning, her eyes wide with fear and her grip on Katie's arm viselike.

"Perhaps we should speak on the street."

Irritation flashed over Mr. Wilson's face, but he recomposed his features into the perfect picture of sympathy.

"We have found your friend, Mrs. Ables."

"Jan? Is he all right? Can I see him?"

"I'm afraid not. We dragged his body out of the Thames last

night. We think he'd been in there for several weeks."

Her head swam. How awful. She wished she hadn't listened to Alice's fears, because she'd be sitting down and not standing on the high street when the tears inevitably sprang into her eyes.

"Last time you saw him, did you have any worries for his mental state? Did he say or do anything to suggest that he might take his own life?"

"Absolutely not! He was planning on coming to my sister's wedding."

Mr. Wilson nodded sadly. "Are you sure you don't want to talk about this in the car?"

Alice's grip reminded her to say no. She shook her head.

"I'm afraid your friend attracted the attention of the NKVD. Do you know who they are?"

She shook her head again, trying to listen instead of imagining the terrible scene of Jan being dragged from the river.

"In Russian, it means the People's Commissariat for Internal Affairs. Basically, the Soviet Secret Police."

"I don't understand. He's Polish." Was Polish.

"The Soviets are the new authorities in Poland, and they were following Jan."

"But why would they care about a pilot?"

"We aren't entirely sure. Can you remember what he told you about his family?"

She tried to push the terrible thoughts of Jan's drenched body out of her mind and focus on Wilson's questions. She tried to think. He'd never mentioned a wife, but what about the rest of his family?

"He mentioned a brother, I think, and I think his father was a scientist. Perhaps a professor. I don't really recall."

Wilson nodded, as though he already knew what she'd told him. "We think the papers you saw in that tin will tell us more. You still haven't found them?"

"No. Nothing."

"You mentioned that a friend of yours who spoke Polish had read the papers. Do you think she could tell us what they said?"

Katie turned to Alice, whose eyes were as wide as saucers. Alice trembled when Mr. Wilson's attention set on her.

"I'm sorry. I can't." Alice turned, about to run away, when two men appeared, apparently from nowhere, and hemmed her in.

Pale and trembling, Alice shook her head. "I don't want trouble."

"It won't be trouble, Alice," Katie reassured. "It might help find out what happened to Jan."

Alice glanced around furtively. Katie was almost certain she was looking for an escape route.

"But you don't understand. You can't. None of you can."

"Perhaps you would like to discuss it at my office?" Mr. Wilson indicated the car again. "I promise that you'll be safe."

Alice pleaded with her eyes. Her grip on Katie's arm was so tight by now that Katie was sure she would have a bruise tomorrow.

She wrenched Alice's fingers off her arm and squeezed her friend's hand. "I'll come with you. There's safety in numbers, right?"

Alice looked far from reassured but had no choice than to allow herself to be bundled into the backseat. After barely five minutes of driving, they arrived at another Mayfair address, near Hyde Park. Mr. Wilson and the men with him guided them into an office building and up the stairs to what Katie assumed was Mr. Wilson's office. Alice kept her arm tightly tucked through Katie's the whole time.

"Tea?" Mr. Wilson offered once they were settled in chairs on the other side of his desk.

"Don't take their food and drink!" Alice hissed in Katie's ear.

"No thank you."

Mr. Wilson poured himself some tea. Then he took a biscuit

from the tray next to the teapot, dunked it in the tea, and shoved it into his mouth, with a pointed glance at Alice. He meant no harm.

"Now, Alice, isn't it?"

Alice only nodded, offering no further information about her surname. However, Katie now suspected Mr. Wilson had known her name all along.

"Mrs. Ables said she showed you the paper Jan left."

"I only saw one page, and only a short look."

"And what did the paper say?"

"*Shchtishla Taina*." Alice spoke the Polish words in a small voice, then translated for Katie's benefit. "Most Secret."

"And what else did they say?"

Alice's shoulders sagged. "I only saw the first page."

Katie thought back to when she had shown Alice the papers. "You did flick through though."

Alice glared at Katie but seemed to decide that she had no choice but to tell them everything. "It was a scientific paper. Physics or chemistry. I'm not sure."

"Do you remember the title?"

Alice shook her head, in consideration this time, not fear. "Not completely, because I didn't understand what it meant. And after I saw it was secret, I didn't want to understand it."

"Any of the words you recognized would help," Mr. Wilson prompted.

"Something about"—she repeated the words to herself in Polish, probably searching for their English translation—"a sustained chain reaction."

Mr. Wilson nodded gravely. He didn't look surprised, which made Katie wonder if he'd known all along.

"Thank you, Alice. You rather confirmed what we suspected."

"What did you suspect?" Katie insisted he tell. She wasn't going to be dragged all this way to be kept in the dark.

"We think, although we aren't sure, that Jan's father gave him a scientific paper he'd been working on in 1939 about atomic energy."

Katie's brow furrowed. "What's that?"

"It's the science behind the bomb recently dropped on Japan."

A strange feeling stole into Katie's stomach. "Why would Jan have that?"

Mr. Wilson shrugged. "There's a lot that's speculation here. His father probably hoped Jan would keep it safe for him or at least keep it out of the hands of the enemies of Poland. Perhaps he intended Jan to give it to the British or the French when the Polish Air Force evacuated. We don't really know what was going on in either of their minds six years ago, and his father died during the war." He sighed. "But we know the Soviets wanted the paper back."

"Soviets?"

"I'm afraid they were allies in the last war, but they'll be the enemy in the next. They don't have a bomb like the one the Americans dropped yet, and they are desperate to get one."

"Are you saying they killed Jan to get the paper?"

"We don't know. But the British government will likely provide for the pilots who fought with us here, allowing them to immigrate with top priority. We know that the Soviets wanted him home and were threatening not to let his wife join him here if he didn't provide the paper."

She remembered the other documents in the tin. The identity documents with false names. "Was he planning to help her escape?"

"I think it's likely. But I'm afraid I've told you as much as I can for now. You understand, don't you, Mrs. Ables, that you can't mention anything I've said here today to anyone."

Katie paused. She'd signed the Official Secrets Act like everyone else when she'd joined the WAAF. But this was different. Personal.

"Jan is dead. I understand I shouldn't mention the paper, but he has friends that should know. They'll want to remember him."

Mr. Wilson pursed his lips and nodded. "Only that then. You can say he was murdered by street thugs. No mention of the paper, all right?"

She nodded and hurried out of the room.

"So what do you lads have to confess?"

Jonty crossed his arms across his chest, schooling his face into a stern expression. Having been a boy himself, he understood what he was looking at. Charlie and John stood before him, eyes downcast and shifting from side to side. A sure sign of guilt.

But exactly what they were guilty of—or thought they were guilty of—Jonty wasn't sure.

Charlie elbowed John. "You say it. I'm not going to."

"You're older than me!"

"Only by a year."

Jonty made a show of raising his eyebrows and tapping his foot. It helped him not to laugh at the display. "Out with it!"

Finally John accepted that, as the older of the two, it was his responsibility to confess. He cleared his throat and shook his shoulders. "We took the tin."

"The tin?"

"Yes. The biscuit tin Katie left on her bed when you went away for that fancy wedding. The one she keeps in her sewing basket."

That tin. Well, that certainly explained the mystery. Jonty scrambled to say something appropriately disciplinary. "You shouldn't have done that."

"We know." John wore his contrite face well.

But Charlie couldn't keep it up. "We shouldn't have taken it. But Katie was so hoity-toity about that wedding and her stupid hat. And then we found out she got biscuits as well, and didn't share them like she normally would."

Charlie's indignation was so comical, Jonty had to bite back a smile. "The tin didn't contain biscuits, did it?"

"Well, no. But we didn't find that out until later. We just swiped it from her sewing basket. Why would anyone keep papers like that in a biscuit tin?"

"So what did you do with it? Do you have the tin now?"

"We were going to give it back, but Katie was so fierce about it. I thought she was going to wallop me. So we buried it in the backyard."

"I think you should unbury it then, don't you? While you are doing that, I am going to be thinking up an appropriate punishment."

Jonty managed to hide his smile until the boys left, fearing the worst. Given the particular nature of the sin, he'd already decided that a week of washing dishes for their mother and sister was penance enough, but he wasn't going to tell them that just yet. Letting them sweat a bit would probably be for the best.

That night, after the culprits had gone to bed, he presented the tin to Katie. Bill was in one of his gregarious moods and had offered to take Martha out to the Empire to see a show. Martha knew to take full advantage of the good times when they came, so Jonty and Katie were alone. She sewed, he read the newspaper. Jonty's heart almost burst with happiness as he played the role of father, wife by his side and sleeping bairns upstairs.

As she worked, he told her the whole sorry story about her brothers. Something must be wrong, because she didn't laugh at their childish motivations like she normally would. She simply took the tin when he produced it with a flourish, placing it in her lap and staring down at it for a long while.

"I saw Mr. Wilson again today. It's why I was late home. I was at his office."

"Is he MI5, like we thought?"

She nodded. "But, Jonty, Jan's dead."

"Dead?" The box in her lap suddenly looked twice its weight.

He gave himself a mental clip over the ear for not noticing something was wrong sooner.

She explained about Mr. Wilson's office, something about Soviet Secret Police and how she'd finally discovered what the paper said.

"Mr. Wilson said I can't tell anyone. I figured you already know about the paper, so I can tell you. But all I can say to anyone else is that he was murdered by thugs. It doesn't seem right when there's so much more to the story."

"That's a heavy secret to bear, but I'm glad you told me. Have you told your neighbors?"

"Not yet. I couldn't work out what to say when I got home, so I didn't even tell Mum. What am I going to tell Mrs. G when she gets back?" Her face crumpled. "He was such a good friend to me, Jonty."

His name dissolved into sobs. What else could he do except drop the newspaper, pull her to her feet, and hold her close. When the sobbing subsided, she pulled away. "Sorry. I feel like I'm doing that lot lately."

"I don't mind, Katie-my-love. I'm just happy to be the one who gets to hold you."

She smiled, like he was her hero. He basked in her radiance, settling on the sofa while she worked away at her sewing.

It was becoming more and more difficult not to reach for her each night when she slipped into bed beside him. He'd made her a promise, and he wouldn't break it, but he couldn't control his subconscious, could he? Each night his mind replayed that moment from their day at the beach, when Katie had pulled his face down to hers. His dreams allowed many different variations of the kiss. Some sweet, some decidedly more passionate.

Sometimes he wondered whether the kiss itself was a dream, since nothing else had changed between them. Although come to think of it, one thing had changed. Katie always retired after him. She was staying up late to sew, as though another wedding were on the way.

"What are you sewing, Katie-my-love? Is that for your work?"

Something fine, by the look of the silk in her lap. And was that lace?

She shook her head. "This is for me."

He recalled the way she'd been able to turn RAF escape maps into underwear. He'd never seen anything more alluring in his whole life than Katie in those silky smalls.

"Will I get to see this?" He managed to get the words out through his suddenly parched mouth.

"When it's ready."

She kept her eyes down and smiled into her work. Eventually, and probably because he didn't look away from her, she slowly lifted her eyes to his. "I think you're going to like it a lot, Jonty."

Her shy smile made him want to leap across the room and cover her head to toe in kisses. He willed her to say more, but she simply went back to her work, so he was left wondering about it. And wonder he did. All he could think about was how he badly wanted to run his fingers through her curls, to feel their softness. How curious he was about what the feel of her porcelain skin under his calloused fingers would be like. How he wanted to kiss those beautiful lips of hers. And not just her lips. Her jaw. And her neck. And that spot just below her ear and—

A knock at the door provided the distraction he needed. He hurried to answer. A telegram delivery boy stood on the other side.

"Are you Jonathan Ables?"

"I am."

A boy presented him with an envelope marked *TELEGRAM* and scurried off. Jonty took out the slip.

From: Royal Infirmary in Edinburgh.
To: Jonathon Ables.
HAMISH MUNRO VERY ILL STOP ASKING FOR YOU STOP PLEASE COME ASAP STOP

"Who is it?" Katie called him back to the sitting room. He read her the message.

"Will you go?"

"He must be at death's door if he's in a hospital." Jonty couldn't remember his uncle ever paying for a doctor in the whole time that he'd lived with the man, no matter how serious the injury. That was saying something, considering the tremor in his hands didn't mix well with the sharp instruments used in carpentry.

He sighed. The last thing he wanted to do was spend a night away from Katie, but his uncle had no other family and had likely pushed away any friends he'd once had. "I think I need to. I might very well be all the man has left in the world. I'll go and pack."

Christian charity, more than any affection or goodwill, motivated his steps toward the train station the next morning. He made it in good time. So good that he was able to catch the earlier train. He ducked and weaved between other travelers, settling in his seat before the conductor blew his whistle, with enough time to gaze out over the other passengers making their farewells. In hindsight, Jonty couldn't explain why one particular scene on the platform outside his window caught his eye.

The scene was unremarkable. A man kissing his wife's cheek as she held a baby in her arms. But something was wrong with the picture. There was nothing dramatic about the people or eye catching about the family group. The pair were surrounded by several children, including a child just old enough to toddle among them. A common vignette at a train station, surely. Just another father saying goodbye to his wife and children. Perhaps it was Jonty's longing to one day have a family like that of his own that made him focus on them.

But when the man turned away from his family toward the train, Jonty realized why he'd taken notice.

The man in the scene was Bill Baines.

CHAPTER TWENTY-EIGHT

Wednesday, 22 August 1945

"Bed eighteen."

The nurse pointed Jonty down a corridor toward an open ward that smelled like antiseptic. Jonty hated the smell. It made his palms sweat and brought back the tangible memory of lying in a hospital bed.

He felt anew the burns on his face and neck, the pain of the grafts and physical therapy that had helped heal them. He almost turned and hotfooted back out to the train station.

Hamish Munro had never given him anything. Why should Jonty try to give him comfort in his dying moments, especially when it came at such an emotional cost? Jonty ignored the proverbial devil on his shoulder that told him leaving now was fine. His uncle was dying and this was the right thing to do.

Hamish lay in the bed, the yellow of his skin more pronounced against the white of the sheet. He appeared asleep, but he was so still that Jonty wondered if he had died already without anyone noticing.

Jonty reached out to touch his uncle's arm. Still warm, thankfully.

The old man stirred, but only slightly, opening his eyes just enough to register Jonty was near. "You again? Why are you here?"

Why had he expected that his uncle would be any different on his deathbed to how he'd been his whole life? "I'm your next of kin. The hospital notified me you were dying."

"I didn't ask them to."

Jonty shrugged. "Yet I came. Can I get you anything?"

"I don't suppose you want to sneak me in a drink, do you? The matron frowns on it but—"

Jonty couldn't believe his ears. "No, Uncle!"

Hamish deflated, appearing to sink into the bed. The monster from his childhood was gone. Now he was just a man. A sick, frail, lonely man. "Then leave me alone."

"Are you in pain?"

Hamish harrumphed. Jonty decided that silence was preferable to his uncle's deathbed belligerence, so he didn't ask any more questions. He simply sat and turned his mind to silent prayer. For his uncle's soul and for his own patience. He sat like that all afternoon and well into the evening, occasionally offering his uncle water—only water, despite the man's protestations—to drink.

His eyes wandered to the other patients in the large room, five in total, but all as sick as his uncle, so the only sounds were raspy breaths and murmured words. Occasionally nurses came and went, but none of the other men had visitors.

Jonty's mind turned back to the thoughts that had occupied him during the train ride north. He'd seen Bill Baines at the station. There was no shadow of doubt in Jonty's mind that it had been his father-in-law on that platform. He'd spent the long hours of travel trying to figure out why he'd appeared to be playing the role of father to an entirely different family. A sick feeling—one that had nothing to do with the smell of antiseptic hanging in the air—crept into his stomach. Jonty would have to get the truth of the matter when he got back to Hackney. But it would likely mean a confrontation with Bill.

A nurse in a starched cap and veil checked Hamish's pulse, drawing Jonty away from his future worry and into his present one.

"It won't be long now," she said with soft sympathy in her words.

Jonty nodded, but he wasn't sure that he believed her. Even though Hamish lay there helpless, the man had fought all his life. Jonty was sure he'd fight now too.

"It's good that you came. He's been asking for you."

Jonty's eyebrows shot up in surprise. "Has he?"

She smiled kindly and nodded. "And he's more peaceful now that you are here."

The room dropped back to silence when the nurse left. Jonty studied his uncle, using what were likely to be his last glances of the man alive to try to have sympathy, to understand him.

"Under the bed." His uncle murmured the words.

Jonty thought he was imagining them. "What?"

"Under the bed." The words were more labored this time, but still understandable. He stared at the old man. Was he in some kind of delirium?

The man said no more, so Jonty took the words literally. He crouched down and looked under the hospital bed. All he saw was a beat-up grayish suitcase. It probably contained the man's worldly possessions. How sad it was that he'd brought them to the end.

But since it was the only thing under the bed, he reached for the handle and pulled it out. It wasn't heavy or large, but a few things rattled about in it, as though it wasn't packed to the brim with clothes.

He rested the case on his knees and unfastened the latches. When he lifted the lid, all he saw at first was paperwork. Then his eyes fell on a book, one that he hadn't seen since he was eleven but was as familiar to him as though he'd seen it yesterday.

The slim blue book of poetry belonged to his mother. She had told him once it was a gift for her seventeenth birthday. Sure enough, when Jonty reached for the book, running his hands over the cloth of the cover, he opened it to see her name written in faded black cursive writing.

Holding the treasured book, his eyes traveled to the other items in the suitcase. A photograph and bundle of papers. He took them up. The photograph was of his mother and father, with a baby. He flipped it over to see "My happy family" written on the back, with the date. His mother had written those words, judging by that hand. But the bundle of papers looked more official than the book and photograph.

The papers were tied with string. He pulled, and it easily released the documents. Hamish Munro's last will and testament, and the deed to the shop and the flat above it.

Jonty's eyes flew up to his uncle. The man's eyes were open but empty.

"Uncle?" He stood, forgetting the suitcase and its contents, laying his hands on his uncle's arm and giving it a little shake.

Gone.

He sat back in his chair, staring at the pitiful old man. No, at his body. Jonty's mind reeled. All afternoon he'd been waiting for this moment, but he hadn't been paying attention when it had happened.

He shook his head. The old codger had no doubt planned it that way. Crafty till the end.

Jonty called the nurse from her station, who came over, checked for vitals, and confirmed the time of his passing.

"Did he give it to you? He said he had something for you."

"I think so."

"He made us send word to you, you know. Said he had something that was yours and wasn't about to shuffle off without giving it to you."

"He said that? That many words at once?"

She gave a sad smile. "That's the way some men like it. Do you have a place to stay tonight?"

He glanced down at the documents in his hands. "Yes. I think I do."

"You look happy!" Collette remarked. "You're glowing. You're not pregnant, are you?"

"Collette!" She rolled her eyes at Collette's vulgarity. Little did Collette know that if she was with child, she wouldn't be glowing . . . she'd be green. Not that she could say anything. "Asking those sorts of questions will get you into trouble!"

Collette shrugged, completely unabashed. "If you are so happy, you can pin this monstrosity on the mannequin. I will measure the Lady Beasley when she comes."

"No, thank you." Katie added sweetness to her put-on smile. "And Marina Hardie's ball gown is not a monstrosity!"

"So have you heard any more about your friend?" Alice murmured so Collette couldn't hear.

Katie shook her head. "Nothing more. But I've telephoned Mr. Wilson to tell him we found the tin, and I'm still waiting to hear back."

"And is your nightdress ready yet?"

Katie grinned. "No, but I'm getting close." It was set to be as exquisite as the things she sold here, but even more beautiful because every stitch was sewn with hope and a promise of happiness. Her skin tingled just thinking about the feel of the silk. "I've had extra time lately."

Jonty had been gone for nearly a week. He's sent a telegram to say that his uncle had passed away and he had meetings with solicitors he had to see to, as well as something about his uncle's shop. She missed him. His patient ear listening to her talk about the girls in the shop, his steady breath when she woke up in the night.

"I have no idea why the woman chose lilac," Collette muttered. "Not everyone can wear it."

Katie rolled her eyes. Madame always chose colors well. The dress would suit Marina's dark hair and pale skin perfectly.

"And the peignoir we are making is also . . ." Collette didn't finish the sentence, except for the expression of disgust she wore.

The bell on the front door tinkled downstairs, and Katie prepared herself to be summoned to meet Lady Cavendish.

"I think they are both beautiful." Alice ventured her opinion, only to bite her lip once Collette shot her a fearsome glare.

"What would you know?" Collette snapped.

Madame's voice came up the stairs.

"Kat-reen, can you come here please?"

Katie looked at Alice and shrugged. Madame rarely did anything as unrefined as calling up the stairs. That was why she had the bell. Katie headed down the stairs, light and happy, but froze in her steps when she saw Marina Hardie speaking with Madame.

When Marina saw Katie, she pointed her finger. Her face turned so vicious that Katie thought she heard her snarl. She looked ready to gouge Katie's eyes out.

"Her. The blonde. She is the one having an affair with my husband!"

"Is this true, Kat-reen?" Madame asked, her facial expression a picture of shock and disappointment.

Katie glanced at her employer's playacting. She understood very well that Madame's feelings about extramarital relations were just as French as Collette's. Madame didn't care whether a woman bought lingerie for her husband or her lover, as long as she paid her bill on time. She probably couldn't care two hoots about Katie's morals. But she might care very much about losing a customer, especially when Marina's ballgown was set to be just as showstopping as Grace's wedding dress.

"No. It's not true." She tried to sound clear and assured, but it didn't feel like it worked. Her throat constricted so that her voice came out small and tight. She shifted on her feet under the gaze of the other two women in the boutique. An invisible string pulled taut between Katie and Marina.

"I saw you with him!"

Katie took a step backward. Marina could easily lunge at her. Instead, she suffocated a scream in the back of her throat. "Coming out of this very shop, carrying on as though he was your own husband!"

"It wasn't me."

"How could it be anyone but you? You even admitted you were old friends when he and I were in here together!" She turned to Madame. "I want her sacked."

"But she is one of my very best seamstresses."

"If you don't sack her, I'll tell everyone I had to cancel my order due to incompetence."

Horror washed over Madame's features.

"And I won't pay."

Madame turned green, and not just at Marina's threat. Lady Cavendish was standing in the doorway of the salon.

Marina Hardie's unscheduled visit—and the unpredictable glint in her eyes—upset Madame's carefully curated illusion of elegant exclusivity, and now there was a customer to witness it. The desperation in Marina's eyes might be dangerous, but Katie also realized it was the kind of look a trapped animal gets.

"Lady Cavendish, how lovely to see you!" Madame strode over to Lady Cavendish, who, in the pecking order of customers, outranked the Australian High Commissioner's daughter. She clearly intended to blame Marina for upsetting the store's equilibrium. "Mrs. Hardie just called in from out of the blue to check in on her gown. She's Australian, after all."

The insult landed as Madame intended it to. Marina composed herself.

Katie took pity on Marina. She moved closer and kept her voice low as she spoke. "It wasn't me. I despise your husband. But

I think have some answers for you. There's a café on the corner called Levinson's. You can meet me there when I finish work."

Stylish, elegant, and blessed with every worldly charm, the shape of Marina's mouth was the only clue to the turmoil beneath her perfectly made-up surface. She was biting her lip. But she soon forced her mouth into a smile.

"I'll be there."

Katie couldn't afford Levinson's. She only knew of it because it was open when she left work, and she often walked by on her way to the tube. The pot of tea Marina ordered sat between them, as did the information Katie had just shared about Collette and Jimmy. The brew had gone cold in their cups.

"I am sorry to accuse you. I thought it must be you because you knew him. I didn't realize there would be another."

Marina touched the rim of her eye to prevent the tears there rolling down her face in public. Katie looked down at her hands, twisting her wedding ring around her finger. She still hadn't decided if she would tell Marina everything about her history with Jimmy. Hadn't the poor woman had enough of a shock for one day?

"What can you tell me about my husband during the war?"

Maybe if Marina had asked something else, asked in a different way, Katie wouldn't have felt compelled to tell the truth exactly as she knew it. She didn't feel bad for Jimmy's sake, but poor Marina obviously had no idea. Wasn't it better that Marina knew exactly who she'd married?

She poured out the story of her time at Bottesford, including the awful bet he'd made and that night outside the pub.

"I fell pregnant."

Horror spread across Marina's face. Her hand slipped protectively to her own waistline. Katie recognized the gesture. She done that plenty of times when she was pregnant with Betty.

"But I married a very good man, who knew about it all and promised to take care of us both."

And he did. In so many ways.

"Does the child look like James?"

Katie sighed at Marina's use of present tense, and steeled herself for her answer. "She died soon after she was born. Her heart wasn't strong."

"I'm so sorry," Marina whispered. "How terrible."

"I hadn't seen Jimmy for years until I saw him with Collette. I didn't know he was married until I saw you in the shop."

And I hope I never see him again.

Hopefully, Katie's look made it clear that she never wanted anything more to do with Jimmy Hardie. Marina Hardie stared dejectedly into her tea for thirty seconds before squaring her shoulders. Katie didn't know what conclusions she'd come to.

"Thank you for tea, Mrs. Ables." She stood, laying some coins on the table between them, more than ample to cover the cost of the untouched pot. "This afternoon has been . . . illuminating."

CHAPTER TWENTY-NINE

Wednesday, 29 August 1945

Big Ben chimed out four o'clock in the distance as Jonty emerged from the underground. He was earlier than planned. Nervous energy powered his every step. Jonty felt out of place among the toffs of Mayfair. He wasn't sure if the startled looks were because of his scars, like they usually were, or because they were suspicious that he would pilfer something and slip it into the overlarge bag he carried.

He had planned a surprise for Katie this evening. This time they really would go dancing and to dinner at a nice restaurant. And if she was amenable, they could stay the night in a hotel. Away from rambunctious brothers and interrupting fathers and mothers who guessed too much. But really, that was only the beginning of the surprises. Tonight he would fill her in on everything that had happened while he was in Edinburgh.

Uncle Hamish had left Jonty everything, so he and Katie were now the owners of his furniture shop and the flat above it. As well as that, it turned out that his uncle's miserly ways in life had made him quite rich in death. The bank had advanced Jonty some of his portion, which would fund this evening's entertainments, but there was plenty left over. Enough that he'd quit his job at Liverpool Street Station to begin a new life in Edinburgh. If Katie would agree to come.

That was a big if.

But things couldn't continue as they were. Not when her father was—well, Jonty didn't know what he was, but he was lying about where he was disappearing to. And Jonty couldn't escape the dreadful feeling that it wasn't just Katie's family he was lying to.

The small suitcase he carried clanged against his thigh as he walked. Lucy had helped him slip all the things Katie would need for a date into a small bag. He asked especially that she include the dress Katie had made for Grace Deroy's wedding. It really was the bonniest thing he'd ever seen her wearing. He'd ignored Lucy's knowing smile when she'd announced that she'd included a few other items she thought he might like. Still, he hoped she'd meant the slip made out of silk maps.

The bell tinkled as he pushed open the door for Madame Martin's boutique. Jonty's only knowledge of sewing was what he had gleaned from Katie. Even so, he knew this was a fine place with a rich clientele.

"Can I help you, sir?"

A beautifully dressed woman with a French accent spoke up from behind a small desk with a telephone on it. This must be Madame Martin. Katie often came home full of details about what the French woman wore. He did listen, even if he didn't understand the finer points.

"Yes. I'm looking for someone who works here. Katherine Ables?" He supposed she used that name here.

The French woman frowned, eyeing his scars. The woman's lips tightened in thorough disapproval, like she was swallowing a wedge of lemon but didn't want anyone to know.

"Again? I hire her to be a seamstress, not to cause trouble."

What did she mean by that? And what kind of trouble had Katie been causing?

"I do not allow my girls to take calls from gentlemen during the working day."

"She's my wife."

He got the impression that Madame found that even worse. She took him by the elbow and dragged him to a far corner of the store. No doubt she was hoping to conceal him should any customers walk in. He understood why. He truly didn't belong in a fancy place like this.

"Wait back here. Don't touch anything."

He shrugged, resigned to the fact that he would never be part of any fashionable set despite the fact he could afford to shop in Mayfair now. He'd never been in a place like this. The items around him were foreign and decidedly feminine. Slips and nighties hung on a rack concealed from the front of the store by a blue curtain. A fortune's worth of silk stockings and knickers sat folded into shelves. All things he'd seen plenty of times on pinup girls, but only glimpsed in real life. Everywhere he looked, his eyes fell on something he felt like he shouldn't be looking at, certainly not with his wife only a few meters away.

Despite the woman's stern warning not to touch, Jonty removed one of the hangers from the rack to get a better view of the nightie. The workmanship was exquisite, even he could see that. Had Katie made it? His lips tugged up at the recollection that she was making something like this for herself. He quickly shoved the smile and the garment away when he heard footsteps on the stairs.

"I told you not to touch, Mr. Ables!"

Had she seen him or had she guessed? It didn't matter . . . He felt the heat creeping into his face, regardless.

"Jonty?" Katie's face was all surprise. "You're home!"

She smiled that infectious, glowing smile that made him want to bask in its radiance. Until he realized her employer was watching them closely.

He cleared his throat. "Hello, Katie-my-love."

"Talk outside and make it quick," Madame Martin said. "We have important work this afternoon."

Without words, Katie took him by the elbow and escorted him outside and two doors down the street. He couldn't help but grin at her, on the cusp of enacting his brilliant idea, as he was.

"I'm so happy you're home. But what are you doing here? We're not allowed to have personal visits."

"I've come to give you this."

He handed her the case he carried, packed by Lucy. She stared at it like he was handing her some kind of explosive that she'd be crazy to accept.

"What is it?"

"It's what you need to put on after work so that we can go out for dinner. Lucy packed it with everything she thought you'd need."

"Really?"

He grinned, happy with himself for having surprised her.

"Courtesy of my uncle."

Maybe there wasn't quite enough money to be extravagant every night of the week, but there was enough for this.

"Your uncle?"

"I'll explain everything at dinner."

He leaned a little closer, took her hand, and pressed the handle of the case into it, enjoying the hitch of her breath as he did. "Tonight is for us." He kept his hand on hers, itching to lean in a little closer and press a kiss on her cheek. "See you after work."

His eyes traced after her as she hurried back into the store, case in hand. Just before she disappeared inside, she glanced back at him and smiled. Not in that tight, apologetic, long-suffering way she often did, but in a way that lit up her entire face with excitement and happiness.

It melted him. "I'll be waiting across the street when you finish."

Jonty was waiting outside Chez Martin, excited about the night ahead, when he heard a voice he had hoped never to hear again. It sliced down his spine.

"Jonty Ables."

He hadn't seen Jimmy Hardie for years. Despite being stocky and well built, Hardie's dark hair and calculating eyes gave him a snakelike quality. He couldn't remember now if he'd always thought that or if it was just after Jimmy had been so despicable to Katie that he had formed his opinion.

He shook the man's offered hand, even though he was sure Hardie didn't deserve the sign of respect. But they'd risked their lives together, and that bond couldn't easily be dismissed. But what was he doing here?

"Demobbed?" Hardie inquired.

"I fell from the sky too many times, and they decided I was a liability. You?"

Hardie had been the bombardier in their crew of seven men, the one who'd lined up the targets and dropped the bombs. Jonty wondered if he felt an extra level of guilt.

"Finished my tour. But decided to stay. Married the Australian High Commissioner's daughter, would you believe?"

Poor woman. Did Hardie's wife know what she'd married?

"I'm going into the family business."

"What business is that then?" Jonty glanced at the shop door, mind racing. What would Katie do if she saw Hardie here?

"Politics."

His eyes landed back on Hardie. "Figures. I imagine you've got a natural talent for it."

Jimmy didn't deflect or defend himself, but Jonty had the distinct impression that he was drawing back, getting ready to strike.

"Katie told me about the baby."

He'd spoken to Katie? When?

Jimmy obviously saw the surprise in Jonty's eyes, because he went to work like the serpent in the garden of Eden. "She didn't tell you? We had a nice little catch-up in the park." The way he emphasized the word *catch-up* landed like a kick in Jonty's guts, just like Hardie intended it to. "She's still very pretty, isn't she?"

Jonty gritted his teeth. What exactly was Hardie playing at? Right now he couldn't see Jimmy as anything more than a cold-blooded creature.

"I wonder why she stays with you? Now that she's not pregnant with my kid, I mean? With those looks, she could do much better, couldn't she?"

Hardie already knew Katie was Jonty's weak spot, but he was pressing Jonty's buttons, testing him for vulnerability.

"What are you doing here, Hardie?"

Hardie's too-innocent expression was carefully designed to create doubt in Jonty's mind.

"Just remembering old times, mate. Particularly that time outside the pub in Bottesford when Katie and I . . ."

He wouldn't let Jimmy finish that thought. He lunged at him, grabbing him by the shirt and shoving him up against the stone wall of the building, not caring what polite society said or did around him.

"That's my wife you're talking about."

He spat the words into Hardie's face, low and fierce. Enough to get looks and murmurs as the good people of Mayfair stepped around them.

Hardie held his smirk. "Yeah? Well, your wife"—he spat the word as though it were a filthy insult—"went and told mine everything, didn't she? And I've come to have a little word with her about that."

Jonty's grip on Hardie's shirt tightened, his breath shallow and ragged with rage so that he couldn't speak. Still, Hardie smirked, enjoying getting under his skin.

"Look, here she comes now."

Hardie directed his words over Jonty's shoulder. Surely it was a bluff, the kind of feint a boxer gives when he wants to land a blow. Jonty couldn't help but look though. Hardie had been telling the truth. Katie stood in the doorway of Chez Martin. Horror and disbelief were both written across her face.

Hardie took his chance. "Give Katie a kiss for me," he hissed.

Then he landed a real punch to Jonty's stomach, causing Jonty to double over in pain.

But Jonty swung back around, landing the punch of his life on Hardie's jaw. He was preparing for another, when he felt the cold hand of a passing constable on his shoulder.

CHAPTER THIRTY

To Katie's utter humiliation, all her colleagues watched from the front windows of the boutique as Jonty and Jimmy were hauled away by local constables. She'd finished changing into her new dress, just in time to see the end of it for herself.

"Is that your husband, Kat-reen?"

"Yes." Her mind spun. What had Jimmy said to Jonty? It didn't take much to guess. Probably something about her. Something vile and insulting. That would explain Jonty's reaction.

She sighed, pinching the bridge of her nose, trying to come to grips with the dramatic turn her evening had taken. She'd bubbled with excitement all afternoon. Jonty being back was surprising enough, but she also tingled with the thrill of knowing that he'd planned a surprise for them. A surprise that involved a beautiful dress and a suitcase for an overnight stay.

She guessed that would be canceled now. Ruined by Jimmy. She would likely have to collect Jonty from the local police station after this.

Madame's fierce gaze pierced through Katie. "I can't keep having scandals erupting around you, Kat-reen. It's not good for my business."

"I know, Madame. It won't happen again."

"But it has happened twice in the last week."

Collette and Alice both watched the dressing down with wide eyes.

"I know. But I smoothed everything over with Mrs. Hardie."

Katie tried to keep her accent in place, but it slipped in her desperation to keep her job.

"How?" Collette's question slipped out as curiosity got the better of her.

Katie glanced between her employer and her colleague, trying to choose her words carefully. "I told her about the kind of man Jimmy was when I knew him during the war."

"What did you say?" Madame asked with words.

Collette demanded an answer with her eyes.

"I . . . I told her that he was a man who couldn't be trusted."

"Did you tell her about him and me?" Collette demanded.

Katie nodded. Collette gasped.

Katie smoothed her hands down the front of her beautiful dress. "And about him and me."

"What?!" Madame and Collette cried, their French accents ringing out in perfect unison.

She gave them the bare bones of her story. "I wouldn't be surprised if he decided to confront me for telling his wife. Luckily, my husband happened to be there." She held her chin high, hoping that was the truth of the matter.

"You might have ruined everything," Collette murmured. "He was going to leave her for me."

Katie rolled her eyes. How could Collette be so blind? "No, Collette. If he says that, he's lying. Trust me. His wife is wealthy and powerful. You are a seamstress. He'll have his fun with you while it lasts, but he's not going to leave her."

Collette scoffed and wrinkled her nose.

"Girls, stop this bickering," Madame commanded. "It is not becoming to do this where people can see us."

Madame ushered them to the back of the store.

"Now, this could not come at a worse time. We have another customer due in fifteen minutes, and this one is the most important we have ever had. Katie, I want you here to take the measurements."

Katie frowned. "But, Madame, it's after hours." *And I think I have an appointment to bail my husband out of the lockup.*

Madame shot her a sharp look.

"Princess Elizabeth's lady-in-waiting is coming. If she likes what she sees, we might be commissioned to make a gown for the princess herself." The news ricocheted through the group. "Can you not stay for that?"

Two weeks ago Katie would have given anything to work on a dress for one of the princesses. She would have said yes immediately and found a way to make it up to Jonty later. But something had shifted. She couldn't exactly say when.

"No, Madame. I'm afraid I can't stay."

"Then I'm afraid I'm going to have to let you go."

Madame's words hit her like a slap in the face.

Collette raised her proud little chin and looked down her nose at Katie. Alice looked like she might cry.

"But I haven't done anything wrong!" Katie pleaded.

"Be that as it may, your scandals are too much. In France, maybe I could overlook a brawl or an accusation from an upset wife. But this is England. I have seen plenty of other talented seamstresses while I have been looking for Françoise's replacement. Any of them can fill in for you."

Katie stood stunned by her dramatic change in fortunes this afternoon. "I will give you your pay for the rest of the week, but after that, your services are no longer required."

Jonty had been ready to kill Hardie. So it was actually a mercy that a passing member of the Metropolitan Police had arrested them both for disturbing public order. And put them in separate cells.

He bent double, resting his elbows on his knees. Katie was probably furious at him, angry he had embarrassed her by fighting in front of her workplace. She might even be inclined to make him stay in a cell overnight, if the glimpse he'd caught of her face as he was dragged away was anything to go by.

When the sergeant came for him, he took one look at Jonty's demob suit and rolled his eyes. "The war is over, mate. Remember that." He probably thought Jonty was another maladjusted soldier bringing his troubles to the high street of Mayfair. Little did he know.

A different but equally stern-faced sergeant attended to procedural matters, filling out almost as many forms as Jonty had signed when he'd enlisted. "You'll get off with a fine and warning this time, but next time there'll be a court appearance."

Next, he was sent to a cashier to pay the fine. His jaw tightened. He hated handing the money he had in his pocket for dinner over to pay fines, but it had to be done, or he would never get home to Katie. And right now she was the one he wanted to see. They had a long conversation ahead of them.

Katie waited for him in the foyer of the police station. She looked exquisite, dressed in the blue dress Lucy had packed. Pity there would be no date now. She hurried to him but stopped short of embracing him.

"Are you all right? Did Jimmy hurt you?"

"I've felt worse."

"What happened?"

"Jimmy couldn't keep his mouth shut."

"I thought it was something like that. So I suppose our date is off?"

"I'm afraid so. I had to pay a fine before they would release me." He let his eyes skim down her figure and back up again, hoping his gaze conveyed just how much he appreciated what he saw. "I'm so sorry, my love. You do look bonny."

"That's all right. I'm just glad you weren't hurt."

She slipped her arm through his and led him out of the station. They accidentally blocked the path of a well-dressed woman in an elegant gown as she tried to enter. The woman looked scared and definitely out of place.

"Excuse me."

She met Katie's gaze. Then she paled, as though she had just realized she was in some kind of horror story. She looked Katie up and down, then turned to Jonty. She paled further when she saw him, his mangled face no doubt adding to her fear. Then her eyes flicked back to Katie.

"Mrs. Ables."

Jonty's jaw almost dropped to the ground when she addressed his wife.

"I didn't expect to see you here." She raised an eyebrow.

Katie gave a tight nod. "This is my husband. Jonty, this is Marina Hardie, Jimmy's wife."

This was Jimmy's wife? And how did Katie know that? Had what Jimmy said been true? His brain reeled.

Marina Hardie carried herself in a way that suggested she hadn't known a day's hardship in her life, and dressed to prove it. Yet here she was about to bail her husband out of jail.

"You know each other?" He glanced between them. He wanted to know more but was scared of what he would find out if he asked.

"We've met, briefly," Marina said tightly.

"She mistook me for Jimmy's mistress, so I had to set her straight about how I know him." Katie spoke quietly and matter of factly.

"You gave her *all* the details?"

Katie nodded.

He blew out his breath through his teeth. The hissing sound made the woman flinch. Part of him wanted to rub in her face the truth about Jimmy's character. But even in the kind of elegant dress that would usually have Katie in raptures, she looked so pitiful under the bare light of the police station foyer. Jonty wouldn't be surprised if Hardie had used his serpentine skills on her too. She might have fine clothes and money, but she was still a victim of his wiles.

"Well, now you know the kind of man you married." He took Katie by the arm and stalked out of the police station, leaving Marina Hardie in his wake.

CHAPTER THIRTY-ONE

For a couple with so much to say to each other, the journey home from the police station was quiet. Unasked questions hung in the air between them. Once or twice he thought Katie would explain how she knew Hardie's wife. But even though she breathed in to speak, she offered nothing. Jonty thought his mind might burst from everything he had to tell her, but it wasn't until they arrived at the door of six Ivy Street that either spoke.

"I lost my job," Katie murmured. "Madame wasn't happy that I wanted to leave to bail you out instead of helping her win a commission to dress Princess Elizabeth."

Jonty's heart did a funny jump in his chest at the knowledge she'd chosen him over the job she loved. "She said I had too many scandals erupting around me. It's so unfair, because I haven't done anything wrong."

"I want to hear all about it, Katie-my-love. Firsthand. From you."

"Tea?"

He nodded. "It's for the best, I think."

Katie opened the front door, but what she saw in the sitting room stopped her from heading through to the kitchen.

"Mrs. G! You're home!"

He followed Katie in to see Mrs. G sitting on the sofa, having tea with Bill and Martha. Katie rushed over to embrace her.

"Where have you been? Have you heard the terrible news about Jan?"

"What about Jan?" Bill asked.

"He's dead, Dad." The audible gasp from everyone in the room informed Jonty that Katie had kept the news about Jan to herself while he'd been away. "I found out last week, but I haven't known how to tell people."

"What happened to him?" Bill asked.

From his position by the door, Jonty observed the conversation. That glimpse of Bill on the train station had given him new eyes for the man. News came tumbling out of Katie. Only Jonty knew how carefully she was walking that tightrope between truth and lie.

"He was murdered."

"Murdered?" Bill and Mrs. G spoke in unison, both paling to the same degree. Mrs. G's hand flew to her heart.

"Do they know who did it?" Bill asked.

"They say it was thugs."

Jonty noticed the minute hesitation before the lie, but he doubted anyone else did.

"Oh, Jan." Mrs. G's tears flowed. "My poor boy."

She repeated herself over and over as the different waves of grief hit her. Katie grasped the older woman's hands. Martha disappeared to the kitchen and quickly returned with a small bottle of medicinal brandy. She added a slosh to Mrs. G's tea and her own.

Bill grabbed up the bottle and took a swig. "What's being done to find the reprobates who killed him?" His forehead creased in a frown.

"I don't know." Katie shrugged, giving a sideways glance toward Mrs. G, whose initial shock had subsided into vacant sadness.

"How did you find this all out, Katie?" Martha pushed a cup of tea into her neighbor's hands. "Drink."

"I met a man at Grace Deroy's wedding. He investigates things like—"

"The man who came the other day?" Bill interrupted before she could finish explaining. "Does he work with the police?"

"Sort of." Katie bit her lip while she decided exactly how much truth to put into her lie. She glanced at Jonty before continuing with her story. "He also told me that Jan was married. Did you know that, Mrs. G?"

Mrs. G's face was hidden behind a teacup, so Jonty couldn't read her reaction. But Bill leaped to his feet, as though he were affronted.

"The man was married and he never said!?"

A scoff exploded out of Jonty. He hadn't meant it to, but he couldn't help his physical reaction to Bill's hypocrisy. All eyes in the room turned toward Jonty, who was forced to defend himself with sarcasm. "Imagine being married and not telling those nearest and dearest to you!"

Jonty looked directly at Bill and watched the words land on Bill's guilty conscience.

"I knew." Mrs. G stole everyone's attention back. "I don't know what she's going to do now."

While the woman gathered around to comfort Mrs. G, Jonty kept his eyes on Bill.

His father-in-law wasn't distracted by the weeping woman. He kept a dark glare directed Jonty's way. Which told Jonty all he needed to know. He'd been right to jump to conclusions about what he had seen on the train platform.

He decided then and there to get Katie out from under his roof for good.

"Jonty, what are you doing?"

When they entered their bedroom, Jonty immediately began packing his suitcase.

"I'm packing, Katie." He collected the items he brought home from the demobilization center, as well as the few other items he owned. Everything fit in the rucksack that he'd arrived at the station with not so many weeks ago.

"I was going to tell you tonight. My uncle left me his shop and the flat above it."

She became still and quiet as he looked around for anything he might have forgotten.

"So are you leaving me now?" The floor felt as though it were falling out from under her feet.

"No!" He ran a hand through his hair, eyes desperate and unbelieving. "How can you think that? I want us to go there to-gether. It's a nice flat that we can make our own. Be husband and wife properly, ye ken? No more secrets. No more interference."

Panic clutched at her chest. Her face must have shown it, because he huffed out a laugh, sinking down onto the bed. Then he reached out his hand, indicating she sit next to him. She did, her thigh close but not touching his.

"That wouldn't be such a bad thing, would it?"

"I just need a bit more time." She couldn't explain it, but with every stitch of her nightgown she was readying herself. It was a slow process, but it was nearly done. Jonty glanced away. He couldn't possibly understand. "I'm trying to be the wife you deserve, Jonty."

"Ooch, Katie-my-love, you are the wife of my dreams. But we need more than dreams, ye ken?"

She did. And she didn't. Her head was swimming with every-thing that had happened in the last few hours.

"Do you want to tell me about Hardie? He said you met with

him?"

"Hardie?" He must have thought she was trying to conceal having met with Jimmy.

"I didn't mean to hide the fact that I saw him, but I suppose he just wasn't important to me anymore. The longer I left it, the less important he became to me. To us."

She explained how she'd seen him with Collette just before Grace's wedding. "I knew he saw me, but I thought he didn't recognize me. And then with the wedding, I was so distracted—so happy—that I didn't even think about him until he ambushed me in the park."

"Ambushed you?" Jonty scowled.

"He must have followed me."

She paused, perhaps for too long, because Jonty's face creased with worry about what might come next.

"Nothing bad happened." She rushed on when she realized the suspense she'd created. "He wanted to know about Betty. Not because he cared but because he wanted to know if a little Jimmy Hardie look-alike was going to ruin his chances at a political career." Just recalling his callousness made her stomach sour.

"When did you meet his wife?"

Katie sighed. "She's a customer. She came in after Grace's wedding, with him in tow. She suspected something, I suppose. Then when you were away, she showed up again. Demanded that Madame fire me. But she'd confused me and Collette. I decided she needed to know what she'd married and told her everything."

She could still clearly picture Marina's stricken face sitting across from her in Levinson's.

Jonty harrumphed. "Poor woman. Shackled to that snake for life."

"I think she's rich in her own right. Her father is a diplomat, the Australian High Commissioner. She could leave him." She shrugged off the thought. "You know, I hope we don't find out. I want to forget all about him . . . I saw you punch him. I've never seen you in a fight. Not even at Bottesford."

She didn't like violence, but she loved him for defending her.

He smiled briefly, then frowned. "I thought I was quite self-controlled. I wanted to wring his neck."

"I can't say I blame you. But I'm glad you didn't. If you did that, we could never forget him."

Silence took over. Silence she wanted to fill with touch. With another kiss like the one from the beach. With more. She took a deep breath and reached over to put her hand on his knee. A tiny, tentative attempt to show him what she felt. When he took her hand in his, she tried to smile. But he lifted her hand to his mouth and kissed her fingertips. Then he gently placed it back in her lap. The rejection stung, and heat crept into her face.

"We can't keep living as we are, ye ken? Come with me to Edinburgh."

"I can't. Not yet."

"Please, Katie." A shadow crossed his face. "I . . . I'm worried it's not safe here."

"Safe? What do you mean? If you are worried about Jimmy, then I don't think—"

"Not Jimmy." He ran his hand through his hair. "Do you not wonder where your father goes when he's away?"

A chill ran down her spine. "What do you know?"

He shook his head. "Nothing certain. But I am going to Edinburgh, and I don't feel good about leaving you with him."

"If it's not safe for me, it's not safe for Mum and the boys, and I won't leave them."

He thought about that for a long time before coming to some kind of conclusion in his mind. "I'm going to Edinburgh in the morning, Katie-my-love. You can join me when you are ready. But once you do, I want us to be husband and wife properly. In every possible way, ye ken?"

Her face warmed. Every bit of fear and anxiety that she was channeling into her nearly finished nightgown exploded in her heart like a seam bursting. What if God had cursed her for her mistake with Jimmy and so all her babies were destined to die? What if it ruined them?

What if it didn't? What if there was a chance of a happy family with Jonty?

What if the way her pulse raced just thinking about it wasn't fear but something else entirely?

Jonty placed his hands on her arms, just below her shoulders, drew her toward him, and kissed her forehead, which felt incredibly chaste considering what he'd just said. "You are the love of my life, Katie, but I want our lives to begin. I'll sleep downstairs tonight, my love."

They barely spoke on the way to King's Cross Station the next morning. They must look like any other couple in London walking arm in arm. But no one could see just how heavy her heart was. Jonty, however, had a spring in his step.

"Do you really have to go?"

He nodded, sad resolution filled his eyes. "But I'll be waiting for you, Katie-my-love. I do hope you'll come soon."

"Jonty, I don't understand why—"

He stopped her words by suddenly sweeping his arm about her waist and pulling her against him, his lips pressed firmly on hers.

Urgent and full of emotion, he kept his mouth on hers until she shut her eyes and relaxed. Her hands came to rest on his upper arms as he deepened the kiss. Warmth bloomed inside her and expanded to fill her whole body. Somewhere far, far away, a whistle blew, and the stationmaster announced the final boarding call for the train to Edinburgh.

When he pulled away, she wanted to draw him back to her body and soul and stay trapped inside that kiss for the rest of the day, for the rest of her life.

But the cool air of the station, not to mention the rest of London going about its business around them, reminded her that she couldn't. Breathless and weak kneed, her hands shot to her own face to conceal the flush in her cheeks.

He took one of her hands and pressed a key into it. Still without speaking, he closed her fingers around the key, drew the fist to his lips, and kissed it. Then he let go, straightened his trilby, and bent to pick up his suitcase.

"Come to me soon, Katie-my-love." Then he turned and boarded the train.

Her gaze traced the carriage windows until he appeared next to one and locked his eyes on her.

They stayed that way as the train moved away.

CHAPTER THIRTY-TWO

Thursday, 30 August 1945

Heavy steps drew her back home, and her sadness grew with every mile Jonty traveled farther away from her. She'd only been to Edinburgh that one time to see his uncle, and now she felt as though her heart belonged there, because it belonged with Jonty.

Aching for a cup of tea, she almost didn't notice the familiar black car parked on the corner. She expected Mr. Wilson to be in the sitting room when she arrived home, but instead the house was filled with the sound of Mum busy in the kitchen and the boys playing out back.

Katie stood at the kitchen door just watching Mum. How many times had she seen her mother working in this way? Likely thousands. Always busy. Always working at something to care for her family. And always alone. Dad was never with her. Not really, except when he came home to demand what was his.

Mum must have sensed her presence. She turned around.

"Hello, Katie. Where've you been?"

"Seeing Jonty off. He's headed back to Edinburgh."

"Again?"

Katie nodded, lips pressing together to stop them from saying more.

"Fancy a cup of tea then?"

Katie sat at the kitchen table while Mum prepared the tea, swirling the pot three times to the right and once to the left to help it brew faster.

"Mum, what would you say if I moved away? Would you be all right?"

"Are you and Jonty thinking of moving out?"

She nodded again, not wanting to admit the reality of the situation. Jonty had already moved.

"Well, I'd be sad not to have you here, but you're a married woman. It's a good thing for you to start a new home with your husband. Where would you go?"

"Edinburgh. Maybe. Nothing is decided. But his uncle left him a flat, so we'd have a place to ourselves."

"Now that's a good thing. Provide some privacy for you to start a family of your own."

Katie was not prepared for a talk like that with Mum. No thank you. She moved the conversation on quickly. "You'd really be all right? Dad can be so unpredictable."

"Don't you worry about me, Katie. I've had a lot of practice handling your father."

A knock at the front door cut off all the questions she wanted to ask Mum. Katie rose to answer it. "Hello, Mr. Wilson! I thought I saw your car. Have you just been at Mrs. Grabowski's?"

"In a manner of speaking. Can I come in?"

He took off his hat as he entered. She stepped back to allow him in, noticing for the first time the two men behind him, who waited outside. She ushered him into the sitting room.

"She isn't in trouble, is she?" Mum asked from the kitchen.

"The opposite. She's been helping me. And I have some answers about your friend."

She indicated that he should sit. "Did the NK-whatsi-call-it get to him? The Secret Police?"

Wilson sat and smiled kindly at her. "Is anyone else home beside your mum? Your husband or dad?"

"Just Mum in the kitchen. But my husband is in Edinburgh. I never know where Dad is."

"Could you call your mum in?"

Katie didn't have to call. Mum was already at the doorway. Katie made the introductions. She noticed the tension in Mum's shoulders, starkly contrasting with her loose, easy posture of a few moments ago.

"Mr. Wilson investigates things. He has news about Jan."

"Please sit, Mrs. Baines." Mum obeyed but didn't lose the tense posture. Mr. Wilson continued. "I'm afraid the explanation for Jan's disappearance is much more mundane than we first thought."

"So no Soviets then?" Katie tried to lighten the heavy mood that had settled.

"Well, we do believe that Jan was being followed by the Soviet Secret Police, like I said. But we think he knew it, and that made him incredibly aware of his surroundings. That led him to see things that he might not normally see."

"I don't understand." Katie glanced at Mum, who was staring at Mr. Wilson with a look Katie couldn't interpret.

"A man slipping away to visit his second family, for instance." Mr. Wilson directed his words at Mum.

"Second family? What do you mean?" Katie asked.

"Should I explain it, Mrs. Baines? Or will you?"

Suddenly tired and worn, Mum shrugged. "You can do it. I've wasted enough of my words on that man."

"I'm afraid your father is a bigamist, Mrs. Ables. He has two wives. Two families, in fact."

"What?" She spun round to Mum. "I don't understand." But one look at Mum's face and it was clear that Mum knew exactly what Mr. Wilson was talking about. The tea turned over in Katie's stomach. "What does he mean, Mum?"

Mum was silent. Mr. Wilson hurried things along, offering an explanation. Of sorts. But Katie didn't take her eyes off Mum.

"Your father has been living a double life, Mrs. Ables. For quite some time now. He has another wife in Surrey, whom he regularly visits."

"Did you know?" Katie forced out a whisper.

Mum nodded, sitting with a resigned kind of calm that Katie certainly didn't feel. "Dad has another wife?"

Katie addressed Mum, but Mr. Wilson answered. "Another family, in fact."

"That's where he was disappearing off to?" Katie's mind reeled. "And you knew?"

Mum rubbed her brow, taking a deep breath that Katie hoped would exhale an explanation.

"He always had a roving eye. I would have been better off not marrying him. But how could I not when I was already carrying you? He left when Lucy was little. Went to work at a factory in Kingston. It was hard on my own with four little mouths to feed."

Katie remembered. She'd been five or six at the time.

"I thought it was over. But after about five or six years, he begged me to take him back. I was happy not to be doing everything on my own. He would disappear for long stretches still, and I thought he was drinking, but I had babies again and was too busy to worry about it."

Mum told the story matter of factly, breaking Katie's world apart as she rewrote their family history.

"During the war, when he was working as a fire warden, he got injured one night. The hospital called one of us, while his friends called the other. So I rocked up to find another woman comforting Bill."

"Who was she?"

"Delia her name was. Still is, as far as I can tell. She has six by him. The youngest is just a babe."

Katie did the horrifying mathematics. He'd been living this double life for most of Katie's own.

"And you never said anything."

Mum shrugged. "What could I say, Katie?"

"Is that where he is now?" Mr. Wilson asked.

Katie had almost forgotten he was here, such was the intensity of Mum's revelations.

"I don't know where he is," Mum said. "After you and Jonty went upstairs last night, he left. I figured he'd gone back to her place. That's what he usually does when things get too much here."

Katie thought back to the lead up to Lucy's wedding and how Mum and Mrs. G had both asked if they'd checked "the usual places." Now she knew what that meant. "Mrs. Grabowski knew too?"

"And Sarah. They were the only ones."

"I'm afraid that's not true." Mr. Wilson broke in. "Jan knew too."

"Jan?"

"Like I said, we think he had become observant. Perhaps he followed Bill and learned his secret. Perhaps he ran into him with his other family accidentally. But we believe Bill killed him on the morning of your sister's wedding."

This was too much.

"Wait. You're saying that Dad murdered Jan?"

"Yes. He strangled Jan, then pushed him into the river. It's a fairly common assassination method for the Soviets, which was why we were confused. But in your father's case, we think it was just opportunistic."

"But what about the passports and the papers? From the tin? I thought you said that Russians or Soviets were after him."

She pressed for some hole in Mr. Wilson's story. Something that might prove her father innocent. The thought of Dad killing Jan—and with his bare hands—was too much to bear.

"Do you have it?"

"Yes." She reached into her sewing basket, where she had safely stashed the tin after Jonty made the boys return it. She handed it to Mr. Wilson, hopeful it contained something that might change his mind about Dad.

Mr. Wilson worked off the lid and looked inside. "This rather confirms our suspicions, I'm afraid." He took out the papers. "Jan was using this scientific paper as leverage to get the Soviet authorities to allow his wife to leave."

"I suppose that's why he had all new documents in the name of Adam and Emmaline Kent made up, right?"

"Yes. And he was successful. He smuggled her here. All he had left to do was collect his documents, hand the paper over, and start his new life. But he was interrupted."

"I don't understand."

"I have someone I think will help." Mr. Wilson strode to the front door.

Katie and Mum stayed seated, unable to speak. Mum's eyes were cast down to the carpet, no doubt trying to reconcile this new information with what she knew of her husband. Katie's mind simply spun through all she'd learned in the last few moments.

Mr. Wilson returned to the room. A thin blonde woman in a blue suit, worn around the cuffs, followed. Katie recognized the woman from the identity photographs in the tin.

"Mrs. Ables, this is Katarzyna Delovski, Jan's wife. He gave Mrs. Grabowski money to rent a cottage for them, and that's where she's been for the last month. Hiding with her daughter in Dorset, waiting for him."

"Her daughter? Mrs. Grabowski was Jan's mother-in-law?"

Mr. Wilson nodded. "I think he gave you the tin with the

forged papers and the scientific work so that Mrs. Grabowski would have access to it. But suspicion wouldn't fall on her if it was found."

"So you're saying he used me?"

"I wouldn't put it quite like that. I would say he trusted you."

Katie nodded, trying not to dissolve into tears with so many people in the room. She saw the resemblance to Mrs. G immediately. "Do you speak English?"

"A little. You can call me Kasia. Our names mean the same thing, I think."

Katie nodded. "Yes, I suppose they do." Jan often told her he liked her name. Now she knew why. "Jan was a good friend of mine. I'm so sorry . . . about everything."

They didn't need a common language for Katie to understand the woman's pain. And right now, amid the swirl of feelings in the room, she couldn't cope with more. She turned to Mr. Wilson.

"Will you give the paper to the Soviets?" After what he'd said in his office, she understood that he didn't see the Soviets as being on the same side anymore. He wouldn't want them to get their hands on anything that helped them develop a bomb like the ones that had cowered Japan.

He kept his gaze level. "I can't say." She knew he meant no.

"If you don't, will she be safe here? Because Jan was brave to do what he did. For us during the war and for her. And you owe it to him to protect her." She was speaking out of turn, but she didn't care. In this moment, so many things felt wrong, and if she could make just one of them right, she would.

"I'll make sure of it, Mrs. Ables."

CHAPTER THIRTY-THREE

Saturday, 1 September 1945

The very first thing that Jonty wanted to address was the smell. He threw open the windows to the flat and scrubbed every surface until his hands were raw from the caustic soap. A lady sold him potpourri, which he placed in small bowls in every room. The lavender hung in the air like his hope that Katie would come soon. Each day he picked fresh flowers from the park and put them in a vase on the kitchen table, just in case today was the day that Katie should come.

She didn't.

Next, he looked at the soft furnishings, most of which had been in place since he was a boy. The carpets were ragged and torn and likely responsible for the lingering smell of mildew. They were easy to remove, and he spent hours on his hands and knees sanding and polishing the wood underneath. Once new carpets and rugs were in place, the flat began to feel new. He left the curtains for Katie. She'd no doubt want to choose the fabric and make them herself.

That night he lay in bed—on a new mattress after he'd removed the fetid old one that smelled like his uncle—wondering where Katie was and if she was in bed thinking about him too. He stared at the ceiling, trying to pray, but instead noticed the pattern of mildew there. He'd add painting to his list of jobs for tomorrow.

By day three he'd finished the cleaning upstairs and ventured to the shop below to see what kind of mess was in there. The frosted glass on the door would need replacing, but otherwise, things weren't too bad. The scent of the wood shavings and finishing oils hit his nostrils, and a surge of feeling shot through him. A few months ago, the tangible memory evoked by that smell, one of being a helpless child at the mercy of a miserly man, might have made him shut the shop door forever.

But now he saw himself as a boy in this workshop, spending long hours down here in silence while he watched his uncle. He hadn't been a kind teacher or a patient one, but Jonty had learned. Enough, at least, that he could manage this place. He looked around at the tools and supplies. Hamish had kept his workplace tidy, even if his house was in squalor. Most of what he saw was in good order.

The sound of a knock at the door of the shop made him jump. His heart did a double beat of hope. He flung open the door. But it wasn't Katie on the other side. Instead, an older, plump woman, with a blue hat, met him.

"Are you opening again?" She obviously didn't feel the need for formalities.

He hesitated. Was he? He stammered out some kind of response about how his uncle had died and he was still trying to decide.

"Humpf."

She pursed her lips and gave him a disapproving look before she left, as though she couldn't abide such equivocation.

But as he closed the door and turned back to the store, he

smelled, in the shavings littering the ground, the aroma of possibility.

He picked up the tools.

"BIGAMIST ARRESTED FOR MURDER OF WAR HERO PILOT."

Katie's face burned with shame when she read the headline on the newspaper being read by the man across from her on the train. She tore her eyes away and directed them out the window.

In the last forty-eight hours, every stitch attaching her to Hackney had popped like the seam on a too-tight dress. Scenes from the last day flashed through her mind as London dissolved into country scenery.

Shortly after Mr. Wilson had left, they received the news that Dad had been arrested at home with his other family in Surrey. Less than twenty-four hours later, newspaper reporters came knocking on the door to ask Mum questions. Mrs. Parkin and Mrs. G chased them away with brooms. In her shock, Alberta confided that she was expecting. Katie put on a show of delight for her friend, but inside she ached.

The hardest thing had been telling her brothers about Dad at the same time as telling them that she and Jonty were leaving. She promised on Jonty's behalf that they could come and stay in Edinburgh once she was settled. Then she packed her bag, hugged Mum, and caught the bus to the cemetery.

She laid some fresh flowers on the grave. "I've got to go now, Betty. But just because I'm not here as often doesn't mean I love you any less."

She'd missed the train to Edinburgh but caught one as far as Lincolnshire. After all, there was one person in all this whom she'd been able to tell everything. A friend who listened and counseled in the kind of straight-talking way she needed right now.

"Katie!" Maggie opened the door of her flat, her jaw slack

with surprise. "What are you doing here?"

Beyond Maggie, Alec sat at the kitchen table, Eadie in his arms. She'd interrupted the family in what was no doubt a precious moment before Alec left them for Australia. Maybe she should have gone straight to Edinburgh.

"I'm sorry to interrupt. I . . . I need a friend right now. I didn't realize Alec would be here."

"Of course. Come in! We have plenty to eat. And in fact, Alec was just about to take Eadie for a walk. Weren't you Alec?"

"Was I?"

"Yes, you were just saying that."

Alec shot his wife a look that said he thought she was crazy before the penny dropped. "Yes, yes I was. The late summer air in England is very good for babies." He cleared his throat. "I'm told." Alec bundled the baby up and made a hasty exit.

Maggie poured tea while Katie poured out her soul, filling Maggie in on all that had happened since their day by the sea. It felt almost like they were back in the WAAF, and Maggie was her corporal, advising on her unwanted pregnancy. Maggie's indignation at Hardie's indiscretions had gratified Katie. But it was hard to admit that Jonty had left and gone to Edinburgh by himself. Tears spilled from her eyes.

"His uncle left him the flat, and a shop, I think, what with everything, we didn't get to talk about it. He said he would stay there . . . and that I can join him when I'm ready."

She explained the nightgown she'd been making with Maggie's material.

Maggie's eyes lit. "Can I see?"

Katie hesitated. She was making this just for Jonty. Did it diminish the value of the gift if she showed it to Maggie? No. She was being silly. It was just a nightie, after all, no different from all the other ones she made at Chez Martin. She drew it out of her suitcase and held it up for Maggie to see. Maggie gasped, eyes coveting every fine detail in the embroidery around the deep neckline.

"Katie, it's exquisite. He's going to love it."

Katie chewed down on her lip. "Do you think so?"

What if Jonty didn't like it? What if he didn't understand all the emotion behind it, the symbolism? Maybe to him it would just look like she had made herself something extravagant when they didn't have much money to spare. She smothered that thought with the knowledge she had gained working at Chez Martin. Husbands and lovers were prepared to pay exorbitant sums for the promise that garments like these held.

"Absolutely. But what about you? Are you ready yet?"

"I don't know. It's like fear and love are doing this kind of tug-of-war inside me."

"Do you love him, Katie?"

She nodded without hesitation.

"Then don't let the fear win." Maggie made it sound so simple when she said it like that. "He's not going to hurt you, like Jimmy did. Or betray you, like your dad did."

"You can't know that." How could anyone know or judge the most intimate moments of another person's marriage?

"I certainly can, because he's neither of those men. It's as clear as day that Jonty Ables loves you enough to move heaven and earth."

"But another baby would—"

"Be a blessing, Katie. I know that your little girl broke your heart into a million pieces, but that was only because you loved her so much. That love in itself was a miracle, considering the circumstances. Hers was a short life, but you filled it with love."

"Do you think if I have other babies they will be sickly and blue too?" She thought about how Mrs. Parkin buried babe after babe in that grave.

"Only God knows that. He numbers our days in his book of life. And even if the number next to our child's name is small, every one of them is precious to him."

Emotion cracked through Maggie's voice to match the tears

sparkling in her eyes. They sat in silence for several moments until they heard Alec fussing at the other side of the door and the cries of a fractious baby whose dinner had no doubt been interrupted.

Maggie headed for the door, where she turned. "Finish your nightdress, Katie. But don't use it as an excuse. Jonty loves you and you love him. That can overcome a lot of things."

CHAPTER THIRTY-FOUR

Sunday, 2 September 1945

Katie slipped the key Jonty had left her into the lock of the Edinburgh flat and took a deep steadying breath. There were no more excuses, no more reasons to delay. And she didn't want to. She missed him. She wanted him with her. Every day. For the rest of her days. Exhaling, she pushed open the door. She picked up her suitcase, heavy with the weight of expectation, and entered.

She expected the house to look the same as it had done when she'd visited Hamish to tell him Jonty was missing. Dark and smelling like an old man who never washed. But instead, the smell of fresh flowers, fresh paint, and furniture polish met her. Jonty had transformed the flat, removing every trace of his sad childhood and creating a home for them.

Her chest suddenly felt too small for all the emotions inside it.

Jonty appeared at the end of the hall. Probably in the kitchen, wiping his hands with a dishcloth. She couldn't read his expression until his face broke out into a smile.

"Welcome home, Katie-my-love."

Her eyes were fixed on him as she carried her case up the hall.

"Here, let me help you!" He jolted into action, hurried up to her, and took the case from her. "Shall I put it in the bedroom?"

"No." She saw the doubt flash in his eyes when she answered too quickly and firmly. "I'll keep it with me."

"You're not thinking of leaving again, are you?"

She shook her head. It held her most beautiful creation, one that she had worked for the last week to perfect. Every stitch was perfect, as fine as any of the things she sold in Madame Martin's.

His lips spread out into a happy smile. "I'll put it in the kitchen then." Before he bent to pick it up, he leaned in close to kiss her cheek.

He lingered at her ear, tickling it with murmured words. "I'm so glad you came, Katie-my-love."

He pulled back and met her eye. Her stomach did a little flip. She wouldn't be surprised if his did too.

She followed him into the small kitchen, noticing a tiny sitting room to the right. Two chairs and a small coffee table. Brand new, from the smell of the varnish that scented the air. And if she wasn't mistaken, Jonty's handiwork. She smiled inwardly, even if she was too nervous to let it reach her face.

A pot of tea sat on the kitchen's small table, along with a plate of half-eaten dry toast, made only slightly less dry by scrapings of margarine.

"Is this your dinner?"

"Would you like me to make you something else? I just wasn't sure when you were coming."

Or if you were coming. He didn't need to say it aloud for her to hear it.

"Toast is fine." She wasn't sure if she could even eat that, with her stomach doing nervous flips the way it was. "Shall I make us a new pot?"

It would give her something to keep her trembling hands

busy. She grabbed the teapot and took it to the sink. With shaky hands, she opened the lid. But the teapot was still warm and half-full, so she didn't waste it.

"I'll make you some toast, Katie-my-love. Then we can sit and talk. Since you are here, the night calls for something special."

He opened a new jar of jam with a flourish and spread it thickly on her slice. A sweet gesture, even if she could only nibble.

Gradually, all the half-conversations, interrupted conversations, and not-started conversations from the last few months came out as they shared several teapots and plates of toast. Jonty's ever friendly conversation calmed her frantic heartbeat. He crept his hand across the table between them and took hers.

She stood up abruptly when they'd exhausted their topics. "Well, I suppose I'll do the dishes then."

But he kept hold of her hand.

"Leave the dishes, my love."

Jonty stood too. So close that her breathing shallowed in her chest at the thought of what came next.

"Are you nervous?"

Did he have to ask? Surely he could hear her heart beating. She nodded in reply, almost imperceptibly. His fingers slipped over her hand and came to rest on her wrist. Callouses tickled the delicate skin above her palm. "Your pulse is racing."

He was so close to her now. His eyes darkened, and she knew he was going to kiss her. And she wanted him to. That familiar heat built in her belly. She swallowed to moisten her mouth.

But instead of kissing her lips, he raised her wrist to his mouth and kissed the delicate skin over her thundering pulse.

"Do you know what they told us when I joined the RAF?" He kept her wrist close so that his breath danced across her skin. What did the RAF have to do with anything right now?

"No." Her voice was little more than a whisper.

"The same part of the brain that controls our fear, controls our desire." He kissed her wrist again, keeping his gaze locked on hers. "So maybe you aren't actually as scared as you think you are."

She didn't know.

She couldn't tell what she thought with him so close, kissing her like that. But she knew she wasn't going to stop him. Deliciously slow, he dropped her wrists, cupped her jaw in his rough hands, and pressed his lips against hers. Soft and undemanding.

The passion from the train station reignited, like a breeze blowing over embers, drawing her into his kiss. She wrapped her arms around him, pulled him closer. His kisses moved from her mouth, along her jaw, down her neck.

Powerful, intoxicating, overwhelming.

And she needed him to stop. Because if he didn't, she wouldn't want him to. She wouldn't have a chance to slip on the nightdress, and all that work, all those hours of sewing, meant to show him how much she loved him in a way that words couldn't, would be in vain.

"Stop." She whispered as he nuzzled into her neck. When he didn't, she said it louder. "Stop. Jonty."

She pushed him back and sucked air into her breathless lungs. But oh how she wanted more of that kiss.

"I'm sorry, Katie." He looked stricken and retreated to the other side of the room. "I didn't mean . . . I would never hurt you."

She knew it now. "I . . . I . . ." How did she say it? "I need to use the bathroom."

Without another word she grabbed her suitcase and fled from the kitchen, leaving a confused Jonty in her wake.

"Are you sure you're all right?"

He paced back and forth in the hallway, past the closed bathroom door, wondering what on earth had gotten into his wife.

"Just give me a moment, Jonty." Breathless, panicked words came through the closed door. Was he really such a beast that he had read the moment incorrectly? What a terrible blunder. Maybe he didn't understand her the way he thought he did. He went to the bedroom and sank down on the end of the bed, newly adorned with side tables he'd made for them with his own hands.

His head fell into his hands amid a prayer that he get this night right. Through his fingers, he caught sight of pale-colored silk in the doorway. His breath caught in his throat.

Why was she torturing him this way? "Katie!"

Her name came out like a growl in his throat, which probably wouldn't help matters. He threw himself backward onto the bed in frustration, catching a glimpse of Katie wearing something made at Chez Martin.

Forget the nightie.

He immediately saw the nightie in his mind.

Focus on the ceiling. Focus on the ceiling. Focus on the ceiling.

"I don't want you to think you have to apologize, Katie!"

"It's not an apology, Jonty. I made this for you. For us."

The words took their time to sink in as Jonty stared at the newly painted ceiling, trying to forget the enticing glimpse he'd seen of her in the doorway. He didn't want to move for fear that this was another dream.

"I never had a proper wedding dress or anything, and so I thought I should make something special."

Barely breathing, he raised himself onto his elbows.

Framed by the doorway, Katie stood clutching her hands in front of her, twisting her fingers together. "Do you like it?"

Surely that was permission to look properly. He let his eyes absorb every detail of her beauty. From the golden curls falling over her shoulders, down to the tips of her toes poking out from under the gown. He took his time, lingering on her curves in the way the garment intended he should. She was so exquisite, he couldn't breathe. Desire thrummed through him. For once, he let it.

"Aye, it's very special." She smiled. His heart burst inside his chest. "Well, turn around and show me the back then."

She let out a nervous giggle but did as he requested. The low back of the gown ended in an alluring V just below her waist. She gave her hips a playful wiggle.

His restraint snapped. He leaped off the bed and closed the distance between them, stopping when he stood impossibly close. But still not close enough. She spun back to face him. He ran his fingertips down her arm to her hand, lacing their fingers together.

She was trembling, but the complexion of her face and décolletage held no hint of red splotches. She didn't recoil when he tentatively ran his fingers along her creamy collarbone. Instead, her breath hitched and her eyes half closed. Jonty wanted to savor every single part of her, every electric caress.

"Are you afraid?"

"No." She shook her head slightly. Each move released more floral notes in her perfume. Not lavender this time. Rose. She nodded too. "And yes."

"You know I won't hurt you, don't you?"

"I do. I want us to be a proper family. To raise our children with all the love and kindness we never had."

"Children?"

Had she said that? More to the point, was he an idiot for pointing out that she had said that, when such talk usually sent her running? Yearning and hope danced in his heart.

"Yes."

He didn't dare to do anything else but share the same breath and listen to both their hearts beating as one.

She acted first, leaning in to touch her lips to his. His arms flew around her, pulling her delicious silk-clad curves into him. He kicked the bedroom door closed, and it didn't open again for a very long time.

Despite sleeping in Jonty's arms for much of the night, Katie woke the next morning alone. She sat up in bed, running her hand through her disheveled curls, letting the delicious memories of the previous night come back to her one by one. Parts of the married-woman code she hadn't understood until now became clear.

Even though it lay discarded on the floor now and she wasn't wearing a stitch, the nightgown had been a triumph. She grinned, throwing herself back onto the pillows. Happiness coursed through her veins in a way it never had before.

Tears came to her eyes unbidden. Then she laughed, treasuring the knowledge she'd gained last night about just how wonderful love could feel.

"What are you laughing about, Katie-my-love?" Jonty appeared in the bedroom doorway, holding a teacup and saucer. She sat up, holding the bedcovers to her chest. His eyes met hers, and a grin the size of Europe spread across his features. "I brought you tea."

She smiled back at him. Her heart beat faster. They stood grinning at each other like two idiots incapable of speech. Until she noticed he'd lost his concentration on the saucer. It had angled downward so that the teacup was now in danger of sliding off.

"Jonty! The tea!"

He recovered just in time and carried the steaming cup to where she sat on the bed. "For you, my wife."

She accepted the cup, her face aching from her smile, but she didn't need relief. Jonty sat on the edge of the bed. He studied her as she sipped, as carefully as she might study a garment when trying to work out the pattern. Then he ran his hand down her arm in an impossibly soft caress, setting off tingles that ricocheted through her body.

"My wife is so beautiful."

The admiration in his gaze was almost too much. It made her

skin warm. She wanted to repay the compliment but couldn't find the right words to express the grateful feeling in her heart. It felt twice its usual size. "Is this the way all our married days are going to begin? With tea brought to me in bed?"

"If you like." The expression on his face told her he would do just about anything for her if she asked right now. "I intend for us to live happily ever after, you know."

She understood the feeling. "We will. I love you, Jonty."

"I love you too, Katie-my-love."

THE END

EPILOGUE

From the doorway, Katie cast her happy gaze about a room strewn with wrapping paper. A sagging pine tree decorated with paper chains sat in the corner of Alec and Maggie's small sitting room. Bing Crosby crooned over the wireless, even though there was absolutely no chance of a white Christmas in this heat.

It felt wrong to celebrate Christmas, complete with roast chicken and plum pudding, on such a hot day. She supposed she'd get used to the reversed seasons eventually. She'd have to, since Australia was to be her new home. No doubt it would be easier to adjust to the temperature once the baby was born and she wasn't the size of a whale.

She and Jonty, with their two little girls in tow, had finally made it to Australia as assisted migrants in July, just in time for little Lily to celebrate her second birthday. There had been a lot of false starts before they'd finally boarded the ship that brought them here. But Katie had been glad about the delays. They meant she wasn't traveling while pregnant with Martha, who was barely a year younger than her sister. Jonty had been incapacitated with seasickness for most of the journey. If she'd had to contend with two children, a poorly husband, and her customary pregnancy illness, she would have been at her wit's end. Luckily, the sickness hadn't been as bad with this pregnancy, which had surprised them on their arrival.

Alec and Maggie wouldn't hear of them staying at the migrant hostel. At first the two families crammed into one ground-floor apartment below Alec's mother. But when Alec and Maggie's third—or fourth, depending on how you counted—baby came along, she moved in with them, giving up her flat to Katie and Jonty. But they'd only be in it another few weeks. They were due to move south to Jindabyne soon, where Jonty was to be employed building a new hydroelectric power plant.

"Why don't you put your feet up, Katie-my-love?" Jonty slid his arms around Katie from behind, resting them on her belly. He leaned his cheek against hers and followed her gaze with his own.

Four contented children—two with ginger hair and two with dark—sat entranced as Father Christmas read them a story in an American accent. Jack Marsden had taken on that role for the day and now looked rather hot dressed in red felt. He and Grace were staying at one of Sydney's luxury hotels. They'd arrived last week in a flurry of glamour, delighted godparents to Eadie, William, and baby Molly.

"Technically, we're traveling to America. But my father said he'd pay for us to go wherever we wanted as a belated wedding present. We figured we'd go a long way round so we could spend Christmas here," Grace had explained. The last week had been full to the brim of reminiscing and recalling their common past, all of which seemed so far behind her now.

"The children look ready to collapse," Katie remarked, looking at the sleepy faces hanging on Santa Claus's every word while they tried to keep their midafternoon eyes open.

"Not just the children. Alec too," Jonty said.

She glanced over at Alec in an armchair. He'd fallen asleep sitting up, head lolled to the side with the kind of tiredness only the parent of a newborn and two toddlers could know.

"That will be us soon."

She felt his broad grin against her cheek. "Aye. It will."

Just then, the baby gave a strong, healthy kick under Jonty's hand, as though he knew they were talking about him. Jonty chuckled. "Now, go and sit down. I'll scoop the girls up and put them to bed when Jack is done."

A surge of feeling overtook her.

"Wait, Jonty." She turned in his arms before she left them, catching him unawares by planting a kiss on his smiling lips. When he pulled back, he met her eyes with a question.

"What was that for?"

"That was because I love you. I am so, so happy. Happy in a way that I once thought I never, ever could be." A lump rose in her throat, but she spoke through it. "Because of you, Jonty. Thank you."

"Ooooch, Katie. I do not think I can take credit for all of it. God has blessed us more richly than we could ever deserve, ye ken? But I'll happily take all your thanks." He leaned in for another lingering kiss. "Merry Christmas, my love."

Katie wandered—or technically, waddled—outside to Maggie and Grace, who were seated in the shade at the far end of the garden, talking in hushed tones while Maggie fed her baby. The friends had been doing a lot of catching up over the last week and still had plenty to say.

Katie heard snippets as she approached.

". . . we've tried everything . . . Different treatments in America . . . Honestly, I'm not sure he minds, not after what happened with his first wife."

They stopped speaking as Katie moved closer. But she understood. More than once she'd seen Grace holding baby Molly, her face a tug-of-war between wonder, jealousy, and hope. Katie figured that things had been more complicated for Grace when it came to starting a family than they had been for either Katie or Maggie.

"I'm glad you're here, Katie." Grace expertly changed the subject when Katie sank down on a wooden outdoor chair opposite them, savoring taking the weight off her swollen feet in the cool afternoon breeze. "I have something to show you two."

Grace reached into her pocket and pulled out a folded newspaper clipping.

"Look what I found among some old newspapers." She unfolded the clipping and held it out for Maggie to see.

"It's us!" Maggie exclaimed, handing over the clipping. "Look, Katie!"

The clipping was from the *Bottesford Gazette* in December 1942, when they had all worked together at the same airfield. Above an article about a hanger dance sat a photo of the three of them dressed in Women's Auxiliary Air Force uniforms. Katie couldn't help but feel like it was taken a lifetime ago, not simply six years before.

"Do you remember that night?" Grace asked.

"Barely," Maggie said, chuckling. "I do remember it rained a lot, so they had to hold dances in freezing hangars to keep all the airmen out of trouble."

Katie remembered that night well. She'd spent it kissing an airman under the mistletoe. But she wasn't about to tell Maggie. Not when Alec was the airman.

"Well," Grace continued, "I managed to track down the photographer who worked at the newspaper at the time. And he still had the negative. So I made these."

As if from nowhere, Grace pulled out two wrapped gifts and presented them each to Maggie and Katie. Maggie handed over her milk-drunk baby to Grace's greedy arms so she and Katie could open the gifts together. Grace had made copies of the photo and framed them in elegant silver frames.

"Oh, how lovely." Maggie hugged Grace.

"Thank you, Grace," Katie murmured.

Katie concentrated on the younger version of herself in the photo, hair neatly pinned up off her collar as it had to be in the WAAF. Her smile was so carefree that she was practically a different person. This was taken before Jimmy, before Betty, and even before Jonty. So many things had happened since. To all of them.

Tears welled in her eyes, surely because she was pregnant and crying at the drop of a hat. But no. It wasn't just that. It was the deep recognition that the silly girl in the photograph—the one who was about to have her heart broken, trampled, and beaten— was going to get what she always wanted.

A happy ending.

If you have enjoyed this book,
please consider leaving an
online review or telling a friend.
This helps other people find the book

AUTHOR'S NOTE

Grief is a sneaky thing. It is tragedy's long tail that hangs around long after the dust has settled on the initial crises. It upsets and disrupts life with its sometimes irrational, sometimes unexpected appearances in the everyday. It takes years to resolve. Grief has been a theme in all the On Victory's Wings books, in one way or another. This wasn't intentional. In fact, when Katie's character arrived on the page in *Heart in the Clouds*, she was a plot device. A useful obstacle in Alec and Maggie's story. I didn't even like her that much! I had no idea that three books later, she would be the vehicle to write about my own grief at laying a child in the grave.

While Katie's story is very different to my own, I still cried a lot writing this book. It was hard work to give it the levity that ultimately a romance requires. If I have succeeded, it is because of the hope I have through Jesus's resurrection that death—that undeniable certainty of the human condition—is not the end. (1 Thessalonian 4:13–14).

For all the historical notes on the story, please visit https://jennifermistmorgan.com/these-long-shadows/.

ACKNOWLEDGMENTS

First and foremost, to my wonderful family. My long-suffering husband and children, who put up with me playing with my imaginary friends for hours on end. Your patience is one of my greatest blessings. And especially to Angie, to whom this book is dedicated. And to my mum and dad, who are the most dedicated PR reps an author can have.

It is truly a joy to collaborate with editor Dori Harrell. She has such wisdom and insight into the whole book-making process. Similarly, Roseanna White's covers for this whole series have been perfection. Thanks also to my agent Rachel McMillan. I promise now to get on to a whole bunch of books for you!

Thank you to my beta reader Jen for helping me smooth out finer points and plot holes. But thank also you to all my readers. I couldn't write if you weren't reading. I am immensely, overwhelming grateful for your time, your interactions on social media, and your reviews.

And at the risk of sounding like a cheesy actor giving an Oscar acceptance speech, thank you, Jesus. The victory I wrote about in this book ultimately has nothing to do with WWII. It is your victory over death itself. To God be the glory.

READ MORE FROM
JENNIFER MISTMORGAN

*Books in the 'On Victory's Wings' series
are easily read as standalone novels*

Heart in the Clouds
The Mapmaker's Secret
These Long Shadows

Read *Finishing School* for FREE

Inverness, Scotland, 1944: In her final weeks of training at a Special Operations Executive Finishing School, Amy Snee's last chance to redeem her career is to parachute behind enemy lines as an SOE wireless operator. She just needs to master Morse code.

Stuart Lewis teaches radio operations, knowing that his bright, brave students won't last more than six weeks behind enemy lines. Can he bring himself to teach Morse to his high school crush, when it means losing her forever? Or can he give her a fighting chance at love?

With rigorous historical detail and compelling characters, this sweet historical romance will delight fans of well-crafted close-door romance.

Ebook and audiobook FREE for newsletter subscribers.